Jamaican

Flowers

A Novel by Jim Moorman

Dedication

Dedicated to my mentor and friend, Bruce McAllister

Prologue

Marcus Bindi's grandfather described the island of Jamaica as a pimple on the face of the planet. Gramps never cared for island living and had a wanderlust Marcus didn't inherit. Marcus was a simple farmer, perfectly content living in what would be the equivalent to a hair on the pimple - the tiny village of Batasee, population thirty. He went to St. Louis after Gramps died and almost joined the old goat. The city of two and a half million gave Marcus a case of hives and a three day bout of diarrhea that had him cursing the elder Bindi the whole plane ride home, most of which he spent in the lavatory of the 737.

On that seemingly uneventful morning, the wind over Batasee blew a gentle five miles per hour north. Marcus Bindi guided his plow as the draft horse that Gramps had left in his will pulled through the stubborn soil. He carried a switch, though he rarely used it. Monk, his horse, worked for beer—Budweiser, in fact. Gramps said Monk was a bona fide Budweiser draft horse who'd been sold off after busting a few barrels of the breweries finest and drinking himself useless. Gramps got him cheap and used him on his farm near St. Louis for a dozen years with little incident, as long as Monk got a cold beer after a day's work.

Marcus hummed "D'yer Mak'er" by Led Zeppelin, and puffed on a sweaty joint his wife Merry rolled for him earlier that morning. All was well when, out of nowhere, Monk reared up on his hindquarters and sent the plow careening toward his head. He dove and dodged the blade by only inches as he buried his face in freshly plowed dirt.

"What de fuck, horse? Fine, I'll get your beer now."

He watched Monk stagger and shuffle sideways across the field, wondering if he'd already discovered the new keg of Bud next to the barn.

"Woman, you tap dat keg?" Marcus shouted to Merry.

Still covered in dirt, Marcus scanned the field, expecting a prompt reply to his question, but received none. Was his weighty wife drunk as well? He decided that perhaps he could use a cold one, too, when he looked up and saw her standing over him, with the pick ax he'd left for her to use in the vegetable garden raised high over her head. He should have known better than to make demands of a three hundred pound menopausal Jamaican woman.

"You not welcome here, demon!" she screamed as she lowered the point of the pick directly into Marcus' shoulder. He cried out in agony and struggled to get to his feet, but before he could, Merry grabbed hold of the ax handle and retrieved her weapon.

"What da matta wit you?" he snapped, clutching his bloody shoulder. "Fine, I'll spread de fertilizer."

Merry grimaced and raised the ax high above her head once more and dropped it squarely atop the skull of her husband. Marcus dropped to his knees and fell face down in a pile of Budweiser stinking horseshit.

"Back to hell with you, demon!" she shrieked as he fell.

Merry brushed the loose dirt from her hands and spit on the ground. Seemingly satisfied with her accomplishment, she turned to head off the field but was met by one of Monk's rear hooves. The drunken beast kicked high and caught her squarely in the forehead. Merry dropped dead instantly.

Demons, dragons, and evil spirits roamed the streets that morning, looking for souls to steal. The farmers wielded sickles and axes, while field hands threw rocks and bottles.

Joseph Simon, the twelve-year-old son of Martin Simon, buried a machete deep into the leg of his mother, begging her to be damned while finishing the last of his icy pop Popsicle. She screamed and waved garlic cloves at the boy, claiming him to be a werewolf and asking Saint Michael to strike him down as he had the dark angel, Lucifer.

Martin Simon couldn't come to the aide of his wife because he was fending for his own life, battling a gang of neighbors who believed him to be a shark that had escaped from the ocean and grown legs. They pelted him relentlessly with rocks in an effort to drive him back to the sea. His only protection was when the gang members looked at each other and realized that they, too, were sea people. Some were crabs, others were squid, but all had transformed into something other than human.

Martin cried as he watched the ground under him move and slither. The soil he tilled not an hour before had suddenly come to life; the once giant rows of dirt were now giant serpents. He fell to his knees and wept. He didn't even see the boulder that crushed his skull— if the crab man or squid man had wielded it, no matter. He and his entire family were dead.

The men on the mountain shelf watched through their telescopes as the final living residents of Batasee faced off. Cash passed hands quickly and the clinking of cocktail glasses could be heard in between bets. Most of the men were middle-aged and accomplished military brass. Few stood with clipboards, but most didn't. They were too busy getting drunk and playing grab-ass with one another.

"Who had zee horse?" the stocky Frenchman asked, clutching a new stack of francs.

"I did," replied the general.

"I didn't see zat one coming," the Frenchman said, laughing as he passed the stack of new bills to the general.

"And to whom do we owe this spectacle?" a voice inquired from the rear of the pack.

The general paused and said, "One of the foremost U.S. experts in the properties of the hallucinogenic. Sad story that he ended up an unfortunate test subject to his own creation."

The men laughed as they sipped their rum drinks and flicked their cigar ashes to the ground.

"We're down to the last two," the Korean shouted excitedly.

The consortium took their respective places and watched intently through their telescopes. It was genocide turned into sport and labeled as science. The men were all military leaders, scientists, and heads of foreign governments gathered to witness the effects of a newly engineered chemical agent.

"Just think, men, no more troops sent into battle. Now, we simply sprinkle a little fairy dust and watch the enemy tear themselves apart."

The group stopped staring long enough to applaud.

A half-mile below, the two remaining villagers faced off in the main square that an hour before had been covered with brown dirt. It was now littered with the bodies of residents and stained red with blood.

Gregory Mandu and Rufus Jones faced each other. Gregory wielded an ax and Rufus, a machete. Gregory struck first, whipping the ax blade across the torso of Rufus.

Rufus jumped backward. "Not today, dragon. Today, I spill your blood and keep my soul!"

With that, Rufus dropped to his knee and spun around, extending the machete and catching the hamstring of his dragon foe. Gregory fell to the ground, and Rufus delivered a swift, fierce blow with the machete that separated Gregory's head from his body.

Rufus crouched, still in attack mode, waiting for the next evil to strike.

"Take him out," the general barked into the walkie-talkie.

The sniper fixed in on Rufus' position and pulled the trigger. Rufus dropped like a sack of potatoes.

The gentlemen toasted.

"Who had him?" the Frenchman asked again.

The men looked at the pieces of paper they had been handed prior to the incident and studied them.

"Ah— it was me," Lee shouted, as excited as a kid at Christmas.

"Wait— I thought I had him," Wayne, the Middle Eastern emir obsessed with ice hockey, protested. He looked for the slip of paper between the lucky Gretzky and Jager cards in his pocket.

Amir Aziz, aka Wayne Aziz, grumbled before body checking the older, yet surprisingly fit, Korean.

Lee, a former Tae Kwon Do champion in his native land, caught his balance and twirled like a ballerina on speed, catching Aziz squarely on the jaw. The emir, believed to be worth several billion, retaliated by grabbing the shirttail of his nimble foe and yanked it over his head in classic enforcer fashion, one even Gordy Howe would have been impressed with. Aziz landed a solid head butt before calling a truce.

The two looked again through the telescopes hoping to properly identify the body.

"He's gone, they shouted in unison.

"Oh, dear," the general said as he dropped his head and crumpled the small piece of paper in his hand.

Chapter 1

I woke up to the smell of smoke and singed hair. I'd be lying if I said it was the first time. My arm was on fire; well, my shirt sleeve anyway. A normal person would have freaked out or at least made some effort to extinguish themselves, but I was plenty stoned and couldn't decide if it was the weed, a new wave of consciousness, or just another monument to my ever-increasing idiocy. I waved my arm in front of my face.

Trippy, I thought, until the flame ate through my sleeve and scorched my elbow. It was real. The pain neurons shoved their way past the weed neurons and trumped the THC running rampant throughout my brain. It hurt like hell, so I screamed. Thank God for the central nervous system. It was my brain's way of protecting me from me.

My office was only a few hundred square feet but I ran through it as if it were an indoor track. I couldn't remember what to do. Stop, drop? Fuck a duck, man. Then I saw the aquarium. With the flick of a wrist the lid flew open and in went my arm. I heard the sizzle of flames and smelled the remaining sleeve as it transformed from a solid to a gas. Good ol' water.

"Ahhh."

I closed my eyes and felt relieved for a half a second until the fish started nibbling at my exposed, half-cooked elbow. I jerked my arm out of the tank and a Jack Dempsey with it.

As I cursed my fish, I noticed that a good portion of my office had combusted.

"No, man. Not the couch."

The couch was one of the few things I owned that I actually gave a shit about. I'd had it since college. It was where I first got laid, first dropped acid, and first heard Zeppelin. More than those impressive milestones, though; it was where I scribbled my first award-winning formula. Sure, it was an old shitty worn out piece of furniture, but the memories that lived in the cracked leather were irreplaceable.

I went back into deranged chicken mode and scooped water into my hands. Short, quick steps, I told myself, as the water dripped through my fingers. I threw what hadn't leaked out on the couch. I swear to God if the fire could have talked, it would have called me a retard. I would have been hard-pressed to argue.

Scrambling, I searched for anything. Where the hell was the fire extinguisher? Did I even own one? As I hunted, the fire spread. I grabbed the half-empty pot of coffee and tossed the hazelnut blend on the couch, expecting a miracle. The brew wasn't that good anyway. I heard the flames laugh at me again – "Retard."

They taunted me, jumping from the couch to the curtains. Ho-leee shit. I'd finally done it. I was going to burn down the goddamn house. Summer told me it would eventually happen, but I'd assured her I wasn't that incompetent. I sensed a heaping plate of crow in my future. The fire was unyielding. Maybe if I pissed on it? I was half unzipped when I remembered the box.

Holy crap. Where was it? The old ratty cigar box was even more important than the couch. Why was I such a moron?

Maybe I if I hadn't taken all those drugs back in college, I wouldn't be such a fuck-up as an adult. Maybe my brain wouldn't be so fried. I had to fit in, though. Any other guy in my shoes would have done the same. Oberlin College, while small, was my chance to be different – cooler. I was cooler all right, so cool that I won the only two major science awards the school offered and graduated a year early.

Natalie, my favorite ex-wife, swore not to blow my cover. To the rest of the kids on campus, I was just another long-haired hippie who dropped a lot of acid and smoked too much weed. Nat was the only one who knew I was just a nerd in sheep's clothing. That's probably why I married her and took a job with NASA after graduation.

Where had I put that goddamn box? I should have been searching for my journal, the one with my bipolar notes, but the cigar box was more important. I needed to find it and get the hell out of there. Smoke had filled the room. I hacked and coughed as I hunted. Nothing else mattered, although the half-eaten sleeve of Oreos looked especially tempting to rescue. I abandoned the thought and marched on, impressed with my willpower, imagining the weed neurons were flipping off the willpower neurons in my brain.

I wasn't normally this brave. My flight response was the one that had kept me alive this long. Marcie, my therapist, told me my tendency to run was caused by panic attacks, a nice way of calling me a pussy. I was a stallion, not a lion, I told her. But what I wouldn't admit was that, as far back as I could remember, I've been afraid, afraid of everything: dying, living, being a father and husband, and failing.

Natalie and the girls were the brave ones. Autumn once saved a litter of kittens from a stray Rottweiler that looked like he could have eaten them – and her - for lunch. Summer was no slouch either. She beat the snot out of the school bully when she was six. The little son of a bitch had taken her sister's milk money. If it were me, I would have given him the money and probably wet myself in the process.

Any other day facing flames like these, I would have run and peed— at least I would have run – but it was the box after all— the one containing the dozen photos and keepsakes from Autumn, my baby girl. An alarm blasted and nearly sent me through the roof. My head smacked the corner of the desk as I jumped. The thump gave me a hell of a case of vertigo. Even through the double vision, I could see that the office had been completely engulfed in flames.

I crouched and hid beneath the desk. Low and fuckin' behold, there it was.

"A lot of good being brave did, you dummy."

I held the box and prayed and coughed and gagged, but mostly I prayed.

"God, we've been here before. A little help, please?"

I apologized for my idiocy and thought about how many times I'd created disasters just like this one. How many apologies could I make? How many chances would I get? Once again, it was God or bust.

Finally, the sprinkler system tripped and the flames died in the rain. I'd totally forgotten that Summer had it installed after my last incident. By the grace of God, and, undoubtedly, the pleading of Autumn on my behalf, I'd live to see another day.

The sound of Summer's voice cut through the alarm and the sprinkler and the reverberations in my head. How the hell was I going to explain this? At least she wasn't hurt. Cringing, I peered over the desk. Her glare said it all. Her mouth didn't even need to move.

"You are a burned out slob who's bloody and useless."

Still stoned, I muttered, "It was an exercise in expanded awareness."

"Setting your office on fire?"

"Pretty progressive, right?"

"No, pretty much bullshit. There is a real scientist in you somewhere, isn't there?"

Christ, she was like my mother, always the hard nose science, never open to new possibilities. If I said anything back to her, I'd better have the math to back it up.

"Just because I've introduced a metaphysical theory into my research doesn't make me any less of a scientist than you."

"But anything metaphysical is still just a philosophy until you prove it. You fell asleep with a lit joint again. Just admit it."

"But why was I smoking it in the first place? I can't create a new chemistry without altering my perceived reality."

"You're reaching, Sonny. How you ever got this theory of yours published is beyond me. Anyway, I figured you'd be looking for this?"

She stood in the doorway wearing rain boots and a poncho, dangling my journal in a freezer bag.

"Can't you call me Dad?"

"When you start acting like one, you can reclaim the title."

The indictment stung, but she'd forgive me - again. I took her hand and dodged puddles where I could. We were headed straight to the lab.

"Thanks to your little experiment, we have over a hundred plants that are now waterlogged and need to be repotted," she said.

Shit. I sensed her aggravation, knowing how hard she'd worked to keep the place running. I half wondered why she hadn't ripped me up one side and down the other. I certainly deserved it, and was it Natalie and not Summer with me now, I'd still be in the office, my ears bleeding from a thousand-decibel tongue-lashing.

"You have a lot of work to do. Better get cracking."

Summer squeezed my shoulder and cracked a half smile before walking away.

I reached into my back pocket and retrieved my cigarette case. I stroked the joint between my thumb and first two fingers like I'd done a thousand times. It was more habit than ritual. The smoke filled my lungs, and I relaxed. It was the only way I could. It'd been one hell of a morning and now was certainly no time to be sober. I needed to forget my idiocy, fear and embarrassment as quickly as humanly possible and a little pinch of Summer's home-grown was just what this doctor ordered.

We grew it for science and to pay the bills, but I smoked it to maintain my sanity. It was more potent than anything commercially available, even the designer Kush, Diesel, and Afghani crap. Our THC content was the stuff of folklore, but my neural receptors had grown accustomed to the potency, and I always needed more. I had to hustle if I planned on maintaining my lavish cannabis lifestyle.

It took me all afternoon, but I did it. Every single marijuana plant we owned had been repotted. New dry soil and a sprinkle of fresh water meant that our research and my consumption could continue. My hands and knees ached, the combination of age and stubbornness. Summer tried to convince me on dozens of occasions to make the change to hydroponics, but being an old school organic guy, I refused. I was now regretting that decision.

Completely exhausted and sore, I collapsed on the couch in the lab and lit up again, satisfying the hypothalamus and reward path of my brain.

"Calgon, take me away," I said as I inhaled the sweet sticky goodness.

I opened the box and leafed through the photos I'd saved, imagining Autumn was with me, joking and finding a way to cheer me up in the wake of today's huge disaster. That was my girl, my Autumn.

I laughed at the goofy little face in the photo with her tongue sticking out. It was her seventh birthday and my only job was to carry her cake from the kitchen to the picnic table, twenty feet, if that. Of course, I failed, tripping over my own two feet. Her smashed confectionery tribute covered the floor. She could have screamed and cried and thrown a tantrum. It's what any normal seven-year-old girl would have done, but not Autumn. She skipped over and pressed her hand print in the frosting, adding a beak to the thumb and some legs under the heel. She wrote: 'Daddy' under it, called me a turkey, and dotted my nose with custard and whipped cream. Goddamn, I missed her.

I could taste the wet salt on my lips as the tear worked its way past the corner of my mouth. Whoever said time heals all wounds was full of shit. They had obviously never met Autumn because time only deepens them. I sunk, clutching the photos close to my chest, pretending they could somehow bring her back. I took another drag on my joint and fired up my iPod. My eyes grew heavy. I let my thoughts drift along to the melodies of the *Rasta Mon* himself, Bob Marley.

As I floated further and further toward a deep sleep, riding the tune of "Duppy Conqueror", flashes of my mother penetrated the iron curtain I'd constructed to keep her far within my psyche. I fought to reclaim my Zen, but the weed was strong and my brain was saturated. She slipped through my mental force field and was now floating with me.

"Mother fucker," I mumbled as my final wave of consciousness transformed into an alpha wave. REM sleep was now in control and I was watching her story play itself out once again.

Chapter 2

It was a Friday afternoon in Charlotte, North Carolina when my mother, Regina Lafleur, walked in on her husband, Mark, having sex with his golf pro. The pro, Jack Thompson, was whipping her husband's ass with a rubber golf grip, shouting, "Hit that long ball, baby!"

Mark shouted back, "Tee it up big, Jack."

Regina watched for a minute or two before clearing her throat. When the startled pair turned to face her, she squinted at her husband, grabbed the bottle of Chanel #5 on the dresser, and fell back into her all-star fast pitch form. She'd led the Lady Rangers to a state softball championship five years earlier, and it was just like riding a bike. The perfume rocketed toward Mark at 80 miles per hour. Even if he wanted to duck, he couldn't.

She looked at her husband lying there bloodied and unconscious, reeking of ladies perfume and man sex, and shook her head in disgust. She thought the bastard might be cheating on her since they hadn't had slept together in months, but she never expected this. What woman in her right mind would? She politely escorted Jack, the pro, out of her house, then packed her things and left for good.

Five months pregnant and alone, Regina was desperate. Left with no alternative, she called the one person in the world she never thought she'd see again— her sister.

My grandparents disowned my Aunt Rosie after she confessed her romantic preference for the fairer sex. She bolted when Regina was a freshman in high school and sought refuge on a lesbian hippie commune in New Mexico. Rosie didn't attend Regina's graduation, fearing confrontation with their folks. Regina was heartbroken, having idolized her older sister for the better part of her life. The fact that Rosie couldn't come back to share in her rite of passage left Regina feeling abandoned and unloved. Newly graduated and off to college, she was miserable and lonely. With Rosie a half a country away, Regina needed to feel special. Mark seemed like an acceptable outlet.

She thought it was ironic that, after all those years playing softball and refusing the advances of many of her teammates, it would be her husband that finally drove her to seek solace with a group of lesbians.

Regina had been wooed by men, and then abandoned no less than 3 times in that last year of their marriage. Robert Denk, the brilliant mathematician and dean of the department, had called her a prodigy, a great thinker wrapped in a beautiful shell. Winston Garfield, the chemistry professor, said Regina had been the finest pupil he'd taught in some years, and William Baxter, the physics professor, had wanted to test the principal of friction and Newton's third law in a physical way with her. How was she to refuse?

They were brilliant and paid attention to her, more than she could say for her parents, her sister, and her husband. Of course, after a few weeks, they'd all managed to find some fault with her, leaving her feeling crappier and lonelier than ever. She actually had no idea which one of them was the father of her unborn child and didn't care to find out. She just knew it wasn't Mark.

It was a teary reunion, and Rosie welcomed Regina with open arms, as did the other two-dozen or so members of the *Shady Lady Outer Space Experience* community. They didn't live far from Roswell and decided that, since being gay wasn't mainstream, it meant they must be alien. Rosie begged for Regina's forgiveness, and with the last bit of love in her aching heart, Regina offered it.

Fully disgusted with men and unwilling to raise a child around them, Regina embraced the community and even discarded her last name. She was now Regina Flowers, structural engineer to the *S.L.O.S.E.* She was beginning to experience a new sense of belonging and acceptance like she'd never known. She'd say that it was no wonder Rosie never wanted to come home. It was such a magical place.

The full ride to UNC had proven valuable. Regina was able to engineer an irrigation system for their crops in the arid conditions and create a geothermal heating/cooling system for all the residents. That's why, after she'd given birth to a baby boy, she was unanimously voted in as a permanent resident and allowed to raise her male child as part of the community. She named me Sunshine Flowers.

I'd grown up like any other kid, or so I thought. I went to school and did my chores just like my buddies. The aunts were always there to help, but I was usually pretty helpless. Blessed with gifted intelligence, I was the typical nerd, which meant I'd gotten my ass kicked plenty. I'd come home from school, bloodied and bruised, but was mostly told by my clan to toughen up— Regina led the charge on that front. It wasn't like most might think growing up in a lesbian commune. Those ladies were as tough, if not tougher, than the dads I'd known.

What nurturing I did receive came from my two favorite aunts, Summer Day and Autumn Night. The star-crossed lovers originally hailed from California and had tried to start a commune there, only to discover most Californians were much too flaky to make the commitment necessary to run a village. Summer and Autumn hitched to New Mexico and met Aunty Ann, the Mother ship of the *S.L.O.C.E.* Between the three of them, they plotted and hatched the plans. They recruited and welcomed other lesbians they deemed responsible enough to contribute to the community.

They called me their indigo child of light and filled my head with images of space, energy, matter, and the powerful forces of love and positivity. They were the ones who bandaged me up and kissed my forehead. They sang, danced, and dreamed with me. It was them, in fact, who had given me my first mind altering hallucinogenic experience.

Natalie loathed them for teaching me to turn on, tune in, and drop out.   She didn't understand. It was never about running away and escaping real life. It was always about opening up to a higher consciousness – tapping into the inner life force and expanding reality. It was this concept that led me to pursue a career in bio-science. I needed to understand the human mind at a much deeper level than they even realized. They'd opened a Pandora's Box in me and I will forever be grateful to them for it. I loved those wonderful, beautiful, hippie ladies more than the rest. That's why I named our twin girls after them. Nat bitched of course. She always bitched, but I'd been annoyingly persistent enough that she finally caved.

If my aunts were my heaven, Regina was my hell. I tried, but never really bonded with her the way other sons bond with their mothers, and it bothered the shit out of me. I did everything to try and win her affection. She was a scientist, so I tried to wow her with my experiments. She told me to give it up and play sports like other boys my age. I'd pick flowers for her, but she'd just complain that they bothered her allergies. I pretended to have nightmares just to have an excuse to crawl into her bed and lay next to her. She bought me a nightlight and instructed me to sleep with Aunt Autumn if I was too scared. She never once gave me a hug, told me she was proud of me, or defended me in an argument. The only good thing she ever did for me was teach me how to swear. The bitch didn't know how to fight but she knew how to curse, an art she'd been taught by her grandmother. She said that a well-placed swear was as damaging as a well-placed punch.

Goddamnit, if she wasn't right. The week after my first lesson, Sheila, the girl who'd been bullying me at school, received a machine-gun style assault of filthy, vile, insulting curses, the likes of which her virgin ears had never heard. She'd made the mistake of humiliating me in front of Sally Swenson, my first crush. She pummeled me into the lockers and called me a dyke. I exploded, jabbing at her self-esteem the way Ali jabbed Frazier. Stick and jab, stick and jab.

"Queen Queefer and her merry band of bitches. Too fat to fuck, they cum so haaaard when they punch nerdy little boys half their size. Please don't eat me or sit on me. I might suffocate in your giant, gaping asshole."

She didn't know what hit her. I kept at it.

"Your gnarly gash is so overflowing with yeast, you'd score an 'A' in Home Ec just by walking past the door. Your crabs are even disgusted by your nasty snatch. "

It was harsh for sure, and no nine-year-old should be dishing or receiving that kind of verbal beating, but it was the only weapon in my arsenal. It pained me deeply to unleash such overwhelming negativity, but I couldn't go home black and blue another day. Regina would kill me. So I did what I did and said what I said.

Sheila Pinter cried that day. She cried and screamed that she hated me. Then she ran away. I'd finally won, but at what cost?

Sally Swenson laughed like the other kids, but she was horrified. I could see it in their eyes. What Regina had failed to tell me was that it wasn't the cursing at all. It was the crowd the cursing attracted. As I laid into Sheila with my filth, the other kids ate it up, snickered and even cheered me on. For the rest of middle school, Sheila was known as Queen Queefer, and nobody dared cross me again. The ridicule would be too much.

I never told the aunts about it, but I told Regina. She said she was proud of me, and even though I felt sick to my stomach for having hurt that girl so deeply, I made swearing the thing that bonded my mother and me together. Even now, when I unleash a string of curses in a fit, I feel bad, but the whisper in my ear, telling me she's proud, subconsciously keeps me going. Marcie the shrink says I'm really fucked up.

She was my mom, though. I'd have cursed out every teacher, kid, aunt, and passer-by if she asked me to. I wanted so badly to believe that I wasn't the son she didn't want or was too jaded to love. The aunts told me that I was just a reminder of a bad time in her life. But I was just a kid – her kid. I wanted to be the best part of her life, not the worst. Then she fell in love with Neptune Blue, a girl seven years her junior, who appeared out of nowhere one eerie afternoon in May.

It rained that day. It never rains in the desert.

From then on, Regina spent most of her time bickering with the art major from Berkeley about the merits of math and science over arts and music.

As always, I fiercely defended my mother.

Neptune would just say, "What do you know? You're just a stupid little kid."

I wanted to tell her that I had an IQ of 164, and that she could go suck a big bag of dicks, but it wouldn't have mattered. Regina would have scolded me for insulting her and holding my IQ (which she took full credit for) over her girlfriend. It was like that a lot. Neptune attacked, I defended, and Regina diffused the situation at my expense.

That's why, on a hot Friday afternoon in July, when Regina and Neptune left the commune, I had my first panic attack. I had a budding scientific career ahead of me, and I unleashed a mouth full of profanity, but that didn't make being abandoned feel any better. I wanted her to be my mom. I wanted to know that I mattered in her eyes. Even though the aunts were there for me, each time I'd realize that I didn't mean shit to my own mother, I'd start hyperventilating. The attacks persisted and still occur. I never saw the bitch again.

The girls would ask about their grandmother from time to time growing up. I couldn't say much without panicking. Autumn would always stop me. She'd hold my hand and cry for me.

But all Summer would say was, "Toughen up."

I smiled as I thought about my girls in that dream; Autumn, like the aunts, and Summer, like my mom, the commune, my work, and my life. The images all floated by, one after another, like a slide show set to "No Woman No Cry". It was my life and I loved it because, even with all the crap my mom had put me

through, I had my girls. I had a reason to live and be happy -
until that Friday afternoon in Jamaica when I got the call that
Autumn was gone.

Now I only hear Natalie's voice in my head, telling me over
and over that my baby is dead. My dream had become a fucking
nightmare. The nightmare was real, though, and it haunted every
moment of my existence. The weed numbed the pain and let me
tolerate the next inevitable horrible minute. I wanted to wake so
badly, to see my Autumn, to hug her and tell her what an awful
nightmare I'd had. She would hold my hand and cry with me.
Then I hear the chorus:

Little darling don't shed no tears
No, woman, no cry
Hey little sister, don't shed no tears,
No, woman, no cry.

I felt the cold water on my face and my stoned mind told me
they were icy tears. "You're not serious?" Summer exclaimed.

Back to reality, I thought, wringing the chilly wake-up call
from my goatee. As a former state swimming champ, I was used
to the water, and even bragged to my buddies that at age forty-
something, I still clocked fifty laps a week. But the fire sprinkler
and a glass of ice water to the head was a far cry from the pool.
The air held the familiar scent of charred clothing. I glanced
down and watched the water form a puddle around the freshly
extinguished sweater, another monument to my carelessness.

Somebody lock me up, I thought. I'm going to burn the
place to the fucking ground before this day ends.

"Twice in one day?" Summer yelled, more frustrated than angry.

I nodded remorsefully, disgusted with myself once again.

"I remember when I used to smoke this stuff for fun," I said, trying to light the soggy butt.

"I miss her, too, but you can't keep setting things on fire."

My surviving daughter sat next to me and tucked her head into my shoulder.

Pot was the vice. It's what I needed to keep going. It helped me not care. It made life fuzzier, more tolerable. It went against everything the aunts taught me about enlightenment and higher consciousness, but I didn't care. I was now just another stoner trying to stay numb.

"Here. Use this from now on. It's fairly fireproof."

Summer handed me a small glass pipe. I recognized it instantly. It was a gift I'd given the girls for their college graduation. It'd been custom designed just for them: a cheery blossom branch wrapped around the stem.

After they were born, I had the girls' baby footprints tattooed on my back, a cherry blossom tree wound around them. I told them the cherry blossom was beautiful, yet fleeting, just like each stage of their lives. It was my reminder to never take them for granted. I remember it as one of the greatest pains of my life, and I question whether or not I lived up to my promise. I handed the pipe back to Summer.

"You keep it. I get the hint."

Summer tucked it back into her purse and then remembered her original reason for coming down.

"Mike called."

I looked at my watch and tapped the crystal, wondering if it still even worked. It was a shitty Timex I'd gotten as a gift from the *American Journal of Science* for an award- winning article I'd written for them on the positive effects of epilepsy drugs in treating bipolar disorder. The journal made a heap of cash in sales and gave me a fucking Timex. To hell with it, I thought, and pitched the waterlogged timepiece right in the trash.

"What day is it?" I asked as I dried my face and tied my ponytail back into its proper form.

"The 13th of February," Summer replied. "Friday."

Chapter 3

I knew exactly how Mike would be killing time while he awaited my arrival: flipping through the pages of the current issue of *Scientific Mind*, cursing the journal for his lack of mentions, while Candy, or Jade, or Christi with an 'i', would be massaging his shoulders and fellating him under his desk through his tailored Armani trousers.

Mike was tops in his field, having just won an award for a breakthrough in bipolar rapid cycling treatment, much of which was taken from my research. He was highly regarded as one of the best clinical psychiatrists in all of Ohio, probably the entire Midwest. As long as he kept the hospital in grant money, the fact that he was a narcissistic adrenalin junkie didn't matter much to his colleagues. The son of a bitch was as much a car salesman as he was a scientist, and I envied him a little. He was one of the cool kids, one of the guys I'd always wanted to be. While I'd been dealt brains in spades, I'd been left short-suited in the confidence department.

My last visit had been a month earlier. When I kicked through his door, he was the big blind in a five-hundred-dollar online poker tournament and had just flopped the set, making his pocket kings a sure winner. My hands were full. I'd forgotten that I'd been wearing my steel-toed boots. The kick made a hell of a racket and startled his 'visitors'.

"Sonny, about damn time," he barked as I made my grand entrance.

Candy, September's flavor of the month, must have thought me some crazed killer hippie. Who could blame her? I'd be nervous, too. I'm six-feet, three inches of lanky freak. With my hair loose I look like a young Gandalf from *Lord of the Rings*, which is why I like to keep it tied back. Damn Hollywood. I mumble because I'm usually high, and my fashions are scoffed at by even the most bedraggled of Cleveland's homeless. Mike knew me, so he was used to what I call my eccentricity. Candy didn't, so she squeezed the shit out of his right trapezoid, pinching a nerve that sent a jolt of pain shooting down his arm, forcing him to involuntarily click the left mouse button and fold his hand. At the same time, Tiffany, also startled by my entrance, clamped down on Mike's penis. I didn't need to see it to know it hurt. Karma probably owed him anyway. I just shook my head and watched the scene play out.

"Ahhhh," he screamed, violently thrusting his hips forward, ramming Tiffany's head against the mahogany desk, and rendering her completely unconscious.

"Nice work, Flowers. Do you see what you've done?"

"Me?" I said, still in disbelief that a former student and current colleague of mine could be so audacious.

Mike stood and dabbed the blood from his crotch. Candy fanned her hand in front of Tiffany's face.

"Maybe you should try mouth to mouth?" I quipped, knowing damn well that the unconscious one was breathing just fine.

Their dads must have been goddamn proud of these girls. Hell, I'd watched enough Dr. Phil to guess that the daddy issues were probably what drove them here in the first place. Thank God I was a good father. Yeah, right. But even with my shitty fathering, I had to lend some credit to inherited intelligence. These two were dim, to say the least. Candy raised her eyebrows and looked to me for approval.

What was I supposed to do? I gave her the nod. We stood over her in astonishment as she pressed her lips to her Tiffany's, kissing her wildly.

She stopped to ask, "Am I doing it right?"

"Oh, sure. You're doing great," I said.

"I actually got her for you," Mike whispered.

"Maybe you should have knocked me out?"

I waved Candy off and poured the last of my Fiji water over Tiffany's head. She came to and whacked her head again, but was somehow able to maintain consciousness.

"Pay these girls, and let's get to work," I grumbled.

So, that was Mike Maserati, my research partner and friend. I wasn't exactly renowned for keeping great company, having dealt pot for a good portion of my life. But Mike was a colleague, and one who could actually tolerate me. I still loved the work, and, aside from Summer, there weren't many with whom I could share that love.

On this particular Friday, I walked in and waved to let him know I'd arrived. The girl in his office was turned to the side, but she had brown hair and nice tits, double D's by the look of them. I thought better than to disturb her mid-fellatio, having learned my lesson. If I was ever going to have hope for our young women, I needed to distance myself from any of them associated with Mike.

He caught up with me ten minutes later in the treatment center.

"Feeling more relaxed?' I asked.

"I don't get you, man. You haven't been laid since that broad in Jamaica, right? I thought you could use… well, you know."

I loved the kid, but he had zero sense of the meaning of the word boundaries.

"My sex life is none of your fuckin' business," I barked.

He was wounded by my scolding and pouted. I should have just gone about my business and ignored him, but he looked up to me, for whatever messed up reason. The last thing I wanted was another person in my life who actually gave a shit about me to feel alienated.

"First off, she wasn't some broad. I fell in love with her. Secondly, do you really think getting me a hooker named Candy, who thinks mouth to mouth is French kissing, is going to make some sort of grand difference in my life?"

He cracked a smile, remembering the scene. Even *he* couldn't defend that kind of stupidity. The Jamaican broad he'd referred to was Mia and, in much the same way I tried to use my mind control to keep thoughts of Regina at bay, I did so with Mia.

On the surface, I was annoyed with Mike for having injected himself into my love life, but underneath, it was because he'd opened a wound I thought I'd done a decent job of closing. I did love her. I *do* love her. She's married, though, and lives in Jamaica, fifteen hundred miles from Ohio. She was also the one with whom I'd been merrily banging when the call came in about Autumn. My world crashed in on me that day. After that, there wasn't any room in my heart for Mia or anyone else.

"She's not a hooker. She's a call-girl. Please, give me *some* credit," Mike said.

I shook my head. "You're a good friend, Mike, but when will you grow up?"

"When will I grow up? You should talk."

I gave him a glare. It sent the message.

"What?" he said, acting surprised that the topic wasn't up for discussion. The pushy little bastard pressed on. "You've lost your daughter, your wife has left you, your other daughter is about to leave you, and your work sucks – probably because you can't spend five minutes without getting high."

"What do you mean Summer is about to leave me?"

He waffled, and I shot him another glare. It worked again. He buckled and told me about the fellowship she'd been offered.

"Why she didn't tell me?" I asked aloud.

Mike shrugged. Summer was the reliable one. She didn't typically keep stuff from me, so my feathers had been duly ruffled. Yeah, I'd set some stuff on fire, and I could see that being enough to send her packing. But, from the sound of it, the fellowship was something that had long preceded my unintended attempt at arson.

I wasn't naive. Her leaving was going to happen at some point. I was just hoping the business would keep her around. Sure, I'd treated her differently than Autumn; but I'd never admit it to anyone, at least not out loud. She was so much like Regina, and, if that wasn't bad enough, she was Autumn's twin. God has one fucked up sense of humor. She loved me more than anything, but just happened to remind me of the two most painful parts of my life.

Mike changed the subject by bringing me up to speed on the progress he'd been making with Jane, our bipolar test patient. I was uneasy, though. Something about Summer leaving just wasn't sitting well.

"Is she ready?" I asked, somewhat impatiently

"She's ready, Sonny. Work your magic."

I studied Jane's chart. The diagnosis box read, *Adult onset bipolar disorder with schizophrenic tendencies.* Jane's diagnosis was a difficult one to manage. While Autumn was bipolar, she didn't have the crippling paranoia Jane exhibited as the result of her schizophrenic tendencies. As a child, Jane had been an exemplary student and had been offered a full ride to Ohio State in engineering. Shortly after graduating, she began to deteriorate mentally, accusing her family and friends of hacking her computer and stealing the plans she'd designed to hack into the CIA database to expose the covert crimes committed by the agency against American citizens. After a full investigation, the files she'd created were deemed nonsense, and Jane was remanded to the first of several institutions.

Mike, a friend of her father, suggested she be sent to our clinic to undergo experimental treatment using a cocktail of high dose THC and antidepressants as a way to stem some of the paranoia. Her father read my study, called me a quack, and then reluctantly consented. I'd run her through several treatments; she'd shown little in the way of improvement. The treatment was highly suspect among those like Summer - the old-school scientists.

I watched Jane behind a one-way glass window and tried to remain objective, but she reminded me so much of Autumn. I wished I'd known what she'd been like before the disease had gotten hold of her. What could this young, beautiful girl have accomplished in the world? Hopefully, Mike and I would make a breakthrough and give her a chance to still live a normal life.

The concept - my concept - was a good metaphysical theory, one that had been published and embraced by new-age scientists, and demonized by traditional scientists like Summer. My theory is that the brain works like a computer, having both short and long-term data storage and processing power. The operating system is genetics. The programs that run on top of the operating system are life experiences. I believe that all of the chemistry – the type and quantities of neurotransmitters (chemicals) emitted - is set by the genetic operating system and the life experience programs.

When we experience trauma, or have a genetic imbalance that alters the chemistry of our brain, these are bugs or viruses in the brain software. Unlike a computer, we don't have defragmenters or anti-virus programs. Computers speak binary. The brain speaks chemistry and electricity. It also has built-in safety mechanisms to protect us. Patients who experience trauma often repress the memory as a survival technique. Patients who have genetic imbalances will often cease to store processed information in long-term memory.

I believe that in order to clean and reprogram the brain, we have to convince it that the traumatic experience either never existed, or was inconsequential in the patient's life. Sounds easy, right? It's not. The problem is that, because of the brain's survival ability, it has to *experience* a new event. It can't just see or hear it. It will know it is being tricked. We use highly concentrated THC to send a patient into a new reality where we manipulate the limbic system. If we convince the brain the experience in the altered reality is authentic, our hope is that the chemical memory will be stored and used in the normal reality, thereby altering the patient's personality in the real world, hopefully for the better.

The problem is that while THC and pot can alter the senses, the experiences aren't stored in short-term memory. That's why

Summer and I have been working with hybrid strains and high-dose THC. Our hope is that the higher concentration chemical will remain attached to the neuron long enough for the memory to be stored. Summer, the botanist, is the pot girl, I'm the brain guy, and Mike is the cognitive expert who creates the new experiences.

After the theory was published, Summer said, "Well it's creative, I'll give you that. When you flop, maybe you can write a book about it just like the mosquito DNA in *Jurassic Park*."

Summer – my partner, my keeper, and my daughter. Could she really be leaving me? I thought about my mom again, about Natalie and Autumn, and now Summer. I felt the old familiar quickening of my pulse and knew that a panic attack was on its way. I reached for a joint. I patted every pocket a dozen times, my pulse racing each time I discovered one empty. I remembered the breathing exercises Summer taught me. I closed my eyes and took several long, slow deep breaths. I could feel my heart begin to settle, but the anxiety, the impossibly nervous energy, persisted. I needed to hurry up and get back to the car. I must have left the case on the passenger seat.

I gave Mike the thumbs up and watched as he instructed the orderly, Charlie Casper, to enter the room. Charlie's job was to antagonize Jane and get her to the point of physical violence or, at the very least, a state of complete loss of emotional control. We needed her brain chemicals, or juices, flowing before inducing the TCH delusion. Charlie was the best. Jane hated him. She called him the black devil because he was the one who administered her meds. He was a real pro, though, and had handled the best of them.

Mike had shared with me that earlier that day Charlie had received a lap dance from one of the female patients. She was a sixty-three-year-old schizophrenic. One of her six personalities was Ginger, an exotic dancer transplanted to Ohio from Florida. The young orderly could have been repulsed, refused her advances, or laughed her off, but good ol' Charlie simply indulged her persona and slipped a crisp one dollar bill under her bra strap. Ginger used the dollar to buy a soda from the vending machine. She then shook it, opened it, and sprayed it all over Charlie, calling him a pervert and demanding he be terminated. He had asked for a raise.

Jane had obviously heard the story and taunted Charlie as he entered. She bent over, grabbed her ankles and shook her ass. I tried not to laugh but it was funny as hell. Poor Charlie. I felt like I was in some sort of loony bin peep show.

"Where's my dollar, Charlie, you asshole?" Jane asked in her most sultry tone.

The level five trigger Charlie used was that three CIA agents were outside waiting for her. He told her that they'd be moving her to Virginia to conduct experiments.

Jane went ballistic. She burst into tears, fell to the ground, curled her head in her arm and sobbed, cursing the cruel orderly. I slipped in past Charlie and whispered a word of thanks as he exited. He gave me a look that let me know he hadn't been happy with the assignment, but was glad to do his part if it meant helping Jane.

The twenty-five-year-old patient clung to me like a terrified child. I held her tight, trying to remember that her fear was real and that, in her mind, Charlie was the enemy.

"Please don't let them take me, Sonny."

I shushed her softly and assured her that I'd keep her safe. It was a skill, and as the father of twin girls, one in which I'd been quite accomplished.

"Here you go, sweetie, smoke a little of this. It might make you feel better."

Jane took the joint and puffed on it a couple times. Within a minute she transformed. She was as stoned as any human had ever been, maybe even more so. I guided her to the couch and told her to close her eyes. Mike took over and walked her through a gentle hypnosis regimen to get her to relax. Then he dove into what he'd created as a proprietary treatment for our patient study. It was quite impressive and I prayed it would work.

As he spoke, she wore a soft smile and her eyes held a serenity I hadn't yet experienced in our treatments together. She looked like Autumn. Mike finished and played an audio recording that would last three more hours.

"How did she respond when you questioned her?"

Mike looked bummed. "She doesn't seem to be accepting new reality."

I was disappointed again. We were getting a deep response, but we were still unable to embed into her short-term memory. If only Mia were here, I thought. She'd embraced my theory and, as a well-respected bio-scientist, thought to introduce an orchid resin to the THC base to extend the bonding time. She hypothesized that the while the THC was potent enough, it wasn't bonding to the neuro-receptor long enough to induce a memory or experience.

"What else did she say?" I asked

"She wanted chocolate chip cookies."

"Note the munchies."

I scratched my head, wondering what Summer might suggest as a direction for the next treatment. She'd probably just tell me to scrap it all. The anxiety I'd experienced in the observation room still hadn't subsided and was now getting worse. I wasn't sharp. Mike was right. My work wasn't what it once was. I needed Summer.

"Mike, go ahead and get her back on her normal dose of lithium, and I'll tell Summer to raise the THC dosage a bit to see if we can't mimic agonists for CB1 receptors in the hippocampus area to reduce the short-term memory loss."

"Will do, Sonny. Somebody's here to see you."

I hoped it was Summer. I wasn't at all confident about my recommended therapy, but she would be. While I'd never told her directly, she was, without a doubt, more intellectually gifted than I'd ever been – even sober. She inherited my brains, but she also got Natalie and my mother's strong will. Her ambition was admirable, but her aggressive tendencies needed work. Patience was not a virtue in which she placed an ounce of value.

I packed my bag and felt a bit of relief knowing that I would soon be back to the car and my vice. Then, home to straighten things out with Summer over dinner. A heart-to-heart with her had been long overdue. She'd try to brush me off, but I needed to be persistent if I was going to get her to stick around.

Chapter 4

"Hello, handsome," the sultry voice whispered in the darkness.

It was Friday the 13th. I'd expected something, but I wasn't expecting this. Her voice was unmistakable, the one that pulled me from Autumn when she needed me most.

"I'm not interested," I snapped.

My heart was really racing now. I hurried my pace, hoping to make it to the car before a full on attack ensued. She kept pace. She was on a mission.

"You don't even know what I'm going to ask."

I knew exactly what she was going to ask, and my answer was a firm no. I only prayed that, this time around, the choice would be mine to make. I had been promised a reprieve for cooperating last time, yet here she was. They weren't going to blackmail me again. I pulled out my hand held recorder and spoke into it, all I could think to keep myself composed. My voice cracked. I sensed her close behind. Her footsteps echoed in my ears like clanging cymbals.

"Jane exhibited rapid cycling once again, the depressive mode being the dominant phase. Reduce delta 9 THC to .05 MG and increase pollinate .02 MG. Next time, use dye marker and MRI after inhalation to isolate cannabinoid receptors affected. Note any activity in the limbic path…"

She double-stepped and caught up.

"Sonny, wait one minute. Please?"

I kept walking, my forehead beaded with sweat and my palms were slick. I struggled to hold on to the recorder. I clicked the pause button as I made my way out the exit.

"I served my time. I participated in your trial and made my contribution. I was misled, and my research was abused. Now, if you'll excuse me, I have a call-girl waiting on me."

Why did I say it? She had a thing for me. Was my inner six-year-old trying to hurt her? I didn't hate her for what she did, although Natalie told me I should. I just didn't want anything to do with her, or the government, ever again.

"Sonny Flowers, stop. That's a direct order."

"Major," I said, "you forget, I'm not one of your foot soldiers."

I heaved the steel door open and inhaled the crisp fall air eagerly, thankful to have made it out of the building without hyperventilating. I was halfway across the parking lot when she shouted, "What call-girl?"

"Candy," I yelled back and slammed my door.

I fumbled for my keys, turned the ignition, and depressed the cigarette lighter in the dash. Thankfully, the case was right where I'd left it. The pop of the lighter told me I was only seconds from the relief I needed. Why did Mike have to tell me about Summer's fellowship? I hadn't taken but two drags when I saw her in my side view mirror. Like Mike, she wasn't going to back off. I rolled down my window and watched the plume of smoke billow out of the cabin of my Prius to greet her. She coughed and waved her hand in front of her face, annoyed at my immaturity. Her aggravation brought me satisfaction.

"Sonny, please. It's Mia. She's been exposed."

I looked at her for the first time and tried desperately to think of something harsh enough to send her away.

"Not my problem," was all I could muster. The weed was doing its job, but I wasn't as quick-witted as I'd hoped. Better than a panic attack, I told myself.

"You don't mean that, Sonny. You're the only one who can help us. Hodges has made a mess. We need you— Mia needs you."

I sensed the urgency and passion in her voice. Deep down, she was concerned, but not about Mia. Mia was the bait, tempting as hell, but I refused.

"Hodges is an asshole and a shitty scientist to boot. Sorry to say it, but Mia is probably fucked. Call Rhonda Callahan. She might be able to help."

I felt a pang of remorse. Even if I could help, I had other priorities, with Summer at the top of the list. I looked in the rearview as I drove away. She was defeated, and I felt good. Well, my inner six-year-old felt good anyway. She no longer held any power over me. The realization felt invigorating. I couldn't wait to get home and reclaim my daughter. I was going to be the dad she wanted and deserved.

Chapter 5

Summer Flowers collected the photos from the couch in the lab, the ones Sonny was leafing through when she woke him. It had been months since Autumn's death, but Summer still sensed her twin everywhere. They had been born only moments apart and, while a few ticks of the secondhand separated their bodies, they were still attached at the soul. Summer remembered feeling Autumn's pain toward the end, and knew Autumn had felt hers. Summer dismissed it and focused on her work, pretending that the pain Autumn was feeling wasn't real, that it was just a mood swing, or a case of the blues. But she knew better. The guilt of it hung over her daily like a storm cloud. She tried to convince herself otherwise, but knew in her heart the dark truth - she wanted Autumn gone.

Summer couldn't compete with her sister. Autumn had been sprung from the stars and Summer the earth. Her father had compared Autumn to his beloved aunts, and she to the mother who'd abandoned him. Her heart sank, knowing that, by letting Autumn continue down her clouded path, she'd only confirmed her father's assertion. The worst of it was that, with Autumn gone, Sonny was supposed to find solace in her, the surviving daughter. He hadn't. Instead, he crawled into a shell and closed himself off.

Her eyes welled up as she looked at the photo of all of them: Autumn, Sonny, Natalie, and her at Cedar Point. It was one of those nostalgic photos where they all dressed like Cleveland Indians and stood in goofy poses. She shook her head as she studied it, realizing that her gaze was on Sonny. His was on Autumn.

"Story of my life," she mumbled and wondered if he could ever love her even half as much.

She jumped at the sound of the doorbell. Panic set in as she looked at the hundred pot plants in the lab. She flipped the lights, and locked the door, doing her best to compose herself as she walked to the front door. Getting busted was not an option. While she and Sonny were scientists, marijuana, for better or worse, was still illegal in Ohio, even for medicinal purposes. If the Feds had ever raided their farm, she knew that both she and her father would never again see the outside of a jail cell. She slipped the 9mm into her pants and crossed her fingers as she opened the door.

"What the fuck you doing, old man?" she barked at a septuagenarian standing on her stoop. She forced her way out, staring him down and backing him up. He stumbled down the stairs and lost his fez as he grabbed the railing. "Did I tell you it was okay to come to the house, you decrepit old codger?"

The old man stammered and tried to speak. "Mayor Clemens told me…"

"Fuck Mayor Clemens. The rule is that you go to the barn. Do you hear me? Go to the BARN."

The old man sprinted toward the barn on the far end of the property. Summer retrieved the burgundy fez and followed behind. She could see the other three members of the Wellington Elks waiting at the main door, here for their weekly pickup. Her heart raced, half angry and half panicked. *Thank God it was only an Elk*, she thought. Her nightmares about a Fed backing her father into a corner and inducing one of his infamous panic attacks had been a regular occurrence. She knew that, if the nightmare were to ever come true, her father would crack.

"Jack? You tell this jackass to come up to the house?"

"Please, Summer, call me Mr. Mayor in front of the others."

"Fuck you, Jack. Answer the question."

Summer dusted off Sheriff Connley's fez and stared him down before handing it back. The hard ass bitch act had been difficult at first, but after some practice, she found that it actually suited her.

"Apologies, ma'am," the sheriff muttered, placing his fez back atop his crown.

The barn door opened behind her. Summer shuffled ninja-like behind it and jumped the intruder upon his entry. She pressed the barrel of the Glock 9mm hard against his temple.

"And just who the fuck do you think you are?" she whispered hard in his ear.

"Whoa. Whoa. He's with us," Jack Clemens shouted

Summer pushed the ancient bag of bones toward the others, feeling a little guilty as she watched him scramble to retrieve the hearing aid that had fallen to the ground, his hands shaking.

She couldn't show an ounce of fear. *Fear and doubt smell like death,* she told herself. It was a control mechanism, like one she would use in an experiment. She couldn't introduce any variable outside the control, or chaos would ensue and the experiment would fail. This was real life, though, not an experiment, which made the act all that much more important. She furrowed her brow and waited for one of them to make a move. They might be old, but they could still take her if they wanted.

"This is Moe Conrad. He represents Elks in North and South Carolina. We're expanding distribution."

Summer stared at the five of them, guessing their combined age to be somewhere around 360 years old. It wasn't the distribution channel she'd imagined when she and Sonny first started selling pot commercially, but, boy, were they effective. The Wellington Ohio Elks chapter had effectively sealed Wellington as the pot capital of Ohio, very possibly the pot capital of the five surrounding states, averaging sales of over a million a month.

"Not sure we can meet production demands to expand distribution," Summer said, settling down a bit, feeling like she had them under control.

"What if we buy you some more land?" Clemens asked.

"I'd have to hire on a few more deputies to patrol and enforce," Sheriff Connley chimed in.

"No," Summer said, running the figures in her head. "Let's not be greedy. We have a good thing going here."

"Where's your dad?" Tony Jordan piped in.

The seventy-four-year-old banker was her least favorite. It was probably his idea to expand in the first place.

"You boys know who runs things around here? Don't make me pop a cap in your knee to remind you, Tony."

She cringed at the thought of actually hurting one of them. Summer was tough, but had never been violent. It was one of the commonalities she had shared with Autumn.

The others stared at Tony furiously, letting him know that another word from him meant pissing off their supplier even more. Summer used to kiss their asses when she and Sonny first started, posing as the sweet daughter of the man in charge. That lasted until the operation began pulling in a quarter million a month. The old pervs had hit hard on her, barking orders, and sometimes even smacking her ass, but once they hit 200k, she knew that she had them by the balls. If they even looked at her wrong, she shorted their supply by half. They had all become accustomed to living lavishly in a short time. She had to maintain a firm hand. Her dad could never play this role, but it was necessary, and one that complimented the inherited Regina Flowers aspect of her personality.

"We're short this week, boys," she snapped.

"Aw, Tony. You had to say something, didn't you?" Connley barked.

Summer smirked. "Next time you want to expand, come see me first before you bring any new old blood around."

They all nodded.

"So, do I need to kill this guy?" she asked, amused as she watched him fumble with his hearing aid again, guessing that he wanted to make sure he had heard her correctly.

Summer walked over to Moe, slid the barrel of the gun up his leg, over his stomach, and then buried the tip deep in his sternum. She watched the blood drain from his face and wondered if he soiled himself. She loved manhandling the old crooked shysters even if she knew she'd never be able to pull a trigger.

"Just fucking with you, old timer," she said and gave him a peck on the cheek.

The Elks all breathed a collective sigh of relief as Summer handed them the two loaded duffel bags.

"The barn next time, eh, Sheriff?" she said as she walked out.

She watched her father pull up the drive as the Elks loaded their Cadillac. The sheriff and the banker stood guard as the mayor and postmaster stuffed the bags in the trunk. Moe sat in the passenger seat, still trembling after his encounter with the younger Flowers.

Sonny parked and started toward the house on foot. Summer could sense his anxiety and knew that he was trying his best to avoid having to talk to them. Nothing was more certain to send him into a panic attack than a visit from Regina's father.

"Hey, what's the big idea? You don't even stop to say hello?" Mayor Clemens barked.

Summer hurried her pace, trying to intercept the old bulldogs and usher them along. She knew that her father was fragile, and it bothered her to see him bullied by men that they had made wealthy.

"Hi, Gramps," she heard him say.

"Sonny, you need to get a handle on that daughter of yours. She shorted us again this week on purpose, and, on top of that, she showed me no respect in front of my peers."

Sonny just stood and nodded. She guessed he was too high to give a shit.

"Hell, if it weren't for me, you would probably be in a New Mexico jail. All those years I raised you by myself. After that no good daughter of mine ran out on you, and this is the thanks I get?"

Summer made the last few steps and stood next to her father, wondering what his response might be, guessing that she would have to intercede and play the bitch as always. It was a rarity that Sonny ever stood his ground, especially anyone that reminded him of his mom.

"Summer tells me you guys broke the million dollar mark last month. I'd say that's gratitude enough, wouldn't you?"

Jack huffed and puffed as his Elk buddies sneered. "I guess I should expect as much. How can you keep your daughter in line when you can't even take care of yourself? Look at you. You're a mess."

"Hit the road, Jack, unless you want me to short you next week, too?" Summer said, motioning for them to move along.

Try as he might, he no longer held any power over them. She knew that it ate the old goat up, but in the end, the money spoke louder than his need to control them.

"Was Jack busting your chops, telling you what a bitch I am?" Summer asked as she watched the Caddy drive off.

"You know Jack, always bitching about something."

"Well, thanks for sticking up for me."

She could tell that her father wasn't sure if she was being sincere or sarcastic. She cringed a little, knowing that her tone was sarcastic. It was a bad habit – a defense mechanism. She was happy, though. He stuck up for her, something he rarely did.

"Stop shorting those guys, eh? We have plenty," Sonny said.

Summer huffed. "How about you decide how much to give them when you actually start giving a shit about the business?"

She was still in bitch mode and felt bad, but there was truth in her statement. She wanted to soften it up, but when her mouth opened to say something reassuring, she couldn't stop herself.

"Who do you think pays the bills, grows the weed, and manages the house around here?" she barked. "Which, by the way, you set on fire today. Don't think I forgot."

What little light had appeared behind his eyes had now been extinguished. She made her point and had maintained her position as alpha female again, but at the price of their bond. She could have been sweet to him. She could have been positive, but for whatever reason, she couldn't bring herself to do it. It was easier to be angry. She felt a pinch in her gut. It would have taken a tiny effort to apologize, and doing so would have made a huge difference, but the Hum-V making its way up the drive, with its lights blaring, killed that possibility.

"Now just who the fuck is this?"

Sonny scolded her.

"Do you have to curse like that all the time? You're supposed to be a lady. And don't you even think about whipping out that gun."

Summer furrowed her brow. "I'll damn well use it if I have to," she said, but inside, it felt nice to hear him take charge for a change. "Besides, I learned all my best profanity from you." She thought it a nice compliment.

A woman stepped out of the vehicle and approached them. She was pretty, Summer thought, in an unassuming sort of way. She wore Army fatigues and donned a beret over, what Summer guessed, was longer hair pulled up in a bun. Her cheekbones were high and her eyebrows were well-manicured, as were her fingernails. Her uniform hid her curves, but Summer could tell that the woman was tall and lean, probably well-muscled. She marched more than she walked, but Summer guessed she was probably quite graceful in heels.

"Listen to me, Sonny. This isn't a game. We need you back in Jamaica ASAP." Her voice was feminine and soft, but her tone was stern, likely the result of having to learn how to issue orders to men who would sooner hit on her than follow her into battle.

Summer pulled out the 9mm pistol, without hesitation, a direct violation of her father's request. She wasn't sure whether she had done it to get a rise out of Sonny, or whether it was just a force of habit; the byproduct of trying to protect their illegal operation.

"Back off, bitch," Summer shouted.

Christine paused, looking more irritated than scared, and in two moves had Summer disarmed and on her back. The major pressed her boot into Summer's neck and twisted her wrist. Summer groaned. The incapacitated girl looked at her dad and made a silent plea for help.

He shook his head and said, "Don't say I didn't warn you."

"You must be Summer?" Christine asked in a cordial tone.

Summer managed to choke out a "yes" before being released from the hold.

The major directed her attention back to Sonny.

"The plane leaves tomorrow morning. Can I count on you to be there?"

"No," her father said.

Summer caught her breath and whispered, "I'll do it. I'll go."

She didn't even know what it was she was agreeing to do, but she knew the government was asking and her dad was saying no. That was all she needed. She had a penance to pay and guilt that she needed to expunge. Whatever this woman wanted probably had to do with the project her dad had been working on when Autumn died. It would be her chance to finish what Sonny had started and maybe mean that Autumn's death wasn't in vain.

"Summer, you're not going anywhere," Sonny snapped.

Major Smith interjected, "You are absolutely welcome to go, Summer. I've followed your work and know that you are as capable as your father. Plane leaves out of Burke Lakefront at seven a.m. sharp."

The major didn't waste any time. She got back in the truck and sped off. Summer, still planted on her ass, looked up at Sonny and said, "I think that went well."

Chapter 6

I slammed the office door and plopped down on my once dry leather captain's chair. Water oozed out of the cushion and dripped on the paper scattered below. I didn't care. I listened to the tap-tap-tap of the droplets against the floor and just let the water soak into my shorts, ever mindful that my ass would soon be chapped. Damn it, Summer, what were you thinking? Jamaica was no place for a sheltered girl like her. She'd be a lamb sent to slaughter.

The day I'd agreed to work for the US government was as clear in my mind as if it were yesterday. Special Agent Jerome Tuley had been kind enough to inform me that the Wellington Sheriff had sold over twenty pounds of marijuana to an undercover agent over a six-month period.

At least the prick had the decency to buy me a cup of coffee.

I'd met a few agents over the years and knew that Feds didn't buy you coffee unless they wanted something. Ol' Jerome could have slapped the cuffs on me at any time, but he didn't. He just sat there, in his cheap blue suit and gaudy golden necktie, sipping his latte trying to pretend that he knew the first thing about me. Tuley smiled and framed his hands across his face.

"The headlines would have read— 'Feds bust Midwest Kingpin.'"

"But they didn't," I said.

"No, they didn't. You're much too valuable to be sitting in a jail cell, Sonny."

There it was. He needed me. The government needed me. I was about to be blackmailed, and there wasn't a goddamn thing I could do about it. I listened as he tried to sell me on my own brilliance. At least he read my paper, although he butchered the basic idea and mispronounced the scientific name for THC, Tetrahydrocannabinol. He was probably a negotiator. Guys like Tuly were trained to talk people off the ledge and convince them to do Uncle Sam's bidding, but all I saw was a half-rate used car salesman.

"What would you say to a bribe? Would a million do it?" I asked.

It was brazen, but I guessed it was a safe question over coffee.

Tuley choked. A million dollars to a guy like him meant early retirement in the Bahamas or at least a nicer suit. He smiled as he wiped the foam from his upper lip. I saw the greed in his eyes and, for a moment, thought I had him.

"Would if I could, Sonny. Problem is that I can't sell it. Too many in the agency know about you."

"What then? How many do I need to pay?"

Tuley broke off a piece of his oatmeal raisin cookie and offered me half. I declined. He shook his head, letting me know that bribes were off the table.

"What do you want, Agent Tuley?"

My high was fading, and my heart was beating crazy. I wouldn't last. I was likely seven minutes away from a doozy of a panic attack.

"We've been working with the military to develop some new chemical agents. Your theory intrigued us. We'd like you to go to Jamaica and work with some of our people to explore other applications."

"You're not really asking," I said.

"Plane leaves in the morning— zero seven hundred hours."

I held the cookie over Tuley's latte and squeezed. As the crumbs filled his glass, I said, "You're one hell of an elegant asshole, Special Agent Tuley."

Tuley stood and dusted himself off. "See you in the morning, Dr. Flowers"

I stared at Autumn's smile in the photo on my desk. She was so happy that day—

the last day I ever saw her. Would today be the last day I'd see Summer? I pulled out the .38 I kept under my desk, wondering if she and the rest of the world wouldn't be better off without me. Twirling the pistol around my finger, I did my best Lone Ranger impression. A single bullet fell from my fingers into the chamber. I spun the cylinder and snapped it into place then pressed the cold steel to my temple. I'm a drug dealer in my forties who's seen better days. My work sucks, and I can't function without weed. Natalie and Autumn are gone. One pull of the trigger meant seeing Autumn again.

But what if I didn't? She was in heaven, wasn't she? Her suicide was the result of a mental disorder. Surely God wouldn't punish her for that? I wasn't sick, though, but often wished I was. I couldn't take the chance. I'd rather suffer through the rest of this life than be separated from Autumn for all eternity.

What the hell? The drywall, like everything else in the office, was drenched. Framed pics and diplomas fell to the floor. All but one landed face down. The lone image that stared up at me was Summer's six-year-old hand prints. Written below them:

My hands right now seem so small,
but I'm growing every day.
Soon you won't remember,
when they were this way.
So someday when you're feeling blue,
tired, angry, or sad,
Just look at these little hands of mine,
and remember I love you, Dad.

I'd seen it ten times a day but hadn't read it in ages.

"What the hell am I doing?" I heard myself say aloud.

With a renewed sense of purpose, I lazily aimed the gun at the far wall, sighting up an Indians' pennant. This was going to be a hard lesson. If the bullet was in the chamber, I'd lose a treasured keepsake and be thankful it wasn't my head. If not, I'd have won this round of Russian roulette. I pulled the trigger and jumped. The bullet whizzed out in a flash, piercing the front of the ninety gallon fish tank positioned three feet below the pennant.

"Fuck me," I shouted as I watched the tank explode.

The torrent of water further soaked the already drenched office. I saved the few fish I could and then decided it was time to get back to Jamaica and face my demons; only, this time, with Summer in tow.

Chapter 7

I thrashed relentlessly. I couldn't sleep. Punching my pillow and angrily tugging the blanket wasn't helping. I hadn't slept soundly since Natalie and I cursed her as I flailed about. I'd bought not one, not two, but three mattresses in six months hoping one of them would give me a decent night's sleep. I thought about throwing this one out the window, but I was too tired and too lazy.

I lit up a joint and started humming a Bob Marley tune, "Redemption Song". Due to my recent penchant for pyromania and fearing the wrath of Summer, I was careful to crush my spliff in an ashtray after a few puffs. I started to drift and was surprised to hear that Bob Marley had been replaced by Dave Matthews. He was a favorite of Autumn's. She'd turned me on to him shortly before my last trip to Jamaica. There had been many days I'd play Floyd, Zeppelin and Marley for her, and she'd play Dave, Big Head Todd, and Lenny Kravitz for me. We loved music, the way it could transport us and lend new insight to problems, people, and places; one of our dozen common bonds, and a pastime I'd enjoyed often with my aunts growing up.

"The music," they told me, "is like riding an airplane to higher consciousness. Without it, we have to walk."

Autumn really dug that concept. I remember her getting really into this tune called "Dancing Nancies". Dave asked the question in the song: *Could I have been anyone other than me? Could I have been your little brother?* It was deep, and I was surely stoned when she played it for me, but now I wonder if she wasn't trying to tell me something, like she wanted to be someone else that day? She sang along with Dave as she flew to that higher plane. I just watched her. She seemed so peaceful. She sang, *Dark clouds may hang on me sometimes, but I'll work it out.* I should have seen it.

How could I have known that she was anything but? I should have sensed her sadness, but I didn't. I can see it in Jane, but I couldn't see it in my little girl – the despair. Summer tried to tell me. Natalie tried to tell me. Everyone tried to tell me, but I was too damn worried about rotting in a jail cell, so I ignored them, just took off, thinking that I was protecting them when really I was only pushing her over the edge. I went to Jamaica to work for the fucking government and fell in love with a married woman.

What I didn't want to believe was that, while I was doing my own thing, Autumn was back in Ohio swallowing a bottle of pain pills. I blamed Jamaica, Mia, and the government, but it never had anything to do with them. Marcie said it didn't even have anything to do with me, but I refused to believe her. I could have done something. Maybe the right word? Maybe a hug or the right song? I should have, at the very least, just been there.

I didn't want to go back there to that place and that work. The ghosts of Jamaica haunted me. The island wind would whisper reminders of my sins and the Caribbean sun would scorch my soul. Why the hell did Summer say she'd go? I feigned ignorance. It was just one more opportunity for her to try and prove herself to me. She had nothing to prove, but she'd never stop trying. It was my fault – all of it. I admitted it as Dave said, *Falling out of a world of lies, could I have been dancing nancy? Could I have been anyone other than me?*

Summer stared at the blades of the fan on the ceiling gently coaxing the warm air across her face. Her thick blonde hair danced in the man-made breeze and her hazel blue eyes drifted out the window like they'd had on so many nights, catching a glimpse of a shooting star once in a while, knowing full well that it wasn't a star at all, rather a meteorite entering Earth's atmosphere. She remembered the first time she told Autumn the truth about shooting stars. Autumn told her she was more than welcome to believe what she liked as long as she respected her right to believe what she wanted. It was a logical request, so Summer succumbed to her twin.

Summer Flowers was a scientist like her father, but she was also a woman. Logic, reason, and the left side of her brain ruled her, but on nights like this, when she felt especially emotional, it comforted her to know that Autumn might be out there staring at the same shooting star. She still spoke to her in the still of the night, as if she were lying right next to her.

"I should just take the fellowship and get out of Dodge, right?"

"Be with Dad. He needed me for a long time and now he needs you, Summer."

She knew the answer had only been in her mind, but it sounded so real. She scanned the room, expecting to see Autumn. The bedroom door crept closed. *It's just the fan*, Summer thought. The door flung open with a jolt.

"Autumn?" she whispered.

The freshly packed suitcase next to the door caught her eye. She let out a resigning sigh and said,

"Message received. You'd better be right about this"

She closed her eyes and whispered, "This is it, Dad. This is your last chance. *"*

Chapter 8

The car service dropped us at the airport at the ungodly hour of six_a.m. I felt half dead while Summer was exactly the opposite. She bounced around, collecting luggage and taking inventory. My eyes struggled to stay open.

"You getting out, Mr. Flowers?" the driver asked.

"Still trying to decide, Randolph."

"Well it looks like your daughter is raring to go. Where you two heading anyway? Africa?"

"I wish," I said laughing.

Summer looked ridiculous, like she was about to set off on safari, so I understood why he'd guessed Africa. She wore khaki shorts, an olive green tank top, heavy wool socks and hiking boots. The outfit was finished by a straw cowboy hat that looked like it was more fashion than function. The Jamaican sun would make quick work of her pale Irish skin.

I shook my head as she affixed the backpack to her shoulders and assembled the dolly. Noting my refection in the car window, I laughed at the stark contrast between us. My wardrobe of choice was a pair of frayed, wrinkled khaki shorts, a tee shirt that read *God doesn't kill people— Chuck Norris kills people*, and some old worn out flip-flops. I donned my trusty pair of five-dollar sunglasses. My long hippie hair was in its normal ponytail. I brushed my goatee in place with my fingers and struggled to recall the last time I'd trimmed it. You're a handsome man, I whispered sarcastically. I was feeling pretty good, aside from the fact that I actually had to ride in an airplane. It was a panic attack in waiting. What was worse was that I had depleted my stash of horse tranquilizers and only had my potent weed on which to rely for comfort. I walked past Summer, who was struggling with two huge cases.

"What is all this?" I asked.

"I figured we'd need some of our own equipment."

"Whatever you say, Doc."

She was nothing, if not prepared. I chucked my sea bag over my shoulder and headed toward the terminal.

Christine was sitting alone, drinking coffee and reading the paper. She looked a hell of a lot more relaxed than I felt, probably relieved to have Summer and me back on the project. She hated Hodges almost as much as I did. He was a real horse's ass. Science and research never mix well with ego. Hodges had ego in spades.

"Simon, help her with those, please," Chris ordered the steward. I wondered if she knew how to sound like a normal human being, or if everything that passed her lips had to sound like a boot camp drill instructor?

"That's the plane?" I asked. I felt sick just looking at it.

"It's a Dessault Falcon 2000, the finest craft in private aviation," Chris answered.

She was giddy, like flying was fun for her or something. It looked like something a 747 would have crapped out after a big breakfast. I wasn't sure, but it looked like Buddy Holly and Ritchie Valens had already been seated and were waving to me through the window, laughing.

"I have to go," I snapped.

My stomach was in knots, and I had to puke. Performing my best Bruce Jenner sprint, I kicked off my flip-flops and raced to the men's room, praying I'd make it before hurling all over the terminal.

"He's terrified of flying," I could hear Summer tell Chris. "Come to think of it, he's terrified of most things."

Had I not been in such a rush, I would have attempted to at least try and defend myself. I made it to the stall just in time. Hunched over the airport toilet, I heaved so hard I thought every internal organ south of my diaphragm would come up. My head dripped with cold sweat. I clutched the cold toilet and pressed my head against the side, wishing I could either die or transport myself back into my cozy bed.

As I wished for death, every flight I'd taken in my life replayed itself in my mind. I had flown exactly five times, and three of those resulted in airborne trauma.

The first was when I was eighteen and flew to Ohio from New Mexico. The landing gear froze, and we had to turn back and make an emergency landing. The next was when I flew from

Cleveland to Orlando. A drunken passenger opened the emergency exit at fifteen thousand feet. The moron was sucked out and plummeted to his death while I, and the other fifty-two people on board, held on for dear life. That incident made national news and stayed in the headlines for two whole days before some boy band broke up and stole the spotlight. The ordeal garnered me three free flights anywhere in the world. *Ironic*, I thought. The last time was the flight back from Jamaica to Ohio. It was a private jet that got caught in a tropical storm. Needless to say, it was a bumpy ride.

After that, I swore never again to set foot on an airplane.

"I hope Summer appreciates this," I mumbled.

I reached down and clutched the Saint Anthony medal Autumn had given me as a Father's Day gift when she was ten. She told me Saint Anthony of Padua was the patron saint of lost things, as well as miracles. She even taught me a little jingle: *The object is lost and can't be found. Dear Saint Anthony, take a look around.*

I'd unfortunately uttered the jingle on more occasions than I cared to remember.

"My courage is lost and can't be found. Dear Saint Anthony, take a look around."

I did my best to recompose myself and dragged my ass back out to the bar. They say the Lord, or in my case, Saint Anthony, works in mysterious ways. I don't know if it was the great saint or misfortune, but, as I made my way to the bar, my blood started to boil, anger overriding my anxiety, as I watched some asshole hit on Chris and my daughter at six in the goddamn morning.

The moron sat with his back to me, laying it on thick with Chris.

"You ever hear of the Mile High Club?" I heard him ask.

Summer cringed, visibly disgusted by his advances. I spun the son of a bitch around and clutched him by the nape of his gaudy Hawaiian shirt.

"The smell gave me a clue, but the ugly fucking shirt sealed it."

"Sonny?"

"I'm sure you have better places to be, eh, Trumpet?" I said

I shoved him hard, hoping he wouldn't take a swing. He was spineless, even more so than me, so I pounded my chest harder and hoped he would back down. He stumbled backward, struggling to catch his balance. I could see in his eyes that he wanted to save face, but would he take a swing? He looked at Summer and then back at me. He made the connection and probably thought Chris was my wife. I didn't care.

"I— I'm so sorry."

I had him, so I puffed my chest a little more and made a move. As I did, I felt a twinge of pity for him. He looked terrible. The drugs had definitely aged him. He was a coke man, though, and that shit will age you in a hurry. The guy reminded me of Larry from *Three's Company*, a slimy self-proclaimed ladies' man who wore one too many gold chains and smelled as if he'd bathed in bad cologne.

"Well, I should be going. I have to get ready for a flight. Nice seeing you, Sonny."

With that, Joey Trumpet scurried away, his tail properly affixed between his legs.

"Wow. Where did that come from, Dr. Flowers?" Christine exclaimed.

I'd gone from puking coward to knight in shining armor in the span of ten minutes. I was sure my macho display appealed to Chris' military sensibility, but hoped it wouldn't send the wrong message. I hated the dude. It didn't mean I wanted her.

Summer laughed, probably surprised to see her old man still had some fight left in him. "Our hero," she said in a sarcastically adoring tone. "I take it you know him?"

"Yeah - Joey Trumpet."

I sipped a coffee and explained Joey's real name was Joseph Fineman, the son of a rich Jewish banker, which wasn't necessarily a bad thing. Rich fathers have their perks, which for Joey was great because the idea of actual work never appealed to him.

"His idea of manual labor was having to clean up after a coke party at his Florida Keys beach house."

His habit was so infamous back in the 80's that it was rumored he didn't buy from local guys. He paid the smugglers to cut him a piece right off the plane. Mob found out and got plenty pissed; so much, in fact, that they paid Joey's fashion model step-mother to seduce her step-son. Granted, she was only a few years older than Joey; it wasn't too much of a stretch. The gangsters mailed the incriminating photos to Joey's old man. The dude was humiliated and cut Joey off completely.

The ladies shook their heads. "Unbelievable," Chris muttered.

"Oh, it gets better."

I told them how Joey, in a fit of rage, went to the *New York Times* and ratted out his old man, telling all about the money he'd been cleaning for the same mobsters who'd blackmailed him. He said he had to in order to support the spending habits of a twenty-something fashion model wife. District Attorney cut him a nice deal for cooperating and put him in witness protection.

"Yeah, little Joey put the screws to his old man good, hence his nickname—

Trumpet. The mob eventually caught up with the dad and killed him. Joey inherited a fortune. He's a pilot these days and runs drugs between Jamaica and the keys, a task given to him by the mob as payback for ratting out his old man. People leave him alone for fear of Mafia retaliation, but everyone in the Caribbean knows him as a whistle blower and wouldn't trust him with ten bucks, let alone their friend or daughter."

We boarded our plane and the engines fired up. I clenched the armrest and started reciting my Hail Marys. My palms were a mess of sweat, and my heart raced. Summer held my hand as we ascended. It wasn't until the pilot turned off the fasten seat belt light that I actually took a breath.

"What's that?" Summer asked, pointing to the leather fanny pack around my waist.

"It's my plane crash emergency kit."

She shook her head and unloaded her laptop. "How about briefing me on the project so I know what it is I'm supposed to be doing?"

In all the flight and Joey Trumpet drama, I'd almost forgotten where we were going. I asked Chris to bring Summer up to speed. My head was spinning.

"We've been following your work for a long time now."

"It's okay. We're not in trouble," I assured her. At least, I hoped we weren't.

Chris told her about the sheriff selling to a fed.

"That idiot," Summer groaned. "So that's why you left in such a hurry?"

I nodded.

Chris continued,"We were interested in your dad's theory, and its potential military applications."

"I knew you never should have published that article."

Chris told Summer how it was the government's intent to develop a warfare agent that would aid American soldiers in combat. The marijuana plant's THC bonds to a set of neuro-receptors that reside in the limbic area of the brain, the area that controls pleasure, pain, emotion, and the fight/flight response, as well as memory and motor function.

"I'm well-versed, Major."

I felt bad for Chris. She was bright, but miles out of Summer's league. She might as well have been telling Steve Jobs how iTunes worked. Summer and I let it go. No sense in making her feel bad.

"The only way TCH would help in combat is by binding with CB2 receptors and 'numbing the pain' so to speak."

The major nodded. "Pain management and sensory perception to that pain could potentially be altered to allow soldiers to continue to fight, or flee in situations that would have them traditionally incapacitated."

"But it would have to be extremely high dose THC. Also, the effects you're suggesting wouldn't last very long," said Summer.

"Exactly. That's where the cloning comes in."

I interrupted. "We figured out how to clone a rare Jamaican orchid with our G-420 strain. The orchid resin mutates with the THC crystals and acts almost like superglue, bonding the neurotransmitter to the neuron for extended durations."

I could see the light bulb in her mind illuminate.

"I get it. This is why you've had me working on such high dose THC plants?"

"Yeah, I was hoping we could replicate what I'd done in Jamaica without the orchid resin. Obviously, we can't."

"In such high dosages, short-term tolerance would be all the brain could handle. If bonded longer than a few hours, full blown psychosis would ensue."

"Try minutes, not hours," I said. "I was working on a release compound when I got the call Autumn had…"

Summer squeezed my hand, letting me know I didn't need to finish the thought.

"This would be extremely dangerous if it fell into the wrong hands," Summer said.

"That is why there are only a handful of people involved in the project, you now being one of them. We have to find the right dosage, and we must develop a release compound," Chris said.

Summer solemnly agreed.

"Your journal. That's why you've been so attached. All your notes?"

"Yep."

"Who else is involved?" Summer asked inquisitively.

Chris answered, "Some of the worst kinds of people."

Summer tensed, and rightfully so. "Who was all the pot coming from while you were in Jamaica?"

"His name is Hector Hannasui," Chris said matter-of-fact.

"Is he dangerous?" Summer asked.

"Yes, extremely."

I explained that Hector had gained power by aligning himself with the Rastafarian people. "He's the self-appointed reincarnation of Haile Selassie I, former Emperor of Ethiopia."

Chris told Summer that Rastafarian people believed one day, the second coming of Haile Selassie will unite all African people in a new Ethiopia, or Zion. They believe they are currently trapped in Babylon. Reggae music and marijuana use is heavily tied to the Rastafarian movement. Marijuana is used as a spiritual tool.

"Hector has built up quite a loyal following among the Rasta people," I said.

"Why do they all believe he's the Second Coming?" Summer implored.

"He has a birthmark on his bicep that is the exact shape of Ethiopia. Combine that with a politician's tongue, and you have a ready-made Second Coming."

"He uses his henchmen to do his dirty work, believing himself too holy to indulge in violent behavior."

"He sounds like a real bad ass. I like him already," Summer joked.

"He's not one of the Wellington Elks, Summer. Give him a wide berth."

Christine huffed, "It sure doesn't help that your father fell in love with his wife."

Summer shot me one of her infamous cutting stares.

"Oh, my God. You didn't tell her?" Chris whispered.

I rolled my eyes. Chris was a woman, after all. She'd never admit it, but she enjoyed stirring the pot. I didn't know how to explain it to Summer, so I did what I always did, sloughed it off as no big deal and closed my eyes.

My mind was racing though. I was really on my way back to Mia. It hadn't really set in until that moment, but I'd soon be seeing her again. My heart skipped a joyful beat for the first time in ages. I was terrified about Hector, though. If he knew, Summer and I were headed right into a trap – one we wouldn't likely escape.

Chapter 9

Hector Hannasui strolled casually down the utility path that led back toward Port Antonio, where he resided. Sweat dripped from his brow and fell to the dirt path at his feet. He stopped. His nephew, Max, looked over at him and stared silently, like an obedient dog awaiting a command from his master.

"Maxi, it's hot today, no?"

Max nodded.

"Go back and make sure all of the field workers have enough water. Turn on de fans and mist machines for dem as well."

Max ran back toward the lab and the field, quick to carry out the wishes of his uncle.

Hector resumed his walk and whistled as he did, stopping to breathe in the tropical Jamaican air and absorb his island's energy. Jamaica was Hector Hannasui's island indeed. It was where he was born, raised and would, one day, die. With the exception of college spent abroad, he had never stepped foot off the island and liked that just fine.

The Jamaican kingpin's appearance resembled that of a tropical pimp more so than a powerful drug lord. As looks went, he was considered handsome, and standing at six feet six inches. His shoulders were wide and limbs long and lean, but not skinny. The locals knew not to bother him, but the occasional tourist would ask if Hector was a pro basketball player on vacation in the islands. He would always smile and assure them that, while he was blessed with a big body, little coordination and athletic ability accompanied it.

His white linen trousers fluttered in the slight breeze as he walked, and the bright red oxford remained unbuttoned, revealing a sweat-stained undershirt beneath. A straw fedora completed the ensemble. His sandals kicked up the loose dirt as he walked, and his whistle turned into song. Hector was, without a doubt, the biggest Elvis Presley fan on the island of Jamaica. He sang "Burning Love" and stopped to shuffle his hips as he did. He often felt that if anything could get him off his island, it would be an Elvis convention in Las Vegas.

It wasn't long before the remote path of the Blue Mountains opened and fed into a byway. A woman named Dehlia Storm sat beside a fruit cart, fanning herself more to keep entertained than keep cool. She also found it an effective way to keep the insects at bay.

"Mornin, Mistah Hectah," she shouted as Hector approached

"Girl, you gonna set me on fire. My brain is flaming. I don't know which way to go," he sang, motioning to the fork in the road.

"Som mango dis mornin'?" Dehlia asked, unimpressed by his vocal styling. Hector smiled and nodded. He watched the twenty-three year old Jamaican beauty

lean over as she opened the cooler to retrieve the fruit. Her skin glistened in the morning heat. Thoughts rushed through his head and caught him by surprise. A deeply superstitious man, Hector knew better than to make anything but a friend of a voodoo priestess, even if she were twenty plus years his junior.

Dehlia handed him the fruit and took his money, smiling at him all the while.

"Maybe some ackee for you as well, on da house?" Dehlia asked.

"Not dis mornin'. I got to be gettin' along."

"You gonna meet de Flowah mon?" Dehlia asked as she fanned a couple flies off the mango.

"Notin get past you, woman. Dat voodoo give you de gift of de third eye?"

Dehlia smiled as she fanned and sat back down on the foldout chair next to her stand. "No, mon. I was talkin' to dat nephew of yours."

Hector laughed loud and almost choked as he spit out some of his mango. "You know dat boy got no tongue, right? Unless you cast some spell to make it grow back?"

Dehlia wrinkled her brow and shook her head. "We got our own way a communicatin'."

Hector wondered what that might be as he took another bite of the mango.

"What else he tell you?" Hector asked, more serious now.

Dehlia noticed his change in tone. Though they were friendly, she knew better than to get too friendly with the devil; he would surely turn on her one day, if it served him.

"Well, if you must know, he say dat the Flowah mon need to come back to fix Miss Mia— dat de good doctor up dere do notin' for her. He say dat he tink da doctor up to somting bad."

Hector nodded. He wasn't happy Max was talking to Dehlia, especially about business, but his nephew was right, a keen boy indeed.

"Yes, he shared dat wit me, too. Perhaps I go have a word wit de doctor?"

"Take dis." Dehlia handed him a small pouch she retrieved from the pocket of her cut off jean shorts. "Flowah mon gave dis to me. He said if I eveah got in trouble, just blow the dust toward the bad mon. Nevah breathe it in, he say. He say dat dis powdah come from de secret orchid. He did sometin wit it so dat, when you breathe it in, your body freezes. You can hear, see, taste, smell, and feel everyting, but you can't move."

The big man was surprised, but grateful. While he and Dehlia had never been close, he'd known her since she was a little girl. He also knew that, regardless of their relationship, she likely saw Hodges as a common enemy. His disdain for

Jamaicans was widely known throughout Port Antonio. Nobody liked him.

Hector took the pouch and smiled at her, taking another bite of the mango, wiping his hands against his damp cotton under shirt. He began walking back toward the compound but turned back momentarily to wave a thank you to the young priestess.

"Maxi say he gonna marry me." she shouted at him. Hector kept walking and held up a hand to acknowledge that he heard her, but paid little attention.

Max caught up to his uncle at just about the same spot he'd left. Not looking surprised, he simply strode along beside him as they made their way back to the lab. Hector looked over at his nephew and thought of Dehlia and him together.

"So I hear you gettin' married to dat Dehlia?"

Max smiled big and lowered his head, embarrassed.

Hector sliced a piece of mango and handed it to Max. Max took a bite and began to chew. Hector hated to see the boy eat. He never realized how much people use their tongues until he took Max in his care. Eating was one of those times. Max had to tilt his head slightly as he had no way of moving the food in place. After many years of doing this, he'd become quite adept and made quick work of the mango. He wiped his mouth and tugged on Hectors sleeve for another bite.

"Good news, Maxi," Hector said, as he handed him another slice. "Today, you may get to practice your surgical skills on someone other than the workers."

Hector recalled several years prior, they'd had a particularly harsh summer and many of the field workers had suffered from heat stroke. Hector summoned a doctor to come up and make some recommendations for improving the environment. The mist fans were one of the doctor's recommendations, and Hector was quick to take his advice. Once completed, he had the doctor audit the situation and give his blessing.

One of the workers flipped the switch and watched as the big fan whirled. The doc nodded approvingly, and the mist quickly drew the attention of the field workers. They gathered around it, enjoying its coolness. The fan was a hit, until it began to rumble and shake, the blade working loose from the motor. The doctor, Hector, and Max darted for cover, but the doc didn't make it. The blade flew wildly and hit two workers, killing one and badly, wounding the other.

Before settling into a tree, the blade sliced the doctor in his left leg. Too hurt to aid himself, the doc had to talk someone through the procedure of tending to the field hand, as well as cauterizing his own artery and stitching him back up. Hector was not up to the task. He was a deity, after all. Max, however, heeded the call and was an apt pupil. The doc said he was a natural and should consider medical school.

Since then, Max made it his mission to learn all he could about medicine, anatomy, and surgery. His practical experience consisted mostly of helping field hands who got stung by an insect or cut themselves with a machete, but Max addressed each incident as if it were a life-threatening one.

Max looked at his uncle with raised eyebrow and made some mumbling, grunting sounds. He only attempted to speak when he was very excited; otherwise, he remained completely silent.

"We goin' to have a talk wit de doc, Maxi."

Max frowned. He was a keen young man, as Hector had observed. Hector knew that, before his nephew even started his first day of medical school, he would be violating the Hippocratic Oath to do no harm. Max had been in Hector's care for twelve years. He knew what kind of a man Hector really was, and that it was best to do as he instructed. Hector took great care of Max and promised to send him to medical school, but he sensed Max knew better. Max knew that his place would always be at his uncle's side. Medical school was a carrot Hector could and would dangle in front of Max for the rest of his life.

Chapter 10

"Good afternoon, Dr. Hodges. Please, come sit down."

Hector sat in a chaise lounge under an umbrella in the grassy court yard, humming, *Are you lonesome tonight?* He leaned forward and opened a cigar box filled with cigars and a couple dozen perfectly rolled joints. He raised his eyebrows and offered Hodges his choice.

"No, thank you, sir."

Hodges spoke with a thick British accent, which he commonly referred to as the Queen's English. Surrounded by poor Jamaicans he felt were beneath his pedigree and his intellect, he laid it on particularly thick.

"Do you know why I called you here today?"

Hector's Jamaican accent always disappeared when he discussed business. It was one of the ways his workers knew when and how to draw the line. Max knew simply by the look in his eye.

"Sorry, sir. No, I do not."

"Tell me what you know about the arrival of Sonny Flowers to the island."

"Oh. You needn't worry about that, my lord. I've attended to the matter and have had him dispatched for you," the doctor said proudly. "I was informed that he was to return and made arrangements to ensure that would not happen."

Hector pushed his chair back and stood. He turned his back to the doctor and stared out at the pond. He took a long drag from the joint in his hand and held it for a minute, staring. He exhaled as he turned, catching Hodges off guard. The doctor coughed and choked, but regained composure quickly. Hector walked around the table and knelt before Hodges, opening the palm of his hand to reveal the powder given to him by Dehlia.

"Do you know what this is, Doctor?"

Hodges donned his spectacles and stared at the powder. He studied its make-up, color, and overall texture.

"It appears as though it is some type of pollen, but, without looking at it on my charts and under a microscope, I can't be sure from exactly which plant it was extracted."

"Very good," Hector said, and with that, placed his lips to the edge of his palm and blew the pollen forcefully into the doctor's face.

"Why I . . ." Hodges stammered, but Hector stopped him.

"Doctor, what you have just inhaled should be overpowering you soon. Try to raise your hand for me."

Hodges looked down at his right hand, unable to move it from the armrest. His astonished eyes moved back to Hector.

"You remember my nephew, Max, don't you, Doctor?"

The doctor sat motionless in his seat, unable to respond.

"Don't worry. I understand you can't reply, so I'll do the talking while Max prepares his things."

On the opposite side of Hodges, Max spread open a roll of surgical instruments, given to him as a gift from his uncle.

Hector spoke as Max prepared. "I'm quite disappointed in you, Dr. Hodges. I brought you here a few months ago to help my wife, Mia. You came very highly recommended. I paid you a great deal of money, but you have achieved no results. Not only have you failed me, Doctor, you have also now destroyed the only man who can help me. I realize you have been made aware of certain things, of certain indiscretions between Dr. Flowers and my wife. Those things were not for you to know."

Hector paced and puffed on his joint as he spoke, looking up, quietly collecting the right words. He started to speak, but then interrupted himself. He paused and faced the doctor, realizing that he'd forgotten another important point.

"I also understand you took it upon yourself to forgive a debt owed to me by Joey Fineman?"

Dr. Hodges sat motionless, staring at Hector as he spoke. His lips couldn't quiver. His hands wouldn't shake. He couldn't plea for his life or explain his side of the story. He could only sit and listen.

"Max is studying to become a surgeon, and I believe he will be a good one. I've asked him to show me what he has learned from his books and to elaborate a bit for my understanding. I even asked Max if he could cut out your tongue and attach it to his own severed organ. Unfortunately, he cannot, so, instead, he has offered to show me what he knows of open-heart surgery."

Hector smirked as Hodges' pupils dilated.

"I requested that he not use any anesthetic, but he insisted. I agreed so that you wouldn't pass out from the pain. I want you awake for this, Dr. Hodges, who speaks the Queen's English and looks down on the Jamaican mon."

Beads of sweat trickled down the side of Hodges' face as his eyes stayed glued on Max and the syringe. He did feel the needle pierce the skin under his collarbone. It was excruciating, but he couldn't make a sound. The process repeated along the perimeter of his entire rib cage and above his stomach. Soon, the pain was gone. Unable to move his head, he couldn't see Max working on his torso, only Hector's eyes watching Max glide the scalpel from the base of his neck to either nipple and then back to a point above his naval, forming a perfect diamond. The blood oozed as he worked while Hector sat and sipped a rum drink, admiring his nephew's steady hand and surgical skill.

He went on. "You see, Doctor, the human body has always fascinated me. It is so complex and versatile, yet so fragile. I've often wondered what a live, beating, human heart looks like. Today, we will both be able to see it."

Dr. Hodges heard the cracking and crunching, but still couldn't see what was happening to him. He imagined the noise was the sound of his ribs being split and torn from his sternum. He felt the immense pressure and then a breeze as it blew over the exposed cavity.

"Simply fascinating!" Hector exclaimed, watching Max work.

Max looked up at his uncle and pointed to the garden sprayer. Hector quickly retrieved it for him and Max began pumping. He stood in front of the doctor and surveyed his handy work, then sprayed the torso with water from the pump. Normally, a pump like that would have been used to spray fertilizer on plants, but today it had an altogether different application. Finished, Max spun the doctor around to face his uncle.

Hector stood and marveled at the site before him.

"Doctor, you simply must see this. Max has truly outdone himself, and I couldn't be more proud."

Hector summoned a servant who brought over a large, full-length mirror. Hector moved the mirror in front of the doctor. Tears streamed from the Hodges' eyes and fell off his cheeks to the pools of blood at his feet. He sat motionless, staring at his open torso and his own live beating heart.

Hector put his two hands together and clapped. "Bravo, Max."

The doctor's heart beat faster and the adrenaline pumped through his veins as he waited to die. Max handed his uncle the syringe, still a quarter full of anesthetic. Hector plunged the needle into the right ventricle of the heart and injected a small amount. The heart still pumped, minus that chamber. Within moments, the doctor would suffer a painful heart attack, unable to stop it or look away from his own gruesome death. Hodges began to gasp involuntarily and his body stiffened, the tears still streaming.

Hector plunged the needle into the left atrium and injected more anesthetic. The doctor's heart stopped. Hector and Max stared into the mirror and watched the doctor's eyes as the life slipped away from them. Seconds later, Dr. Hodges was dead and his lifeless head fell forward.

"Dump him in de pond and let my flock of piranha finish him off. I need to be seein' 'bout da Flowah mon."

Chapter 11

Christine Smith sat in her seat and sipped her V8. She tried reading, but couldn't concentrate so she just leaned back and closed her eyes.

Her thoughts drifted to Sonny— they always did. She fell in love with him the first time they met. She imagined their first kiss, what it would be like to wake up lying next to him, and maybe even one day being able to call herself Christine Flowers. *Oh, what a nice ring that has,* she thought. A silly little smile drew a line in her face, but didn't last for more than a few seconds. The plane jolted violently.

Her eyes shot open and she stared at the V8, which floated off the tray and hovered before her. Gripping the arm-rest, she waited for the plane to right itself. The V8 dropped and hit the tray hard, splashing the red juice all over her white blouse. Normally, she would have been angry to see a favorite shirt ruined, but the drop was more violent than any turbulence she'd ever experienced. *Perhaps wind-shear,* she thought. Trying her best to recall lessons from pilot courses she'd taken early in her career left few other options to consider. She didn't need to look over to know Sonny was already hyperventilating, and she debated whether or not to leave her seat. The book said to buckle in and let the pilot do his job. If she moved, she could be thrown or even killed.

Just as she was about to settle back in, she heard a loud pop and a horrific scream. Major Smith opened the visor of her window and looked out at the wing. For a split second, she thought it was a bird hovering just below the wing, and then she saw the familiar pattern of marlin that adorned the gaudy shirt of their pilot, Joey Fineman. His helmet and parachute pack were clear evidence that he had ditched.

Son of a bitch, she thought. Sonny was right. The guy was a real weasel.

Any reservations she had about staying put were quickly dismissed; she began to make her way to the cockpit. As she passed Sonny and Summer, she almost choked on their fear and anxiety. Sonny clutched a holy medal around his neck, and Summer looked at her with the terrified eyes of a daughter trying to remain strong and positive. Simon, the flight attendant, strapped himself in and joined the Flowers in frantic prayer.

Christine flung the door to the cockpit and was thrown back by the force of the wind rushing toward her. She grabbed the back of a seat and righted herself, forcing her way to the controls. Her eyes stung as she gripped the pilot's seat and hunted for the oxygen mask. She located it under the co-pilot's seat and affixed it to her head. The plastic face mask allowed her to see ahead. She forced the door closed and buckled herself in.

The console was a maze of spinning dials and red alarms. She took a deep breath and remembered that getting the plane out of the nosedive and level was first priority. Joey had destroyed several of the controls— an obvious attempt to ensure their demise. She grabbed the yoke and pulled back hard. It took all she had to fight gravity and wind sucking her toward the sea at over 300 miles per hour. A direct impact with the water would kill everyone aboard.

After a minute of fighting, she managed to pull the nose of the plane level. The wind was brutal, battering her like torrential ocean waves beating the face of a rock. She saw the indicator beeping, letting her know engine one was gone. They were at five thousand feet and descending rapidly. She checked engine two and was relieved to see it still cranking, *thank God*. As she reached for the radio to call in their position, the alarm sounded.

Engine two was gone, and they were now gliding through the sky on, quite literally, a wing and a prayer. The horizon provided no sign of land. She would have to attempt to ditch and make an emergency water landing. The odds of surviving a water landing were slim, but it was their only option. Anxiety took hold of her as the plane continued its descent, her arms summoning strength from deep within to pull the yoke back into her belly.

The major drew the flaps and prayed, fighting to keep the nose of the plane up and the wings level. She fought with all she had as the water rapidly approached.

Prepare for impact!

The tail touched first and glided across the glassy ocean for a few seconds before the left wing tilted and caught the water. The force of the ocean against the wing ripped it off completely and spun the fuselage around like a tether ball. The right wing caught next and jolted the plane violently. Like its counterpart, the wing was severed from the body of the craft. Momentum ceased and the fuselage came to a completed stop. Christine had been knocked unconscious, strapped to the pilot's seat.

In the main cabin, water rushed in through the gaping holes that had held the wings in place. The trio of passengers hurried to unbuckle themselves and rushed toward the makeshift exit before the cabin completely filled. Summer and Sonny struggled against the rushing water and almost made it, but, as the sea filled the plane, they found themselves pinned against the ceiling of the cabin. They took one deep breath and, in an instant, were completely submerged. The last thing Summer saw before going under was the sheer look of terror in Sonny's eyes. She didn't know if he was going to make it through this one.

The salt water burned their eyes as they struggled against the foam and bubbles. Summer felt her chest begin to tighten and burn. She struggled not to panic as the pressure in her ears built. She knew they were sinking fast and that it would only take a few more seconds to pass the point of no return. The single thought that comforted her, as she exhaled a small breath of air and popped her ears, was that she might soon be reunited with her twin sister.

Summer found her father in the dark abyss and pulled him toward the exit. She hooked her foot to the opening and pulled him through. Free in the open ocean, they watched the plane sink below them and vanish into the depths, but from the blackness of the water below, something raced up from the darkness toward them. *Shark,* was all she could think. She stiffened and braced for impact, her heart in overdrive, pumping blood and adrenaline to every organ in her body.

The object pounded them hard and rocketed them toward the surface. After what seemed like a year since her last breath, she and Sonny shot through the barrier of the surface and gasped hard. The object burst through the surface. Summer laughed, relieved and thankful to still be alive.

"What's so funny?" Sonny shouted, still gasping for air.

"It's my equipment case – the one you didn't think we needed."

"Yeah. Grab on." Sonny yelled.

"I thought it was a shark."

"Don't look now, but they're not far behind."

Summer looked over her shoulder and saw at least one fin heading toward them.

"Son of a bitch," she exclaimed.

"Over there," Sonny shouted, pointing to a pile of floating debris.

They saw the flight attendant, Simon, about 100 yards away, yelling and splashing. Simon hadn't seen the fin. The splashing and screaming would only make him a more desirable dinner option for the predatory fish, but she was too far from him to help or even signal for him to stop. She tried waving to the terrified steward, but he didn't see her. He didn't see the fins of the shark circling him either. It didn't matter; the one that got him came up from below. Simon disappeared under the water. The screaming suddenly stopped and, in that split second, there was only foreboding silence.

Chapter 12

Summer and I watched in horror as the sharks tore Simon apart, shredding every inch of him in a hellacious feeding frenzy. The blue sea was stained red with the poor bastard's blood. Our turn was coming. I prayed that young steward's sacrifice would spare us but knew better. There would be a dozen of the toothy fuckers on us in minutes.

Summer started to panic. I was worried I'd soon be joining her.

"Did you see what species?" I asked, not sure what else to say.

I knew goddamn well we had at least one, maybe two, tiger sharks in our midst. My hope was that Summer hadn't noticed the broad snout and dark dorsal stripes. Tigers were no joke and came in second to the Great White as the greediest for human scientists. Very few people had ever faced a tiger shark in the open ocean and lived to tell about it. Under water, I might have a chance to at least fend them off. Maybe if they knew we wouldn't be an easy meal, their sense of self-preservation would override their desire to snack on us?

Summer shook her head, letting me know that she hadn't seen anything. I wondered if she was lying, trying to protect me.

This was my chance to fight for her – for us. I bragged to my friends that I still swam fifty laps a week. I'd like to be able to brag that I fought off a tiger shark. The thought of it was almost ridiculous but I needed to convince myself if we were going to have any chance. I was a champion swimmer. I could hold my breath for two minutes. I could do this.

Summer clung to my arm and begged me to stay close. I hadn't been needed by her in a long time and it felt good, but I had to get below and see what was lurking before it was too late. I was just about to dive when we felt the tug on our legs. I almost had a coronary and Summer screamed.

"Jesus, what's the matter with you two? You act like your plane just crashed into the ocean," Chris exclaimed as she popped up behind us.

I was relieved to see her alive and hugged her. She smiled and splashed us playfully.

"Don't do that," Summer snapped.

"What's going on? Are you hurt?"

I told her about Simon and the looming threat below, and it was just then that we sensed the massive object looming below. The fish swam powerfully enough that we felt the drag of the current pull at our feet.

"Yeah, I felt it, too," Chris whispered.

Summer was starting to show signs of shock, chattering teeth and blue lips. She trembled and stammered when she tried to speak. I needed to get her to safety, but there wasn't a goddamn thing in site and every piece of technology we owned was submerged. I felt my plane crash kit around my waist and knew that it only held a couple travel bottles of rum, some weed, and my journal – safe and dry inside a freezer bag. I unclipped the pack and handed it to Summer. After a kiss on the cheek from both of them, I sucked in a huge gulp of air and thrust myself below the glassy blue surface of the Caribbean.

Once underwater, I opened my eyes and blinked a few times. The salty water stung like a motherfucker, and I struggled to see a foot through the murky blue. I was scared, real scared. A shark was heading toward me, but in the murk I had no clue how close he was. I guessed maybe twenty yards away. I felt another one pass under me. My chances of surviving were slim at best. I decided to deal with the fella approaching from the front. I needed to try for his gills. It was probably easier said than done.

I exhaled a small breath and felt slight relief in my lungs. As the bubbles passed in front of my eyes, I prepared for the worst. In a flash, the beast was upon me, its mouth slightly agape, ready to take a chomp out of whatever body part I offered. As he approached, I did my best to angle my body away from his jaws. Miraculously, it worked. I caught the asshole on the snout and reached for his gills. My hand started to bleed. His razor-like scales made me feel like I was holding a cheese grater. I watched him chomp, trying to take a bite out of my leg, or worse, my crotch. I found a gill and thrust my free hand through one of the slits. He hated it and darted off. Score - Sonny one, shark zero.

I shot to the surface and sucked in as much air as my lungs would allow. I was losing steam. My head pounded and every muscle in my body burned. My skin felt like it had been stripped from my skeleton and what remained had been soaked in a tub of habanero peppers. If my new fishy friend decided to come back for round two, he'd feast.

The fin sliced through the surface. That stubborn son of a bitch was probably pissed as hell and was now more vengeful than hungry. I couldn't blame him. I was in his world and had just fucked him up. If it were me, I'd be pissed too. Positioning myself on my back, I floated and waited. My only chance would be to connect with a kick or two. It might buy me another pass, but he'd ultimately be the victor in this fight. I scanned the horizon, hoping to see Summer one last time. God, I wish I would have done more for her.

The fin was moving in fast. I closed my eyes and braced myself. The forty ton humpback broke the ocean's surface and breached as it exhaled a breath that could have rivaled an eruption of Old Faithful. The mammoth whale crashed back to the surface, sending a torrent of waves right at me. The chop tossed me around like a rag doll, dunking me several times. I struggled for breath, swallowing more ocean than air. The whale had done me a solid favor driving the sharks away, but unless help arrived in short order, I was gonna drown.

Chapter 13

I struggled against the current to stay afloat, and used what little voice I had left to call for Summer. My only response was from a couple gulls yakking as they flew overhead. I rubbed my medal: *The girls are lost and can't be found. Please, Saint Anthony, take a look around.*

I'd barely finished the recitation when I heard what sounded like a motor. Normally, I would have told myself it was the weed, but I hadn't been this sober in months. Maybe I was dead? A voice called out, and I guessed for sure it was death. I rolled over. It hurt like hell, so I must have still had a little life left in me. I could barely tread water. As the life ring hurtled toward me, I mumbled my standard thanks to St. Anthony and asked that I not become fish food so close to being rescued.

"Grab on, mate." the stranger shouted.

I accepted the offer and held on as tight as I could. Completely exhausted, I couldn't even try to swim. My rescuer pulled me aboard and gathered the life ring as I collapsed to the deck, coughing out what seemed like a gallon of ocean.

"Out for an afternoon swim?" he asked.

I wanted to laugh. It was pretty funny, but my body, mouth included, simply didn't have the energy.

"There weren't two lovely chippies out swimming with you now were there?"

"Summer?" I mumbled.

"Sure, mate. They're below with my partner. They were the ones who insisted I come looking for you."

I breathed a sigh of relief and extended my arm, a silent plea for help to get me to them.

He was an Aussie, for sure. His accent was unmistakable. He helped me to my feet and carried me toward the cabin. "Bishop is the name, mate. You must be Sonny?"

I nodded, still barely able to speak. Bishop flung the cabin hatch open and helped me down the ladder well. My eyes still stung from the sea salt, but I could clearly see that Summer and Chris were tied and gagged, strapped back to back. My guess was that I'd be joining them momentarily. I wanted to muster strength enough to fight him off, but couldn't.

"Motherfucker," was all I could muster.

Bishop and his first mate just laughed at me. I couldn't even make a fist. My hand was bloody from the shark. It, like every bone in my body, had been rendered useless. I flopped down on the cabin seat and then fell to the floor.

"Should I tie him up, Cap?"

"No," Bishop replied, "this one is no threat."

"Who are you?" I muttered.

"Funny you should ask, mate. I'm a salvage man. My first mate and I work these waters looking for old wrecks, treasure, and the like."

Bishop lit a cigar as he spoke. I wanted to puke.

"I intercepted a radio call about a plane that went down and a man on that plane by the name of Sonny Flowers. Seems you are a valuable asset to a very important man. He even rerouted a transport vessel to see if they could find you. You blokes are lucky we found you first."

I mustered enough energy to flip him the bird.

"I don't want you, mate. Hector does, and I'm sure if he's willing to derail a shipment because of you, he's probably willing to give me whatever is on that boat of his in exchange for you three."

"Ransom?"

"See, Luke, he's a smart guy," Bishop joked to his first mate.

Luke wasn't that tall, but he was menacing. I guessed him to be 185 pounds of solid Jamaican muscle. Brandishing a 9mm nickel-plated pistol, he held the ladies at bay. Chris squirmed and wriggled in her seat a bit, but with just one grunt, not even a word from Luke, she stopped.

I surveyed the cabin, hoping to find something, anything, that could help us – a radio, a club, a handsome young boy for Luke?

"I see you looking around. If you're planning on pulling a fast one, I'd advise against it. Luke's got an itchy trigger finger."

Bishop exhaled a puff of cigar smoke in my face. I dry-heaved and spit up a little more ocean.

"Besides, where are you going to run? You want to jump back in that water? It's whale season, you know. All those baby whales and placentas floating around tend to bring in quite the assortment of aggressive sharks. They should call it shark season."

I couldn't argue with the man. Where would we run? Hector's guys would be by soon enough, and it wouldn't take them long to figure out what was happening. I felt a little sorry for Bishop. He thought he could actually negotiate with Hector. He was as good as dead. The thought had barely come to me when I heard shouting on the deck. It sounded like a Jamaican accent and prayed it was Hector.

Bishop peered through the cabin window and started cursing.

"They've boarded. I see three more coming. You guard the bow. If they break through, shoot them."

Luke scurried over toward the forward cabin hatch. Bishop made his way aft. The surly first mate held the pistol out in front of him, but I could see that he was scared. I only prayed that a stray bullet wouldn't catch one of the girls. The sound an AK-47 makes when being fired is very distinctive, and, after three months on Hector's island, I knew it all too well.

The bullets sliced through the door, slivers of shrapnel flew through the cabin. Luke fired four rounds into the opening as one of the crew flung the hatch. I watched Luke's eyes widen as one of Hector's men peppered a dozen bullets into his chest, launching him backward toward the girls. His body lay sprawled, lifeless and limp on the cabin floor, bleeding into the area rug that caught him.

The crewman rushed down, ready to open fire on any other would-be assailants. What they found was me and the girls, waiting to be rescued.

"Sonny, mon. Is dat you?" the gunman asked, looking surprised to see me alive and breathing.

"Get us out of here, Rufus," I whispered.

Rufus Jones signaled to one of his crew to untie the ladies and to put them up on their feet. The gunman stepped over the dead body of the first mate and made quick work of the bindings that held the girls.

"Thank God, you're alive." Chris shouted.

She was going to hug me, and it was going to hurt. She threw her arms around me and told me how happy she was that I hadn't become fish food. I groaned and Rufus pulled her off.

"I thought I lost you, baby," I said to Summer.

She smiled and held my hand. I wished she wouldn't ever let go.

"C'mon, Sonny, mon. We got to get goin' before somebody come and give us a bigga mess."

We made our way topside and were greeted by fifteen of Hector's crew, all of them brandishing machine guns and smiling, showing off their pearly white teeth. Service with a smile, eh?

"What 'bout dis one?" Rufus asked.

Bishop had been restrained by a man who was more gorilla than human. Jesus, the hulkish Jamaican, dug the barrel of the AK into Bishop's side. The Aussie winced in pain.

"Give him to Hector," I said.

Rufus complied and gave the ready.

"What about the boat?" Summer asked

"Don't you worry your pretty little head 'bout dat, young lady. We got dat all figured out," Rufus said as he nodded toward Jesus.

Jesus hoisted the mini rocket launcher over his shoulder and took aim. He fired toward the aft of the ship at the water line. He knew that the rear end would fill and drag the ship down to the bottom, ass end first. He even demanded they wait to depart until he heard the boat scream. Rufus explained that when a ship sinks, the air from the hull whistles as it tries to escape. It's called screaming. Jesus loved hearing the sinking ships scream.

"Okay, men, back to Port Antonio," Rufus shouted.

The engines roared. Rufus pushed the throttle full forward, and our rescue ship began its long journey back to Jamaica.

Chapter 14

I scolded Rufus for making eyes at Summer, then collapsed on the oversized bed in the cabin of the sport yacht. I lit up a spliff from my plane crash emergency kit and took a long drag. The calm rushed through me, settling my nerves and soothing my aches.

"Would you mind some company?" Christine asked.

She crawled in next to me and rubbed my neck and shoulders. I wanted to protest. I knew where it would lead, but my body refused to yield to my better judgment.

"You did good, Smith— landing that plane," I mumbled.

"You did good, Flowers, with those sharks," she retorted.

I handed her my spliff and offered her a hit.

"A peace offering?" she asked.

"Do you want it or not?"

She'd refuse, but I was nothing, if not polite. To my surprise, she took the joint and puffed it lightly, choking, while trying to inhale. I laughed and told her it was nice to hang out with a weed virgin. I had to give her credit, though. At least she tried. My eyes grew heavy and I started to doze off. I didn't even feel her take the joint from my fingers, but awoke to the sight of her inhaling like an old pro. She exhaled a decent plume right in my face.

She stared at me and said," Do you think there will ever be a time when you can look at me without contempt?"

My heart sank. She thought I hated her. I didn't. I hated who she worked for, and I hated that she took me away from Autumn, but I didn't hate her.

"I'm sorry," I said, "I have a lot of respect for you, Chris. You're a tough chic."

She got up and made for the door. Was it something I said? While they weren't sweet nothings, I didn't think an apology and a compliment were harsh words. She closed the door and locked it, then slid back into the bed. Uh oh, I thought. I'm fucked now.

She pulled me close and kissed me. Our lips met, and it felt surprisingly good. I hadn't kissed a woman since Mia. I should have stopped her. I wanted to tell her that I wasn't the man she needed and that my heart wasn't available, but, like a typical guy, I didn't. I just kept kissing her. She unbuttoned her V8 stained blouse and slipped out of her skirt, revealing a body I hadn't expected. Her frame was slighter than I'd imagined and her limbs were long and lean. Her slender fingers glided through my hair. I pulled her in close.

We made love. Her energy was palpable and her eyes let me know that this was something she'd been wanting for a while. Thirty seconds later, I was flush with embarrassment, apologizing profusely. Not only had I been rendered immobile, but I was also in need of a tantric sex refresher course.

"There's something I need to tell you," she whispered.

"Just give me a few minutes. I'll go longer the second time around."

I feared some post-coital confession. I expected her to tell me she loved me, or that she had some dastardly plan to steal me away from Mia. I didn't let her say anything. I should have. I just pulled her in and kissed her again. She welcomed my advances and offered an atta boy when I confidently powered past the forty-five second mark.

Chapter 15

The boat thumped down hard from what I imagined was an unexpected big wave, startling me awake. I rolled over and saw Christine Smith sleeping, her bare back exposed, the sheet pulled down just enough to remind me she was completely naked. I sat on the edge of the bed, not sure if moments or hours had passed. The combination of the weed and exhaustion still had me mentally reeling.

I ran my fingers through my hair and replaced the trademark Sonny Flowers pony tail. As I fastened my belt and grabbed my shirt off the floor, I couldn't help but feel every bit of my age. There wasn't much time for me to wallow as I heard a soft knock at the door. I knew who it was and what the scene would appear to be.

"What's going on, Dad?"

"It isn't what you think," I whispered, "but I liked hearing you call me Dad just then."

Summer saw the major, lying naked on the bed. She shook her head in disgust. I'd let her down yet again.

"She came on strong. I didn't have the energy to refuse."

It was the truth, but the look in her eyes let me know that Summer disapproved all the same.

"First Mom, now Mia? You're all class, Sonny."

There it was again, the sound of my own name pissing me off. Sure, I hated constantly disappointing her, but I'm a grown man, for Christ's sake, capable of making my own decisions. Summer, like my mom, just seemed to constantly remind me of my faults. Who knows, maybe she had a right to be upset? Maybe she didn't? Had I walked in on her and Rufus, I'd be plenty angry, but I can't pretend she's not a grown woman herself. She'd never been one to date, always preferring work. I guess maybe she felt I should do the same?

I was just about to close the door when I heard Chris whisper,

"What's the matter, sweetie?"

"Nothing. We're getting ready to pull into port."

I closed the door and pressed my ear against it, not sure what I was really expecting to hear. Her soft sobs made me feel like an even bigger asshole than I had already. Not only had I just upset the work balance, but I'd managed to agitate both her and Summer with the same act. I only hoped she wouldn't complicate things on the island. I needed to get our work completed then get the hell back home to the real research and real life. My hand clutched the door knob as I wrestled with the idea of apologizing. I'd probably only be leading her on, so I let go and limped topside. Summer was waiting and the island was calling. Hopefully I wouldn't make any more stupid decisions.

Idiocy in Jamaica could mean never seeing home again, only this time, my nonsense might hurt Summer. I couldn't let that happen.

Chapter 16

Summer Flowers walked ahead of her father, still angry with him for his shenanigans with the major.

Summer had seen pictures and read about the beauty of Jamaica, but, until she stepped off the dock that afternoon, she would never have believed it to be real. She marveled at the radiant pink oleander growing overhead and stopped to study the sea grapes hanging near the sand. As she reached for her camera to document the plant life, she found herself in an unexpected tug of war with a very tall slender Jamaican boy. He had a strong hold of her shoulder bag and continued to tug even at her protest. Trying to keep her cool, she tugged back - hard, hoping it would send a message. The boy didn't give.

"Honestly. Do you mind?" Summer barked.

The young man jumped back, startled. After a few second stare-down, he started to slowly reach for the bag again. Summer raised her eyebrow and stiffened her shoulder. He retreated.

"You'll have to excuse my nephew, young lady. He was simply trying to help. I insisted he do so."

Summer found herself staring directly into the dark pits of Hector Hannasui's eyes. The usually emboldened young scientist was taken aback by Hector's imposing size and stature. It had to be him. His presence was very commanding. She stammered and tried to mutter an apology, but he quickly interrupted her.

"Sea grapes are often planted near beaches to stabilize the edge."

Summer watched as Hector plucked two grapes from the tree and offered her one. She pensively accepted, studied him as he closed his eyes, and bit into the fruit, looking as though he were enjoying it for the very first time.

"You must be careful. You see there is a pit in the middle. Just like a beautiful lady— sweet, yet riddled with hidden danger."

Summer nibbled the grape gently as Hector introduced himself.

"You must be Summer? I've heard about you from your father. I must say, you are much more beautiful in person."

Summer smiled, and while she welcomed his introduction, she still felt quite uneasy. Hector was, indeed, a powerful entity on this Earth. He possessed a command of the things around him like no other person she'd ever encountered. She was both intrigued and frightened.

"This is Max, my nephew. Forgive him as he has lost his ability to speak."

"I'm sorry, Max. I didn't mean to . . ."

Max lowered his head and snatched her shoulder bag. Summer didn't protest this time and accepted Hector's arm as he led her toward the waiting vehicle.

"Your chariot, my dear."

Summer squeezed in next to her father.

"Careful, sweetheart. We're not in Kansas anymore."

Summer huffed and brushed Sonny's hand away as they drove off.

The Jeep navigated the dirt roads with reckless abandon. Summer waved the no-see-ums from her face and spit them from her tongue as the driver sped onward. Sonny warned her about the annoying gnats, but, like most things Sonny said, she paid little attention until it smacked her in the face.

The group approached the Hannasui house as the sun began to set behind it. Exhausted and overwhelmed, Summer asked to be shown to her room and left alone for the evening.

"Nonsense, child." Hector snapped at hearing her request. "Dinner will be served in an hour. You are my guest. I expect to see you there."

Summer stiffened. She nodded and swallowed the lump in her throat. She flashed back to her graduation day and remembered telling her father how much she wanted to follow in his footsteps. She remembered Sonny telling her to be careful what she wished for because she just might get it. Sweating and terrified, she wished for nothing more than to get on a plane and head straight back to Ohio.

As she made her way to her room, she couldn't help but marvel at the classic plantation style home. It was almost castle-like with a magnificent spiraling grand staircase and several corridors that led outward from the main foyer. As she made her way down the main hall that led to her room, she heard several muffled voices behind closed doors. A few spoke with heavy Jamaican accents. One in particular caught her ear.

Summer slowed her pace and stopped to listen at one of the bedrooms, feeling a pit in her stomach begin to form. There were two distinct voices, both female, in a very heated discussion. Summer pressed her ear against the antique red door straining to hear more clearly.

"Once Mia . . . recipe . . .what about the girl?" was all she could make out.

"Don't you know it's impolite to eavesdrop?"

Summer, startled, jumped back and spun toward the staircase. Christine Smith had just made her way up, bags in hand, and looked as exhausted as Summer felt.

"C'mon. I think we're down here," she told Summer and beckoned her the opposite way down the hall.

Summer wondered if Chris was awake when she and Sonny had had the exchange on the boat. Judging by Christine's pleasant tone, she guessed not.

Summer tried in vain to place the familiar voice, but simply couldn't in her current state of mind. She felt it would come to her in time and decided a long bath and change of clothes were first on her short list of priorities.

"Chris, do you know which room is my dad's?"

"Hopefully, one on a different floor," Chris said.

Summer didn't press her and felt bad knowing what it was like to be on the receiving end of a Sonny Flowers letdown. The ladies parted ways and entered their respective rooms across from one another.

After a long, hot bath, Summer felt revived and overjoyed to be cleansed of all the salt water and trauma of the day. She looked at her watch and was impressed that she'd left herself fifteen minutes before she was expected at dinner. She stumbled through her bag and retrieved the Ziploc bag also known as Sonny's plane crash kit. She stared at the foggy bag and shook her head.

"Moron," she spoke aloud.

Tipping the bag over, she dumped the contents on the bed.

She collected his drug paraphernalia and set it off to the side, deciding to focus on the mission at hand and familiarize herself with the notes he'd made during his last stay on the island. As she leafed through the sticky pages, she sat puzzled for the first time in as long as she could remember.

The heiress Flowers had been reading Sonny's notes for years and could easily decipher most of his chicken scratch, but the Jamaican project was different. Notes seemed out of place and garbled. She observed that Sonny had begun marking his pages in the corners with numbers and symbols. After several attempts, she decided to give up. Her head fell back on the soft down pillow and stared up at the faux ceiling painted to look like open sky. It was really quite lovely she thought as her eyes began to grow heavy. Closing them and concentrating on the voices behind the red door once more, she attempted to place the sound with a face in her mental Rolodex. She replayed the verse over in her mind, carefully sounding out each word, unable to recognize the voice.

Knock. Knock.

Summer shot up, startled and made her way toward the door, hoping Sonny had come to tell her they could leave, and that he'd fixed Mia. She knew, though, this was a far cry from her new reality. Peering through the one way eye hole, she realized that the knock at the door was actually the door across the hall— Chris Smith's door. She couldn't quite make out the figure standing in the hall in front of her, but was confident it was a man. He was tall and well-tanned, but not Jamaican. She knew he was older because of the chicken skin on the back of his arms and the silvery hair that poked out of the black ball cap on his head.

"I heard you had a close call out there today," the voice said.

"I managed to land the plane, but I wasn't able to further our objective. I think the key will be uncovering whatever is inside the head of Mia Hannasui."

Summer made a mental recording of the conversation and another to keep Chris at a distance. If only Sonny's journal were more legible, she thought, she might be able to beat them to the punch. The alarm on her wristwatch sounded unexpectedly.

Chris and the stranger stopped their conversation, and Summer quickly silenced the alarm.

Opening the door, Summer tried to act as casual as possible. After all, the alarm was signaling it was time to leave for dinner. The gentleman at Christine's door was already fifteen steps down the hall, but Summer was happy to catch a clear glimpse of him even though it was from the rear.

"Oh— hi, Chris. Are you heading down for dinner?" Summer asked in the perkiest tone she could muster.

"Y-yeah. Dinner. Right." Chris was clearly distracted, studying the young scientist.

"What do they eat in Jamaica, I wonder?" Summer said, trying her best to mask the new uncertainty that surrounded the major.

Chris smiled and said, "Lizard."

The two walked together, laughing, as they prepared for the Komodo dragon feast awaiting them.

Chapter 17

Hector Hannasui greeted Summer as he greeted all of his guests—

with the diplomacy of a UN ambassador. Showing off his best smile and squinting his eyes just enough to impart genuine sincerity, he had them all fooled.

"Welcome to Jamaica and to my humble home."

The guests looked around and raised their eyebrows at one another, acknowledging that their surroundings were anything but humble. Sonny and Summer were seated across from one another at the formal dining table and Christine was seated next to Summer.

Summer looked uneasy, and Hector sensed it. "Before we begin, I would like to share something with each of you."

Summer wanted to dart a look to her father but restrained herself, still stubbornly extending the cold shoulder. The wait staff presented each of them with a small covered tray.

"Please, uncover your plates," Hector prompted.

The guests smiled as they looked down and saw the single, tightly rolled joint sitting next to a disposable white lighter reading *Welcome to Jamaica* in the middle of their plates. In addition, there was a small piece of paper with an inscription that read:

Let this gift open my mind and soul to a greater spirituality - in Hector's name, we pray.

Hector spoke softly and the slight wrinkles that formed around his eyes as he spoke let Summer know that he meant her no harm.

"My sincerest apologies, Summer, for snapping at you earlier, but this is why I was so insistent on your attending dinner. Please, everyone, recite the enclosed prayer and enjoy."

The guests spoke in unison and watched as Hector delighted in his own self-proclaimed glory. The tropical air in the dining room was humid and heavy. As the group exhaled, the collective smoke filled the space and hung like an early morning fog. Summer's eyes rolled back in her head and she sank heavily into her chair. She watched Sonny shake his head and move his jaw side to side and back and forth, likely trying to regain some of the feeling that had been lost. Christine's neck turned to rubber as her head rolled around almost involuntarily. Hector sat perfectly still and simply closed his eyes.

"I've been smoking weed for a long time," Sonny tried to say the words, but they were slow to form. Finally, he was able to muster, "I can't feel my fucking jaw."

"This is going to radically change the global marijuana market, Sonny," Hector said.

At the same time, Summer regained her bearings in her new altered state and spoke, "W— what is this laced with?" was all she could mutter. Her brain still worked, but her body was not cooperating, a clear indicator of strong CB2 receptor bonding.

"This is the formula Mia was working with before she had her accident," Hector said in a low, seemingly sad voice.

Everything was happening in slow motion as if time itself had gotten stoned with them. Summer looked over to Sonny, unable to stay angry at him in her loose state. "What's in this? It's like nothing we've ever produced."

Sonny shook his head. Stoned and slack-jawed, he was barely able to speak in clear sentences. "No idea, orchid hybrid of some kind. I'd have to see her notes. Where is she?"

Hector didn't answer.

Summer was overwhelmed, more inebriated than she had ever been. She reached out and ran her fingers through the smoke, watching it dance around her hand as if she were willing it to do so. Her mind floated and started to hallucinate. She began to see life in inanimate objects; a vase containing beautiful orchids yawned. She would later learn that what she observed as a yawn was really just a swirl in the ceramic pattern, but for the moment, a yawn it was.

Hector spoke, and it sounded like a record on low speed. He beckoned Sonny and her to sit with him in the courtyard. Her mind was like jiggling Jell-O. She thought she was standing and walking, but then realized she hadn't moved at all. Time didn't exist. Had she been sitting there for an hour or a minute, she wondered.

Next thing she knew, she was hanging onto her dad and walking outside, although it felt more like floating. Their steps were slow and deliberate, and, after what felt like an eternity, they were sitting in a beautiful courtyard with a pond in the back, moonlight glimmering off the surface. It looked like black ice to Summer's stoned mind, and the tree that stood next to it resembled what looked like a mythical sea creature springing from the earth, ready to dive into the black water.

Summer sat silently for a long time, taking in the beauty of the night, watching stars whiz by and small animals scuttle across the yard. The grass danced in the soft breeze and kept her attention for what she thought was a very long time.

Finally, the voices of her father and Hector broke the vigil of the evening. She struggled to maintain focus on the conversation, the dancing grass drawing her back in.

"Hopefully Hodges will keep her occupied. Where is the old bastard anyway?"

She knew her dad was referring to Chris and wondered where she was.

Hector shook his head, "Dr. Hodges is no Sonny Flowers. He had to go, I'm afraid."

"Where is Chris?" Summer asked.

Hector told her that he'd dosed the major's joint with a small amount of Ativan.

"She's sound asleep. I couldn't have her intruding on my time with you and Sonny."

He laughed a deep laugh and Summer thought him insane. Was she supposed to appreciate his action? What did that mean for her and her father? Had they been drugged as well?

"And you expect us to work for you?"

It was probably the weed, and the fact that her mouth typically worked faster than her brain, but she heard herself mutter the question. She regretted it instantly, but before she could apologize, she heard herself blurt out, "How do you expect us to trust you now?"

She could see Hector become irritated. She guessed that he wasn't often grilled by his guests, let alone a feisty American girl. She was expecting the worst and cringed at the thought of what he might do or say to her. What was she thinking? She felt her father's hand on her knee. He squeezed it hard enough to let her know to take it down a notch.

Her host composed himself and smiled, his pearly white teeth a stark contrast to his dark Jamaican skin.

"My apologies, Ms. Flowers. Perhaps this will help regain your trust?"

Hector motioned to the man Summer recognized as Rufus from the boat.

"Bring me dat pirate. Set him up on da pole," Hector ordered.

Rufus nodded obediently and rushed off. Summer reached for her father's hand under the table, sensing something bad was about to happen, praying she wasn't right. Her high was beginning to weaken. The THC slowly released its hold over the neural space it had occupied the last couple of hours and left her relaxed; a little slow, yet more mentally aware.

She thought of the Elks and her father's words, a reminder that Hector couldn't be spoken to like one of them. Here on the island, Hector was king. Summer started to apologize, but Hector held up his index finger. She stopped and bit her tongue. Hector puffed on a cigar while they sat in shared silence, waiting for Rufus to return.

Moments later, Rufus reappeared, shoving the Aussie pirate toward a tall tree stump, scarred and ripped from, what Summer suspected, were many nights like this one. They watched as Rufus wrapped Bishop's arms around the pole and bound his wrists. Bishop, gagged and bound, didn't know where he was and struggled to free himself. He thrashed his body around the pole and frantically rubbed his wrists against the rough bark in an attempt to slice through the nylon rope that held him in place.

Rufus whistled. Max, the lanky shy boy who wrestled with her handbag on the beach, appeared in the doorway, solemn, and ready to go to work. Rufus removed the blindfold as Hector approached. The pirate stood frozen, realizing that, not only were there few places for him to hide, there were five sets of eyes on him as well.

"Mistah Bishop, pirates used to steal my shipments. They don't anymore."

Hector moved in close to Bishop's face. Summer could see Bishop wince as the giant man stared deep into his eyes.

Hector spoke softly in the pirate's ear. "*Dey* are too afraid. Are you afraid, Mistah Bishop?"

Bishop, wide eyed and sweating, nodded.

"Good," Hector said and extended his hand toward Max.

Max handed him the bat, and Summer watched as Bishop tried to plead his case through the gag. Hector, completely unaffected, gripped the handle of the aluminum bat tightly and rested it on his shoulder like a lazy batter waiting for a fastball.

He looked into the eyes of Bishop again and said, "Dis will not be pleasant."

With that, Hector swung the bat low and hard. It connected firmly against the side

of Bishop's knee. Bishop screamed into the gag as Summer jumped and cringed. The sound of the bones cracking under the force of the bat made her queasy. Hector made sure to not only inflict as much pain as possible, but to also study her reaction as he did. Summer knew Hector was sizing her up and letting her know through this act of violence that he was in charge and could do as he pleased. He stared at Summer and Sonny, scowling as he unloaded on Bishop's other knee.

Summer sat silently stunned, trying to hold back the tears, her emotions amplified under the power of the weed. How could she feel compassion for a man that held her hostage only a few hours earlier? But it wasn't compassion for Bishop, rather, a deeper fear of Hector.

Bishop lost consciousness. Hector reached into his pocket and retrieved the smelling salts. He waived them under the pirate's nose, and Bishop, revived, came back to life. He moaned and wailed in complete agony, tears streaming down his cheeks, his arms hugging the tree to keep his weight off the broken knees.

Hector held the barrel of the bat in his right hand and the handle in his left. He made sure Summer had a clear view as he drove the base of the handle through the back of Bishop's shoulder. Bishop screamed as his shoulder was dislocated and his rotator cuff ripped. Hector repeated the action on the other shoulder and then handed the bat to Max.

Hector wiped his brow as he headed back to the table. Summer clutched her father, terrified of what might happen to them, forgetting all about his weaknesses, wanting only to feel that her dad would protect her.

"Finish him," Hector ordered Max.

Max unrolled a bullwhip from his waist and flicked his wrist. The whip sliced the humid air and glided effortlessly toward the crippled prisoner. The crack of the whip made Summer jump again— a single tear fell as it connected and Bishop screamed. The gag had been worked loose. Bishop now had the full use of his mouth. It didn't matter, though. He was too far gone. Max continued to lace him with the whip until his body fell limp.

Bloodied and broken, Bishop hung on the post, barely breathing. Max cut the ties on his wrists and watched the once cocky pirate collapse.

"Toss him in," Hector shouted.

Max complied and dragged the pirate to the edge of the black pond, the water still and glassy. It took all of his strength, but he managed to lift the dead weight and launch the limp body into the water.

Summer lost her breath when she saw Bishop regain consciousness and fight to keep his head above water. With both shoulders dislocated and his knees broken, he was barely able to stay afloat. He begged for mercy as he gulped a mouthful of the black water. His head broke the surface again, choking and coughing, but still alive.

Summer looked on in disbelief. *This is inhumane*, she thought. *Why not just shoot him?*

Just then, the water started to bubble and move all around him, almost as if it were boiling. Bishop started screaming, terrified and helpless.

"What's going on? What's happening?" Summer asked frantically.

"It's de piranha— my flock." Hector said matter-of-factly. "If a man robs you and you kick him, he limps away wit your tings. If a man robs you and you shoot him, he is dead. You get your tings, and life goes on. If a man tries to rob you, and you break his arms and legs, whip him and feed him to de piranha, he dies, yes. But word spreads, and no man evah try to rob you again, especially those closest to you. Let dis be a lesson, Sumah Flowah."

Summer watched Bishop struggle for his last breath before the bubbling cauldron sucked him completely under. In just a few minutes, the water would be silent and still once more. Anyone entering the courtyard wouldn't have a clue that, only moments earlier, a man had been viciously tortured and eaten by a school of ravenous fish.

She watched Hector reach into his pocket and retrieve a small envelope which resembled a thank you card. He slid the envelope across the table and said, "Dis is for you. It was with Mia's tings in de lab."

Hector puffed his cigar and leaned back in his chair, dabbing the beads of newly formed sweat from his forehead. He started humming what they were sure was "Return to Sender" by Elvis Presley.

Summer didn't know what to do or what to say. How was what Hector had just done supposed to regain her trust? Was it all just a big show – a display of power?

"He captured and tried to ransom you and your father. He was your enemy. I vanquished him. Now you can trust me once more."

Had she spoken out loud? Was he able to read her thoughts? Could he really be a deity? She felt so uneasy. As if her words weren't enough, now she had reason to fear her thoughts as well. She turned her attention to Sonny.

"Well?"

Sonny handed her the card. Summer opened it and studied the two words – *Serpentine Orchid*. She couldn't be sure, in her state and without her equipment, but she was almost certain the words had been written in blood.

"What do you make of it?" Hector asked as he exhaled.

"I have no clue," Sonny said.

"Nor do I," said Summer.

"Well, you two geniuses had betta figure it out."

Hector rose and departed through the dining room, stopping at the entrance and turning to say, "Dinner is served."

Chapter 18

Where am I?

I was hazy and disoriented when I woke the next morning, much like I had been many of the mornings of my life. I tried moving, but my bones were reluctant and stubborn. I was feeling old and stiff, and not in the good way. I creaked and cracked my way to the bathroom where I ate three Vicodin, the way a kid would eat their Flintstones vitamins. My body was angry and told me that I was in no shape to be moving, so I crawled back under the covers and moaned. Talk about zero to sixty. I went from Ohio sloth to Caribbean swashbuckler and my being was in revolt.

Why was the sun so goddamn bright? The note from Mia stared up at me begging to be deciphered, but I was soundly stumped. What was she trying to tell me? It seemed so ominous, the writing in blood. It was like something out of Hollywood – very dramatic, Mia.

"Sonny? Are you up?" Summer asked, forcing her way into the room. She looked around to see if I had company and looked relieved to see me alone.

"Go away. I'm dying."

"Oh come off it, old man."

She ripped the blankets off of me and opened the blinds.

"What if I had been naked under here?"

"I put you to bed fully clothed. You are not ambitious enough to undress yourself."

"If this is your idea of payback, consider my debt fulfilled."

"I feel great. Maybe you should start taking better care of yourself?"

"Spare me the lecture and kindly hand me a joint?"

She wouldn't humor me. As I got up to collect my doobie, Summer studied the note. I asked her what she made of it.

"Not a clue," Summer replied. "I looked through all of my databases and not a single hit on a serpentine orchid."

I collected my mop of hair, tied it back, and splashed some water on my face. The Vicodin was kicking in. I was finally able to move, albeit slowly. As I emitted the first of, what I guessed would be, several dozen marijuana-laced exhalations that day, an idea formed.

"There's one person who may be able to help. I think we should pay her a visit."

"Her? Some other woman who's smitten with the great and powerful Sonny Flowers?"

I smiled. "You'll like her, smartass. She's a voodoo priestess."

Chapter 19

At the basin of the Blue Mountains, in a small cottage given to her by her Grandmother, Dehlia Storm watched a black-billed Amazon parrot perch itself on a low hanging branch of the Geiger tree near her window. She marveled at the bird and imagined for a moment what it would be like to transform herself into a parrot.

"Would I be able to fly to New Orleans?" she thought aloud.

"What was dat you said, love?" the voice next to her whispered as his hand stroked the small of her back, exposed outside the white linen sheet that covered her.

"Notin. Just dreamin' 'bout finding my fatha again."

"You've never met him. Why would you fret 'bout such tings?"

She turned to him and smiled softly. He was so handsome. Why did she always fall for the wrong men? It was a curse passed to her from her mother, one witch she would never forgive.

"He's all I have left. I have nobody else."

"You have me."

She squinted and pushed him away. "Need I remind you, Rufus Jones, dat you are a married man?"

Rufus sighed heavily and rolled onto his back, wishing he'd never met Dehlia. His life would have been much simpler that way. "Tell me again 'bout New Orleans and your fatha's plantation."

"Oh it's a grand plantation house wit columns and balconies and a paved brick walkway, stretching down between a row of giant magnolia trees with beautiful pink blossoms."

She smiled as she spoke of it, recounting it the way her grandmother described the majestic city in the southern United States to her when she was just a small girl. "It sits on the Mississippi River between New Orleans and Baton Rouge."

"And your fatha?"

"He runs the plantation as an inn. It was left to him by the widow he served there. At night, he plays the spoons for a Zydeco band in the French Quarter."

"I will take you dere and finally get off dis rotten island wit its run down parishes and crummy jobs."

"Poor sweet Rufus, you cannot go wit me. Hector will find you, and he will kill you. You married his niece. You can nevah leave."

"Soon, my love. We will find your fatha and live in New Orleans. I will find a—" Rufus couldn't finish. They heard visitors approaching.

"Oh, no." Dehlia cried. "You must go."

Rufus quickly gathered his things and crept out the front door. He slipped into the thick vegetation surrounding Dehlia's house and disappeared. Hurrying to dress herself, Dehlia slipped on her sandals just as she heard the knock at the door.

"Flowah mon? What you doin' here?"

Dehlia flung herself into his arms, excited to see the only true father figure she'd ever known.

"You must be Summah?" Dehlia asked, giving the blonde beauty a quick up and down.

Summer nodded and smiled halfheartedly.

Dehlia prepared rum drinks for her guests as they made themselves comfortable.

"What is it you do, Dehlia?" Summer asked, dusting off a throw pillow and plopping down on the sofa.

"I'm a voodoo priestess and a farmer. I grow fruit and vegetables and sell dem at de market."

Dehlia smiled, knowing that Summer was skeptical. Dehlia knew that she looked more like a college co-ed than a practitioner of the dark arts.

"Voodoo? Really?" Summer quipped.

The young slender priestess ignored Summer's sarcasm, something she was used to from the science community. Types like Summer were narrow-minded in the ways of spirituality, and impossible to convert. Sonny was different, though. He accepted her for exactly who she was, and she loved him for it. He told her it had been because of the influence of his daughter, Autumn.

"You are very lucky to have a fatha like Sonny. I hope someday when I meet my fatha, he is as good to me as the Flowah mon has been."

Dehlia smiled at him softly and kissed him on the cheek as she handed him the rum punch. Summer rolled her eyes and mumbled under her breath.

"Pay no attention to her, Dehlia. She's mad at me for not being as perfect as she is. According to Summer, I lack backbone and moral fiber."

Dehlia looked down and spoke softly. "We all have our skeletons, Sonny. Don't fret now."

"Oh, like shacking up with Rufus?" Summer jibed.

Dehlia's eyes flamed and it took all she had not to curse the younger Flowers to a

life of loneliness and despair, but she didn't. She loved Sonny, and Summer was his daughter. She saw the pain in Summer's eyes and believed a good person to live inside her—behind all the insecurity. Dehlia closed her eyes and took a long deep breath. She exhaled and turned her attention to Sonny, completely ignoring Summer. "What can I do for you, friend?"

Sonny removed the note from his pocket and handed it to the priestess. "What do you make of this?"

Dehlia left the room and returned a few minutes later with a heavy leather bound book, dusty and aged. The once legible title on the spine had been worn away over time and the pages crinkled as she turned them.

"Dis book is one handed down to me by my great-grandmotha. It have all de history of de island. Not de kine of history seen in school books, but stories of Spanish galleons and buccaneers who loved Indian girls."

Dehlia smiled, ever the romantic, dreaming of being with Rufus in New Orleans.

"What does any of that have to do with us?" Summer asked impatiently.

Dehlia studied one of the illustrations, again trying to not let Summer affect her.

"I knew I'd heard of it before. My grandmotha told me de story."

Sonny listened. Summer looked unenthusiastic.

"She said der was once a ship named *The Serpentine Orchid*. It was captained by a famous buccaneer named Julius Jameson. Captain Jameson led a raid against Spanish town and tried to claim the island of Jamaica for himself. While his ship bombarded de city with heavy cannons, Captain Jameson and a small crew of his finest swordsmen rowed ashore to infiltrate de barracks of the commanding officers."

Sonny lit a joint as Dehlia spoke. He offered the ladies a hit, but both refused. Dehlia continued on.

"Jameson and ten men fought and killed every officer holding de barracks. He was said to be de fiercest pirate in the waters at that time, even more fierce than Morgan. De Spanish were over-matched by his skill and cunning with de exception of one, Maria Paloma. Maria was a striking beauty, a seventeen-year-old duchess betrothed to a Spanish captain named Devante. Jameson cut down Devante as he stood defending his love and kidnapped de girl for himself."

Summer huffed. "I could be in the lab right now."

Dehlia closed her eyes again, this time mumbling a short chant.

"Oh, I think I'm going to be sick." Summer said, clutching her stomach.

"Bathroom is over dere," Dehlia pointed to a room adjacent to the kitchen.

"That wasn't nice," said Sonny.

"De girl had it comin'."

"She'll learn one of these days."

Dehlia smiled and went on. "Legend has it that Jameson and his men collected Maria's dowry along with her and headed back to de ship to continue da barrage from de water. Da bombardment did not last. Two Spanish ships came around from either side of de bay and trapped Jameson. He was forced to flee, but made off wit da girl and da treasure."

Sonny puffed on his joint and interrupted, "You sure you don't want some?"

Dehlia shook her head.

"It wasn't long before Jameson tried to have his way wit Maria, but she was a woman scorned. Her heart belonged to her slain love, Devante. The stories say dat Jameson came into de Captain chamba drunk on rum and didn't notice dat de shape on da bed wasn't Maria. He pulled back de blanket and saw her dowry spread across da bed. He turned just in time to see de dagger pierce him in the throat. She drove it in and whispered dat she would nevah love anotha as she did Devante."

Dehlia stopped momentarily to sigh the sigh of a girl in love. Much like Maria, she loved Rufus Jones. Forbidden, yes, but she didn't care. She continued, listening to Summer in the background, throwing up.

"Maria then pulled out de dagger and drove it into her own heart. Da next day, de two Spanish ships found dem and sank *The Serpentine Orchid* where she stood. All de treasure has been found, but no one evah found da dagger. Some say Maria took it wit her to de otha side to protect her from Captain Jameson."

"What do you think it all means, Dehlia?" Summer asked, returning from the bathroom, wiping her mouth and looking flushed.

"Don't know. Maybe you go out der an see for yourself?"

Summer shrugged.

"You asked about de *Serpentine Orchid*, and now you know. More rum?"

Sonny laughed and extinguished his joint. "You could have just said shipwreck a mile off shore."

Dehlia scrunched her forehead and chanted in a foreign tongue as she flicked some of her drink at Sonny. Dehlia sipped the rum and flipped through the digital photos on Summer's camera, admiring the photographs of the flora and wildlife she snapped on her walk up.

"Very nice," Dehlia said, handing the camera to Summer. "I especially liked de one of de pink hibiscus."

Summer extended a half smile and snatched the camera from Dehlia, shoving it back in her bag and giving her a very insincere, "Nice to meet you."

Summer walked out and Sonny followed. Dehlia grabbed him and pulled him aside.

"You be careful. Dat girl has a lot of anger and sadness inside her, Flowah mon."

"She'll come around. She always does."

Dehlia gave him a kiss on the cheek and watched as he hurried to catch his impatient daughter.

Chapter 20

General Lawrence Chamberlain paced silently, his arms crossed behind his back, one hand clasping the opposite wrist. It wasn't as much pacing as it was marching. His posture was militant and the cadence of his steps matched the ticking of the grandfather clock perfectly.

He practiced as often as he could. The good Lord saw fit to give the general feet that were two sizes too small for a man of his height and weight. The marching was a conscious exercise designed to keep him from literally tripping over his own two feet every step.

"This is a problem," he said as one heel clicked to the ground in time with the clock.

"No problem, General. Sonny will figure it out before de crowd arrives."

Hector leaned back in his chair, feet propped, arms behind his head, and exhaling as he spoke.

"Well, I hope you're right. My intelligence sources tell me he and his daughter haven't even stepped into the lab."

Hector started choking. "Your intelligence sources? You mean dat crazy girl be following Sonny round like a lost puppy? Elvis would call her da devil in disguise."

The general stopped pacing and faced Hector squarely. His face tightened and his eyes fixed on the king of the island like a snake about to strike. Hector, sensing the anger, dropped his feet and spun around in his chair.

"I'll have you know that the little girl you speak of is a major in the United States Army. Furthermore—"

Hector interrupted. "Former. Right, General? You and she are former officers in the U.S. Army."

The general was about to rip Hector up one side and down the other when the door opened.

"What is it, Max?" Hector snapped impatiently.

Max tried to explain what he'd seen to his uncle, but stumbled and stammered so terribly that Hector finally stopped him.

"Write it down, boy."

Max wrote, his hand shaking: *Rufus and Dehlia in love. Sonny to go to Jameson wreck.*

Hector nodded and dismissed Max. He sat silently for a moment, studying the piece of paper in front of him.

"General, I have an idea. Tell your guests to expect a real life demonstration of the formula."

"Very well," barked the general.

Hector leaned back in his chair once more, lifting his heels back to their former resting spot. He studied the blades of the ceiling fan as they slowly circulated the thick Jamaican air and hummed the tune still stuck in his mind.

"That will be all, General. You can go now."

"Just a minute. What is it you're planning?"

"It's best you don't know, General. What you don't know can't be held against you."

"Understood."

And with that, the general excused himself.

"Max," Hector shouted. Max reappeared in a flash and stood silently awaiting his uncle's orders. "Tell me more 'bout what you saw."

Hector puffed on his joint and Max told him everything.

Chapter 21

We didn't say a word to each other on the walk back. Summer was agitated, and I hadn't a clue why. Maybe she was still irritated about Chris and me on the boat, but to act so bitchy was out of character for her.

"What's bothering you, honey?" It was a big risk calling her honey. My trying to act sweet was like salt in a wound to Summer. My little scientist preferred a nod of approval over a term of endearment any day of the week. Still, there had to be something I could say?

She shrugged me off.

"I can't read your mind. You were pretty bitchy to Dehlia and that's not like you."

Summer just kept walking, maintaining her silent vigil.

"Jesus, just let me have it already. Yell at me. Call me an asshole. Tell me what a shitty father I am. Just please don't carry on with the cold shoulder."

I should have kept my mouth shut. My frustration only strengthened her resolve.

"You want some?" I held out the joint as a peace offering.

"No, thanks. I need my brain fully functional. I don't know why you find it so necessary? You aren't nervous or in one of your panicked states."

"What did I do?"

Summer shot me a glare and in her bitchiest tone said, "Well, I need to catalog these photos I took, and we should probably look at Mia and Dr. Hodges' notes before heading out to sea."

I nodded. "You look through the notes. I already know what they say. I'm heading back to my room for a nap."

She shook her head and said, "I don't even know why you bothered to come."

Back in my room, I studied my notes. I didn't need to. I remembered it all, but I wanted to figure out what Mia was trying to tell me. The shipwreck better provide some answers. I read her writing and thought of my beautiful Mia. She used to tell me how much she loved working with me. I told her she was crazy and had island fever, but I loved hearing it. The memory of her perfume, the softness of her perfect skin, and the smile that won my heart still resonated. When would I see her? Was she still even alive? My gut rolled as I considered the possibility that Hector had learned of our affair. He couldn't have known. If he had, I'd already be dead. Maybe he was waiting for the formula to be completed before killing me? Maybe it was all just a grand scheme? What if I was supposed to complete the formula and cure Mia just so Hector could confront us about the affair and THEN kill us?

At least we'd be together, I thought.

"Stop this, Flowers. You are just being paranoid," I told myself.

Unlike some stoners, I'd never been afflicted with pot-induced paranoia, but with a dude like Hector looming, I didn't need the weed to blame. I was plenty paranoid without it.

I hoped Summer was having better luck.

Chapter 22

Summer scoured through her father's notes as she waited for the photos to load. The idea of multiple orchid or multiple marijuana hybrids as potential solutions for their problem seemed logical in theory, but now she needed to prove it. Her botany degree would be an asset as she worked to identify potential candidates. The compound was potent for sure. Hector had given them a mild dose of what she was confident Mia had developed as the production agent.

Why would Mia have dosed herself with a compound that hadn't been fully vetted? Why would she risk her life knowing that a release antidote hadn't yet been developed? Maybe it was all a ploy to get Sonny back to the island? What if the release compound had already been produced? What if Mia hid it out on that shipwreck? Hector would have already found it. It was too simple.

The ding on her computer signaled that the photos had been successfully downloaded. As she sorted them by genus, a practice her father had imparted upon her as an undergrad, one photo stood out. It was the pink hibiscus Dehlia had mentioned liking. Summer felt bad for being snotty with Dehlia. She saw Sonny act around her the same way he had with Autumn. This was supposed to be her time with him and now, separated from all of the reminders of her dead sister, along comes the Jamaican version of Autumn – Dehlia fucking Storm. *Just perfect*, she thought, as she zoomed in on the photo.

Summer cropped the image and gasped when she saw what it revealed. Behind her hibiscus, lying downhill were a pair of eyes staring back at her. She gasped. Had Dehlia known? Is that why she deliberately mentioned it? Her eyes remained glued to the image on the screen as she tried to place the face— it was Max. She was sure of it. He'd been following them.

"That cheeky little shit."

She assumed that he had been privy to their conversation with Dehlia, and assumed the worst. Hector would likely know by now so the sooner she and Sonny made it out to the *Serpentine Orchid*, the better. For all she knew, Hector had a boat with some of his men out there already.

"Chris— wake up." Summer yelled as she pounded on the door.

The major stumbled out, still looking half dead from the night before, and asked what was happening. Summer explained and showed her the image on her laptop.

Chris barked instructions. "Hector has a fleet of speedboats docked across the bay where we landed. He keeps them rigged with dive gear because he transports shipments between the boats and mini-subs. That's how he moves all of his marijuana. Take one of them and get to that wreck."

Christine studied the photo as Summer sped off. Once out of sight, she minimized the photo program and read the open document Summer had forgotten to close.

Summer pounded on Sonny's door.

"C'mon, Sonny. We have to go. Hector knows about the *Serpentine Orchid*."

She explained as they scrambled toward the marina. "You'd think Hector would have already considered the shipwreck?"

"Yeah," Summer said, "but he may have overlooked something we wouldn't."

Sonny agreed and asked Summer if she'd been able to locate anything in her botany database.

"I think I figured out what's missing from the orchid clone."

"The release compound, right? The second flower?"

"Yeah," Summer said, surprised her dad had already figured it out, annoyed that he hadn't mentioned it before.

"I'm hoping Mia found it," he said as they ran toward the boat docks.

"Me, too," said Summer, "and what's more, I hope she left it for us at that shipwreck."

Chapter 23

I pushed the throttle full forward and the boat responded. We were in a race for our lives, or at least that's how it felt. For all I knew, we actually were. The sport cruiser cut through the glassy Caribbean like a Ginsu knife, and, for a split second, I imagined Summer and I were on vacation. While Summer worked below, assembling the dive gear, I raced a pod of spinner dolphin and smiled as a few of them breached in my wake. A short ten minutes later, I found our mark and dropped anchor. The depth gauge read forty-two feet. Not too bad, but still deep enough to get me into trouble.

"There's only enough gear for one of us to go down."

"I'll go. You stay topside and keep a lookout," I said.

No sign of Hector or any of his henchmen. Good thing, too. I was nervous enough just going down solo. What was I looking for again?

"Remember, she wrote the note in blood, so look for anything red or bloody – a note, a flower, anything," Summer instructed.

I nodded and took a test breath from the regulator. As I fell backward off the edge of the boat and started my descent, I could clearly see the wreck. The Jamaican sun and clear water made for great visibility. The aft half of the galleon was buried in the sand, while the fore jutted up toward the surface like it was rising from the bowels of hell itself. I checked my depth gauge – forty-two feet on the button. The shadow of the *Sea Ray* was still visible above.

I swam toward the bow and nearly jumped out of my skin as a twelve-foot tiger shark cruised past. No hello, goodbye, fuck you – nothing. I hadn't noticed at first, but the sombitch had caught himself a sea turtle. I'd about had enough close encounters of the tiger shark kind. Pensively, I poked my nose through the rip in the hull, hoping another set of chompers wouldn't be lying in wait. A puffer and a couple triggers were all that came out to greet me as I worked my way around the wreck. I was two thirds around and hadn't seen a goddamn thing. It was a cool wreck and all, but an old cannon and some broken cleats were the only items of note that crossed my path. Then, just when I was about to call it quits, I saw the Leviathan that adorned the bowsprit. It was an impressive sight for sure, but the orchid it carried in its mouth looked like the real prize.

As I moved in to take a closer look, the sound of a motor and the shadow of another boat above sent my pulse racing. *Fuck*, I hadn't been fast enough. The panic was starting, and I doubted I'd be able to light a joint underwater. I could just see Hector and his men topside. They were probably already boarding or worse, taking Summer. I started sucking air, the stupidest thing a diver can do. Kicking hard, I tried to ascend but only made it a few feet before the depth charge detonated. It was probably a good twenty feet above me, but the force of the explosion was enough to drive me down hard to the sea floor.

I felt like I'd been punched in the sternum. Sand billowed up around me and I was completely disoriented. I could barely make out the sound of splintering wood, but couldn't see what was happening.   Little did I know that the bowsprit of the *Serpentine Orchid* was separating from the main hull. It fell toward me faster than I could swim. I braced for impact.

There I was, soundly pinned against the ocean floor – completely trapped. What was worse - I only had ten minutes of air left in my tank. I'd need at least five to get to the surface. *Don't panic, Sonny*, I told myself, but it was too late. My pulse was racing, this was it. Lights out for good in T-minus-nine minutes. Nobody was coming to rescue me this time. They must have found what they needed, so good riddance to me.

The sand settled and the Leviathan looked me square in the eyes. The orchid appeared plain, nothing special about it. I took short breaths and pressed my hand against my chest. I asked good ol' St. Anthony for help once again, certain that I'd used up what little grace I'd been given.

Next to the head of the Leviathan, a gold object jutted up from the sand. It was the lost dagger Dehlia spoke of – the one Maria used to kill Jameson. What a waste. I'd just made a once in a lifetime treasure find, and in six minutes, I'd be dead. Some other moron would find me holding it and steal it away. Hopefully the locals would contrive some fantastic tale about a curse or some shit like that. Sonny Flowers found it, but the boat wouldn't let him keep it.

I buried the blade against the hull and tried to pry myself out. I looked at my air. Three and a half minutes. I'd resigned myself to defeat when I felt another punch, this time to the head— a second depth charge had detonated. The giant pulse of water destroyed what remained of the *Serpentine Orchid* and snapped the bowsprit in two. The ship had taken the brunt of the impact and had actually shielded me from what would have been certain death.

Free, I kicked as hard as he could. I'll worry about the Benz later. I needed a breath, and I needed to know Summer was okay. My oxygen had run out. I had at least twenty feet to go, and my chest ached from the pressure of the charges. My lungs were on fire. Would I really survive another impossible feat only to die with ten feet to go? Kicking harder, four, three, two. The light was darkening. My lungs were about to explode. Don't black out now. One! I broke through the surface and sucked in as much air as my lungs would allow.

I was dizzy after several more breaths and floated on my back in excruciating pain once again.

"Dad?" I heard her call.

She was alive. Thank Christ. And she called me Dad. Maybe I was dead after all?

Chapter 24

I hugged Summer and busted her chops for looking surprised to see me alive.

"I feel like a cat that just used his ninth life."

She didn't say anything. She just pointed starboard. I expected the worse, Hector with a gun, Rufus with his gang, or Max with his whip. What I hadn't expected to see was Chris Smith, alone and lying dead on the other boat. She was sprawled on the deck, a pistol in her hand.

"Summer?"

"Dad, it was awful. She came out of nowhere and held me at gunpoint." Her voice trembled. "She said she didn't need us anymore and went all crazy telling me if she couldn't have you, nobody would. That's when she dropped the first depth charge."

"It was Chris?"

I couldn't believe it. Yeah, she had a little schoolgirl crush on me, but she wasn't a psycho. At least I didn't think she was. Holy shit. We were in a lot of trouble.

Summer's hands were shaking. I held them and tried to calm her down. She took a breath and nodded. "I ran below before she fired. The spear gun was mixed in with the dive gear, so I grabbed it. I shot her but not before she dropped the second charge."

I played the scene in my mind as she spoke. "It's okay. I'm just glad you're not hurt."

I held her and told her that she did the right thing. What I couldn't figure out was why. It just didn't add up. Chris wouldn't have worked so hard to get me back here to help her only to go crazy in some sort of jealous lovers rage. What had really driven her to drop those charges?

"Sonny Flowers. You need to come with us, please."

I didn't hear them approach. Jesus smiled as he patted the 9mm in his belt. What was it with these guys and their unabashed friendliness? It was like Hector had sent them all to Hilton concierge training.

We boarded his boat and I prepared for the worst once again. It seemed all too common a thought these last couple days. My heart raced and the anxiety bubbled. Get a grip, old man. Summer needs you. I reached out and squeezed her hand.

"Is this it?" she asked.

"No," I said. "If Hector wanted us dead, we would be."

There was only one person waiting for us at the dock.

"He took Rufus, Sonny. Hectah found out about us and he took him," Dehlia said.

It was all falling apart. Hector probably knew everything. It was the only explanation. He'd probably had us under surveillance the entire time. Shit, I wouldn't be surprised if he had audio and video of my affair with Mia. I was starting to think she wasn't even alive, but Aunt Autumn would have told me to trust my gut and my gut told me she was. Maybe it was just because I wanted it so badly to be true. I slipped Jesus a spliff and asked him for a couple minutes with Dehlia. He smiled and gave me the okay. Everybody on the island knew I kept the best stuff for myself, so a joint out of my personal stash was as good to a Rasta as hitting triple sevens on a slot in Vegas.

I grabbed Dehlia's hand and held it against my stomach, unzipping the wetsuit as I did. She pulled away, momentarily thinking the worst of me. I shushed her and told her to trust me. She felt the handle of the dagger and understood my actions.

"Take it. It's yours."

"I know what to do wit dis," she whispered. A hug and a tear-soaked kiss on the cheek were my thanks. I watched her disappear into the dense brush and hoped I'd see her again.

"Was that what I think it was?" Summer asked, having witnessed the exchange.

I nodded and cracked a half a smile. Jesus gave the nod and flicked what remained of the joint into the sea.

"What else did you find down there?" Summer asked.

"Nothing."

She huffed, acting like I was keeping something from her.

"Get in dere," Jesus ordered, pushing us through the door of the lab.

It looked just like I remembered. Closing my eyes, I breathed in the sweet scent of orchid, blooming marijuana, and what I swore was the scent of Mia's perfume. I was pretty sober and surprised at how keen my senses were without the aid of my old botanical friend.

"So I'm curious to know what you found out there."

Huh? So much for my good senses. I hadn't even noticed the old bastard sitting directly across from me in Mia's old chair.

"Who the fuck are *you*, man?" I implored.

"Who the fuck am I? I'm the reason you're here *and* the reason you're still alive."

I tried to turn and leave, pulling Summer along with me but the effort was in vain.

The old dude gave a nod, and Jesus sent the stock of his M-16 squarely into my gut. I doubled over and felt like I was going to puke up my spleen.

"Jesus," I moaned, trying to catch my breath.

The hulkish Jamaican just stood there smiling like an idiot. It made the humiliation and pain that much worse. It took such little effort on his part to inflict so much pain. I'd like to see him try and figure out the Schrodinger Equation.

Summer gasped and tried to come to my aid, but the Jamaican strongman pulled her away.

"Yes, Jesus is his name, Dr. Flowers, and mine is General Chamberlain. You may address me as General or Sir."

"What the fuck do you want, man?"

The general nodded, and Jesus kicked me in the ribs— hard. I regretted my new-found sense of obstinacy.

"What the fuck do you want, General?" I whispered.

"What I want, Dr. Flowers, is for you to finish what you and Mia Hanassui set out to complete. I need that control agent, and I need it in twenty-four hours."

"Never gonna happen — sir."

"If you value your daughter's life, it will, Dr. Flowers."

With that, the general walked out of the lab. Jesus followed, but I could tell that he wasn't happy about having to leave me alive, the sadistic fucker. He was still smiling, though. Go figure.

"Daddy, are you okay?"

"Who was that guy?"

"I saw him talking to Chris when we first got here."

"Chris?"

"Yeah."

"As in Chris Smith the girl you just harpooned to death?"

"Oh, shit," said Summer.

"If he and Chris were in cahoots, he's going to be plenty pissed when he finds out she's dead."

"We'd better get to work and give him what he wants, fast," Summer said, helping me to the workbench.

My eyes sank as I massaged my ribs back into place. I sighed and said, "The problem is that I have no idea where to begin."

Chapter 25

Rufus Jones sat blindfolded, his hands bound behind his back and his feet tied to the legs of the metal-framed chair. He heard light footsteps walking around him and knew who it was without having to see.

"Maxi, I'm sorry, mon. I love her."

Rufus smiled as he thought of his beloved Dehlia, but the smile was quickly wiped away by the forceful backhand of his captor. The sting couldn't suppress his spirit, though it did steal some of the wind from his sail. Rufus just imagined him and Dehlia on the porch of that plantation house in New Orleans. He saw her skipping along in a sundress, excited to be coming home to him.

The door flung open, and a new set of footsteps approached. His blindfold was removed, and, after taking a moment to let his eyes adjust to the light, he focused on the imposing figure before him— Hector Hannassui.

"Should I take you to de courtyard and feed you to de flock?"

Rufus sat silently, waiting for Hector's heavy hand to fall on him, ready for whatever was coming his way.

"Max tells me dat my niece wasn't good enough for you? You had to go aftah dat voodoo girl. Did she cast a spell on you? Was dat it?"

Hector was quite agitated. Rufus knew that no matter what his response, the outcome would likely be the same.

"A spell of love," said Rufus.

"You weren't supposed to fall in love wit her," Hector shouted.

Whack! The force of Hector's punch sent him flying across the room. His head hit the wall and knocked him unconscious.

"Make sure he doesn't die. I need him alive."

Max nodded and righted his one-time friend.

Chapter 26

Summer leafed through notes while I sat at the workspace, remembering my first days on the island. I was angry, having been muscled into a government project and stolen from my family. I was bound and determined to do everything I could to fail miserably. Then Mia walked in. She was so beautiful and, in a flash, all my anger melted away. She was eager and excited. To her, it was a chance to work on something real, not to just clone the next great strain of weed for her sociopath husband. Summer gave me a poke in the ribs. It hurt. Between the depth charges and Jesus' rifle stock, I had at least two broken ribs. Breathing had now become something I no longer cared to do.

"So what do we know for sure?" I asked, trying to forget the pain.

"We know that whatever Mia was dosed with works."

" Shiiit, we don't even know if she's alive. Have you seen her? I haven't."

"This better not be about you missing your girlfriend. Didn't you hear that crazy man? We need to figure this out, Sonny."

I looked around the lab and had forgotten just how many plants were here.

"Well, we have a whole greenhouse behind us. Let's start there."

Summer reluctantly nodded, and we set off with our notes and hand-held recorders. Mia had categorized the inventory and assigned a Dewy Decimal-like marker to each area of the floor. It was actually quite impressive. I was jealous I hadn't thought of it.

"Do you see it?" I shouted to Summer.

"Yes, marijuana is classified with the capital letter M. Orchid is a capital O. Different strains of pot are lowercase letters, and different subspecies of orchid are also lowercase. It also looks like someone added suffixed numerals. Dosages?"

"Yeah, that would be my guess. We need the master list of strains and sub-species."

"I'll look for that while you look for any classification differentiators," Summer shouted.

I walked the aisles and noted all of the category codes. "MOjo-10, MOjo-15, MOjo-20." I recorded as I walked. "MOsz-05, MOsz-10..."

We'd only been at it an hour when the general and Jesus came back to check on our progress. I bit my tongue when the general smirked at me. I wondered what involvement Hector had with him. Summer turned the corner. Jesus snatched her up.

"Let her go, asshole." I shouted, trying to dart in between her and the general. I was slow. My ribs ached. The general laughed and waved me off. I was in no shape to try and fight Jesus, not even on my best day.

"Bring her to me," he ordered.

Summer struggled to free herself from his grip, but it was no use. Jesus simply dragged her over and threw her down hard in front of the general.

I watched as Chamberlain opened the backpack and retrieved two small silver objects from it. They looked like metal dog collars.

"Let go of me, you son of a bitch!" Summer yelled.

I was sure she was wishing she had her Glock handy now.

The fight was useless as the general grabbed her wrist and snapped one of the bracelets around it. He repeated the same on the other wrist. I tried to make a move.

"Uh-uh, Dr. Flowers," the general warned. "You don't want your little girl to lose a hand, now do you?"

I raised my arms in surrender. The general snapped a larger ring around Summer's neck and pushed her toward me.

"What is this?" Summer screamed.

The general beamed. "Why this is the latest in military intelligence interrogation technology."

"A torture device," I said.

"Very good, Doctor. Maybe you are as smart as they claim you to be?"

I grabbed the ring around Summer's neck and tried pulling it apart.

"I wouldn't do that if I were you, Doctor Flowers," said the general.

"These devices are tamper proof. Any detection that they are being meddled with will set them off."

The bastard waved a remote control.

"You see, a timer is set for each. Your daughter's right hand is set for twenty-four hours, her left is thirty-six, and her neck is forty-eight. I have exactly forty-eight hours until some of the world's most powerful military minds arrive to see what you've produced."

"You'll remove the devices if we get you your agent in time?"

"We'll see. I always have the option to manually override the timer. You see, *your* little girl here took the life of *my* little girl."

I felt sick again.

"Chris was your daughter?"

"That's right. So, work fast, Sonny Flowers. I may extend the mercy to your daughter that she didn't extend to mine."

With that, the general pressed a button and the red light on each of the devices illuminated.

"What happens if we don't figure out the formula in time?" Summer asked.

"If the timer or override is triggered, the red light will turn green and set off a small explosive. You'll lose your right hand, Ms. Flowers. A series of lasers will fire after the explosion to cauterize the veins and arteries in the stump. This will keep you from bleeding to death until the next timer is triggered, and so on. Obviously, you can guess what will happen if the ring around your neck is activated. I'd encourage you to get to work and keep your head about you."

He laughed as he said it and slammed the door.

"You sadistic son of a bitch." I screamed, but he was gone.

"Look at you, tough guy." Summer joked.

I saw the fear in her eyes. "I'll figure it out, sweetheart."

She broke down and finally let out all the tears that had been welling up inside of her, for, what I imagined, were years. I hugged her and let her sob. She was human after all. Maybe she wasn't as much like my mom as I thought. Maybe Regina wasn't really that terrible.

Who was I kidding? Of course she was. Summer, though, was my little girl, and any daughter of mine had to have at least some kind of a heart.

"I don't want to die, Daddy."

"I know, baby. I won't let that happen."

Chapter 27

Summer cried a while longer. I struggled to maintain composure. The fact was that we were no further along than we had been since setting foot on the island three days earlier. Mia's note was the link to an antidote. I had to find it, but the stress wasn't helping. My subconscious needed do the work for me. I needed a joint.

I stared at the tray of test tubes that had been hidden in the fridge under the workbench. That had to be it.

"What are they?" Summer asked.

"I think they're liquefactions of the isolated THC and orchid compounds. Look,

they're labeled."

The first label read MOjo.022.

"I think they're dosages," Summer said. "The .022 must be the milligram of orchid pollen." She leafed through a binder next to the tray. "The THC content is the constant and the orchid pollen is the variable. The different specimens of marijuana confirm this because there are a zillion more pot plants than orchids."

I studied the chart and couldn't disagree. "We need to find which one Mia is dosed with in order to create an antidote."

"We need a blood sample," Summer said.

"No time."

I picked up a vial in the fourth row. It was the only one in the tray that matched Mia's writing. I recognized the little loop at the top of the letter O. "This is the one."

"How can you be sure?"

"I can't, but I need you to trust me."

Summer analyzed it and determined it to be a highly concentrated form of the MOjo.55 strain.

"This is the highest THC concentration I've ever seen," she exclaimed. "Is this what Hector gave us the first night?"

"No, if we'd smoked this, we'd be in a state of long-term psychosis. I can't believe she'd take this on her own."

"Are you saying she was dosed with it?"

"It's the only thing that makes sense."

"This is insane. A compound like this is the type of shit that, if you don't have a way to clear it from your brain, would need a lobotomy to fix."

She was right. It was dangerous stuff indeed. It was stronger than the strongest LSD I'd ever seen and could last months, maybe forever.

We needed a double dose of the release compound for Mia.

"What now?" Summer asked

"Now I say we get high."

"What?"

I could see the irritation and disappointment in her face. She thought I was panicking again, and I should have been, but I wasn't. The sad fact was that my sober mind wasn't going to solve this problem.

"I'm going to try something your aunt taught me when I was a kid. It's called lucid dreaming, only I'm going to meditate, or lucid daydream."

Summer shook her head in disgust. "This is your genius plan?"

"Yeah. I fixate my mind on what it is I want and let my subconscious figure it out."

"Great. More of your metaphysical nonsense."

This wasn't science. My idea was preposterous to her, but I hoped she'd go along. I held her hand and held her eyes in mine. "Sometimes you have to feel color in a monochromatic world."

Summer grabbed a vial of the low dose base THC and held it out.

"I hope you're right about this."

"Only one way to find out, right?"

I downed it and closed my eyes.

"So much for living to see my 29th birthday. Bottoms up."

Summer tipped back what remained and, together, we drifted off. I guided her as my aunts had done for me, telling her to empty her mind and let it fill with only things relevant to our mission. I told her to use all of her senses, to let her subconscious do all the work.

"Don't *think*, Summer. *Feel.*"

I urged her to listen to the numbers and science she saw in her mind and touch the results. I focused on Mia. I visualized where we'd been, our conversations, and our tests.

Talk to me, Mia. What is it you need me to find?

Chapter 28

It didn't take long for the euphoria to envelop me. Levar Burton from *Reading Rainbow* started reading my journal as if it were a children's book. I could hear the theme song and see the carton images swirl. My scribbling started to move on the page, sliding and slithering like a thousand tiny snakes. They reformed new words, words I hadn't expected to see.

"Watch out for dat girl. She'd got a lot of anger in her."

Levar said it, but they were Dehlia's words.

"Scram, Levar," I mumbled. "I need Mia."

"I just wanted to make you proud," I heard.

Summer? I couldn't lose her. *Mia, where are you?*

I tried to clear my mind and focus, but random flashes burst in my brain like fireworks. I saw the *Serpentine Orchid*. What did I miss? I saw Hector handing me the note in the courtyard. I saw the letters in red. Was Mia's message an anagram? Was it possible? Was the ship a ploy?

My mind took the note and floated it in a black space. I concentrated hard on the note and only the note. I imagined the blackness turning white as the letters came to life on the blank canvas. They were dripping with blood and melting into the white, the pools of blood morphed into small puddles of hot red wax.

The letters rose up out of the steaming puddles in a different order— a new order. I worked *Serpentine* first.

The letters moved fast now, sliding under and jumping over one another: *Preteens, In - Preteen, Ins - Preteen, Sin - Serene, Pint - Entrees, Pin - Entrees.* Nothing was making sense.

Help me, Mia.

I remembered staring at her on our first orchid hunt together while she stared at the plants.

She smiled at me. "Sonny, are you even working?"

"What am I looking for, exactly?"

I recalled her accent - British with a Jamaican flare, an indication that she hadn't originally hailed from the island, but had been transplanted there.

"You remind me of this plant, Sonny. It's a lily pretending to be an orchid. It tricks the bees into taking its nectar and pollinating the same way they would an orchid. You're a great scientist, but you pretend you're not. Now go find me my orchid."

I barely finished the thought when the letters snapped into place, as if I'd just found the key that unlocked the treasure chest.

Serpentine Orchid – pretense in orchid – the pretend orchid – the lily.

I opened my eyes and wrote it down. As I stumbled down the aisles of the lab, I hoped something would present itself. It seemed like forever. Each aisle the same – pot plant after pot plant. Never thought I'd live to see the day I would be unhappy to see one. Where was it? I was high and wished I wasn't. Would I remember sober? I couldn't remember what the lily looked like. I was headed down the last aisle.

I rubbed my medal and prayed hard: *The lily is lost and can't be found. Dear Saint Anthony, take a look around.*

I opened my eyes and looked up. There it was, hidden among the orchids, doing its job. The Blood lily – the pretend orchid. That's what Mia had been trying to tell me. It was an anagram. *Clever girl.* The Blood lily was the key. The resin from its pollen would release the bond of the orchid resin from the neuron.

I caressed the petals and pulled the potted lily close to my heart. I looked up to the sky and took a deep breath, silently thanking the patron saint of lost things and the daughter who introduced us.

Chapter 29

Summer had fallen asleep. She woke to find her father in a frenzied state at the workbench.

"I figured it out," he said, scanning the tray of vials. She watched, still half asleep, as he lifted the tube from the tray and handed Summer two syringes, one containing the MOjo 55 and one containing the release.

"Give me five minutes, and then inject me with the release compound."

"Wait," Summer interrupted. But it was too late.

She watched her father tip the vial back and down the full contents of the remaining MOjo 55 concentration. Within seconds, he was gone. Summer looked at her watch and knew she couldn't wait five full minutes She uncapped the release compound syringe and wiped Sonny's shoulder with an alcohol swab.

Sonny swatted her hand away hard and shouted, "Who are you?" He was already hallucinating. "What happened to your face?"

She was scared. He stared and squinted at her. She could only imagine what it was he was seeing. For all she knew, he was watching her face contort and melt, her cheeks dripping off of her face, resembling a gooey grilled cheese sandwich. She approached him once again with the syringe and he shuddered. Shaking and screaming, he yelled at her to move back, accusing her of trying to kill him.

"Put the fucking knife away." he said, every muscle in his body tensing as Summer approached. She didn't know what else to do. She edged closer, hoping she would be able to inject him before he planted her on her ass. Once she stepped within striking distance, he swung at her— hard.

"Got to get the hell out of here," he mumbled under his breath.

Summer gathered herself, thankful the release hadn't been shattered. Sonny moved toward the entrance, but then clutched his head in angst. He started to thrash and swat at what Summer guessed were the plants. In his mind, they were probably wrapping themselves around his ankles or creating a wall in front of him. Jesus must have heard Sonny's screams. He opened the door to investigate and found Sonny in all of his craziness.

"Hold him," Summer shouted.

Jesus wrapped Sonny in a bear hug.

"Snakes crushing me. Boa constrictors."

Like a man on PCP, Summer watched her crazed father summon strength, fueled by adrenalin. Sonny shot his arms up through the snake arms of Jesus and threw him to the ground forcefully. He ran like the wind and disappeared into the dense foliage before Jesus knew what hit him, and before Summer could inject him.

Jesus scrambled to his feet and gave chase, but it was in vain.

"De general gone kill me," he said, limping back to the lab.

"Help me," Summer whispered.

Jesus rushed in to find Summer Flowers lying on the ground barely conscious. He knelt beside her and gently lifted her head off the ground, trying to get a grip around her.

Summer opened her eyes and found her mark. Jesus, caught off guard, looked like a deer in the headlights as Summer plunged the syringe into his neck. It was the syringe filled with the MOjo 55.

Once incapacitated, she filled a second syringe with the Ativan Hector used to knock Chris out their first night on the island. The combination of the drugs sent Jesus into a coma almost immediately. With the antidote syringe tucked safely away in one pocket, and the Ativan/MOjo 55 combo in the other, Summer set off to find her father.

Chapter 30

Summer ran toward the main house, her neck and wrists still shackled by the torture devices. *Where could that old fool be,* she thought as she walked, knowing that in his state he was highly paranoid, and, combined with his delusions, would not likely approach her even if their paths crossed.

Thankfully, she realized that they were well under the time allotted by the general to manufacture the agent. With the antidote in hand, she could revive Mia, get the neckband and bracelets off, and satisfy both the general and Hector. She breathed a small sigh of relief, knowing her mission would soon be accomplished.

As she approached the door to the main house, she heard footsteps behind her—

the marching footsteps of a man with feet too small for his body.

The familiar voice spoke. "Just where do you think you're going?"

Summer spun around, her hand around the lethal syringe in her right front pocket.

"Is that my agent?" the general asked in a rather calm tone.

Summer knew this might be her only opportunity to face the general one-on-one, and she knew that with the syringe she held in her hand, she had a chance to kill him if she could get close enough.

Just think of the Elks, she told herself. *Remember how you manhandled them at the last pickup. You can take this old bag of bones.*

She took several steps toward him, getting within five feet or so when he barked at her to stop. The old salt stared her down, studying her movement and her eyes. She guessed he'd fought in his fair share of battles throughout his career. He knew malicious intent when it approached and sensed him looking right through her.

He coyly slid his hand in his pocket and found the remote. He held it in plain view. Summer cringed. She'd either pounce and win, or pounce and die.

"Did Jesus have a fall back in the lab?"

His delivery was as smooth as a five hundred dollar-an-hour lawyer questioning a witness on the stand at a murder trial. He knew what happened, but waited for her answer. She offered none.

"Where's your father?" he fired at her.

Summer paused and refocused, trying to pick the right words, hoping he wouldn't discover any holes in her story. She needed to get a few steps closer. Explaining the correct series of events would either get her the two steps she needed, or it would unravel her and give her nemesis the upper hand.

"My dad overdosed himself to test an antidote. He hit me in a delusional state, and I was knocked unconscious. I woke to see Jesus dead and my father gone."

Summer held her breath waiting for the general's response. He stood silently and maintained his posture.

"So, what's that in your hand?"

"It's the antidote. I was coming here to find Mia. I thought she might be able to help."

"Ah, yes. The ever-popular, Mrs. Hannassui. Does Hector know you've discovered a cure?"

Summer suspected the general had his own agenda, so she lied. "Yes, I phoned him from the lab and told him. He's waiting for me."

The general smiled a sheepish grin and shook his head. "My dear girl, you may be a brilliant scientist, but you're a crummy liar."

Summer knew the jig was up and decided to go for it. She lunged forward, holding the syringe high above her head, praying for an accurate puncture in the general's neck. She knew he would be dead in seconds once the needle pierced his skin, so it was simply a matter of aim and luck.

Her aim looked true, and she was only a few feet away when she let out a horrific scream and fell to the ground. The explosion was small but devastating. Her right hand was gone; she lay writhing in pain as the trigger on the wristband fired of several small lasers that went to work on what was left of her wrist, cauterizing the bloody stump and keeping her from bleeding to death. Once completed, an injection of high dose antibiotics was automatically administered to prevent infection.

"I'm sorry, Summer, you were saying something about Hector?"

The general wiped his face with a handkerchief, cleaning the little bits of bone, flesh, and blood from his cheek and forehead.

Summer couldn't respond. The pain was intense. The general tossed the handkerchief aside and knelt beside her.

"See what happens when we don't trust each other?" he frisked her as he spoke and found the other syringe in her pocket. "Ah, what do we have here? My guess is that this is the real antidote."

The general smiled and stood, placing the syringe in his pocket and marched back several paces.

"Now, I'm going to enjoy watching you die. Consider this payment in kind for killing my daughter."

Summer gasped in pain.

"Not so fast, General. I believe she's suffered enough for one evening, don't you agree?"

Hector's voice was a welcome relief. She fell limp, knowing her rescue had arrived in a most unlikely form.

"It's in his right breast pocket," Summer muttered.

Hector strolled toward the general and placed his hand over the general's heart. He smiled and removed the syringe.

"Excellent. The remote, please?"

"What about my daughter? I want my revenge."

Hector nodded. "Plenty of time for dat, General," and with that, Hector released the devices from Summer's neck and wrists.

"Ms. Flowers and I have an arrangement."

Chapter 31

"Open your eyes."

Mia Hannassoui opened them and looked up at Hector with a sober mind for the first time in weeks. Her face was a sunken hollow shell of its former beauty. Her hair was nappy, her body yearned for a long bath. In spite of her sickly outward appearance, her eyes were bright, still full of life. Hector nodded. It had worked. The antidote was a success.

"Clean yourself up. Dere is work to be done, woman."

Hector walked out of her room and the door closed hard behind him. Reality came rushing back in a very harsh, sudden moment. In the very next moment, however, her heart leapt for she knew her sweet Sonny must be on the island. He was the only reason she could have been revived. She sat up and pulled her knees in close to her chest and rocked herself gently. Sonny was here at last. Her heart filled with both anticipation and fear. Hector's warm reception was indication enough that her worst fears had been realized. She was certain he knew about her affair. She prayed that Sonny was still alive.

Mia felt the warm water of the shower caress her body, as if it were the first time she'd ever felt water against her skin. She adjusted the knob and turned the heat up, letting the steam pour over the top of the glass door. Closing her eyes, she held her head under the shower head. When she opened them, she screamed. The water had turned into fire.

That sadistic son of a bitch.

The flames rained down on her, scorching her skin. She looked at her arms and shuddered. Her skin had begun to blister and bubble under the intense heat. She could smell her hair burning and almost fainted when she looked down to see blood and flesh dripping from her bones seeping slowly down the drain.

Mia stumbled backward and almost fell, but caught herself. When she looked down, she saw that her arm had miraculously been healed, the flames had returned to water. Rushing to the mirror, expecting to see the gruesome remains of her former self, she was shocked to see her body as it was, completely intact with not even the hint of a burn. As she stood in the mirror, she barely recognized herself. Her collarbone protruded, her ribs shone slightly, and bruises revealed themselves prominently on her arms and legs.

"What happened to me? Why don't I remember anything?" she asked aloud. "Will Sonny still think I'm beautiful? Will he still want me?"

She heard a voice in the hallway ask, "Everything okay in dere?"

"I'm okay."

Still trembling and fighting back tears, Mia managed to get to her closet and get dressed. As she made her way to the main dining room, she squinted, the bright hall lights hurting her sensitive eyes. She actually ducked several times, thinking they were lasers shooting at her. The guard escorting her was startled. He gave her a look that begged the question— had she indeed been cured?

"Flashbacks," she told him as they walked.

Hector met them in the courtyard. Mia embraced the familiarity, having spent many nights dreaming of her beloved Sonny under the Jamaican stars above.

"How are you feeling?" Hector asked

"The great Second Coming doesn't know?" she retorted sarcastically.

"Back to your old self, I see."

Mia nodded and rested her head in her hands. She was feeling tepid and very hungry. The servants brought her a plate of berries and cheese. She devoured them, but stopped suddenly when a few of the grapes scuttled across the plate. She jumped back.

"Everting okay?" Hector asked, watching her insane reaction to the lifeless plate.

"I'm having some bad flashbacks. I have no idea how long they'll last."

"Let's ask de doctor?"

Hector nodded and Max disappeared. Mia looked at Hector, watching him study her and wondered what he must be thinking. According to a calendar she had just passed, she'd been in her delusional state a few weeks, but it had felt like years. Now that she was back to somewhat normal, she felt the familiar coldness of his stare and wished, on some level, that she'd never been revived. Her only solace now was knowing that her true love was on the island. Her heart beat faster at the thought of his touch, his kiss, and being held by him one more moment, even if it were her last.

Mia heard Max approaching from behind, but she didn't need to see or hear him. She could always tell Max by his smell. He wore the same cologne every day, Dehlia's favorite, Lacoste.

"Hello, my sweet boy."

Max leaned down and embraced his aunt with the tenderness of a loving son. Mia knew that, as long as there was a breath in Max's body, he'd keep her safe. He knew no other that was as close to a mother as she. She loved him, too, and wished Hector would have simply let him go off to medical school. Hector said he worried Max wouldn't be accepted because of his handicap, but Mia knew better. Hector needed Max to do the dirty work the great Halie Selassie reincarnate could not.

"Mia, meet Dr. Flowers," Hector said jovially.

Mia's face brightened at the mere mention of his name. She turned, expecting to see her beloved Sonny, but was both surprised and confused to see a woman in his place. She extended her right hand, and it was graciously accepted by the visiting doctor. Mia held the stranger's hand and stared in her eyes, wondering if this was another flashback, praying silently it was.

To her chagrin, it wasn't. The woman that stood before her was older than she, but not old by any means. She glanced back at Hector, and judging by the smile on his face, she knew he was in love with her. He stared at Dr. Flowers adoringly and didn't avert his gaze even as Mia looked directly at him.

"Apologies, Mia. Hector misspoke. I haven't officially received my doctorate, and while I am quite capable in your field, I fear I don't have the tenure of my ex-husband, Sonny."

"Mrs. Flowers?" Mia was confused.

"Please, call me Natalie."

Hector invited Natalie to sit with them.

"Mia, I understand you're experiencing some flashbacks? Well, nobody to date has endured the level of psychosis you have for such an extended period. I fear you may have them for quite some time, maybe forever."

Mia listened to Natalie, and could probably ascertain for herself the condition of her brain, but she didn't interrupt. She let her go and simply watched her. What happened in the last month? Where was Sonny? Was he even on the island? Was Natalie the one who discovered the cure? How could that be possible? Was this all just another terrible hallucination?

"I'm sorry, Natalie. Tell me again where you studied?"

Natalie started to speak but was interrupted.

"Oh silly Mia. Did you really think she was a doctor?"

Mia looked at the figure approaching through the doorway. It was dark and she couldn't quite make out who it was, but, as soon as she appeared in the light, she knew in an instant.

"You must be Summer? I've seen pictures."

"I'd shake your hand, but, as you can see, it was recently amputated."

Summer held up her bandaged right arm, showing all in attendance that in spite of her loss, she still had plenty of attitude. She directed her interest to Hector.

"What is to come of the general? Feed him to the flock perhaps?"

Hector motioned for her to come closer. Summer approached and leaned in. Hector embraced her as if she were his own daughter.

"Not yet, child. We still need him, but I will have a talk wit him 'bout your hand."

"Mother," she snipped. "You weren't supposed to be here. It took me a day to place your voice. I heard you talking to someone when I arrived."

"Well, I couldn't very well sit home and let you have all the fun, could I?"

"Ladies, ladies," Hector interjected. "Let's focus, shall we? Since you are both here, let's discuss our business at hand."

"Right," Summer replied in a very formal tone. "Mia? I believe you've engineered some very special hybrids? We're interested in them for production."

Summer leaned in and slid the stub that once held her right hand across the table toward Mia, letting the bandage touch her fingertips. Mia was repulsed and retracted her hand into her lap. Summer laughed.

Mia whispered softly, "Please let this be a delusion."

Chapter 32

Sonny crept through the dark mountainside looking for something, but what exactly was yet to be revealed. The jungle terrain was treacherous in the daylight with a sober mind. At night, under the influence of the most highly potent hallucinogenic concoction known to human kind, it was all together horrific.

He walked with the stealth of a ninja stalking a target, but didn't do so for reasons most might expect. In Sonny's mind, the trees, ground, plants, and wildlife were all animated and alive around him. The dirt under his feet looked and felt like a bed of moving lava. The soil churned under him and tried to suck him into the earth, but he fought hard with each step, pulling his feet from the sinking ground beneath him.

A sober mind watching him would see a gentle, quiet scene with little action. The Jamaican night was a beautiful sight to behold. The stars were bright and crickets chirped, but to Sonny's eyes, the stars were alive— a shower of comets and meteorites bound directly for him. He ducked and dodged to avoid being hit by several in an open field near the foot of the blue mountain passageway he and Summer had navigated the day before.

He didn't see her lurking in the woods near him. When she jumped out to confront who she thought was one of Hector's men coming after her, Sonny screamed in sheer terror and curled up into a ball, his anxiety instinct taking over.

"Sonny?" Dehlia dropped the stick she was carrying and approached him.

Sonny was dripping from head to toe with sweat. His adrenal glands were working overtime, and every nerve in his body was shot to hell. He heard whispers that were over a half mile away and felt vibrations in the ground comparable to what a snake might feel in its belly. The problem was that he had no sense of reality, and everything seemed like a threat.

"What do you want?" Sonny's voice trembled as she approached him. She looked like a she-devil with the face of Neptune Blue, the one who took his mother from him as a young boy.

He cursed and cried, "You had to take her away from me, didn't you? All I ever wanted was for her to love me. She hated me just like you hated me."

Dehlia sensed that something was horribly wrong with him and guessed he had been the victim of the same ill fate Mia suffered. She knew there were limited options and decided to try and talk him through his bad trip.

"Sonny Flowha, my name is Helen, and I'm an angel sent to you by Saint Anthony. You are lost and need help."

Sonny looked at her and, where moments before stood a dark imposing Neptune Blue, now stood an angelic form more beautiful than anything he'd ever seen. Her dark hair flowed and reminded him of his Aunt Summer. A white glow surrounded her and when she smiled, he felt a warm sensation all around him.

"Take my hand," Dehlia instructed him.

Reaching out to take her hand, he watched the white glow transfer to his body and surround him.

"Careful!" he said pointing to the ground. "It's moving."

Dehlia shook her head and said, "As long as you are with me, no harm will come to you. I've stopped the ground from moving. Look now. The ground is still."

Sonny looked down and saw the soil at his feet solid and motionless. He breathed a sigh of relief and smiled. Dehlia guided Sonny through the field toward the path to her house.

"Ahh!" Sonny screamed and ducked out of the line of a falling star.

"The light around us will protect you. Nothing can penetrate the light."

Sonny looked up and delighted watching several stars bounce off the aura around them.

Dehlia was pleased with herself and knew that her mother and grandmother would be proud of her had they been here to witness her quick thinking.

Once home, she knew she wouldn't be able to keep Sonny contained for long. A man with as quick a mind as his would surely be inventing new, creative hallucinations in no time at all.

Then it dawned on her— the powder he gave her. She laid him in her bed and told him to close his eyes and breathe in the angel dust. He did as she instructed, and she gently blew a small amount of the pollen in his face.

He would be immobilized for some time, hopefully enough time for her to hatch a plan. Surely Hector and Max would be looking for Sonny, and it wouldn't take them too long to come knocking on her door. In his state, she couldn't count on his cooperation, so she did what she always did in times of trouble and doubt; she invoked the spirit of her grandmother. Her council was invaluable, but the price she paid for performing such a complicated spiritual ritual was sheer exhaustion. She had no other choice and headed out to the cliff where she arranged the spirit rocks.

Chapter 33

Dawn arrived, and with it, a sense of urgency, importance, and maybe the most subtle feeling – fear. This was the day the dignitaries were to arrive for the dog and pony show. This was the day an unsuspecting village would die.

Mia, feeling more like an indentured servant than a scientist, worked throughout the night alongside Summer to take the most potent strain of the chemical agent and maximize the effects for the most effective result. The most effective result as defined by the rogue general was total and complete psychosis, heavy on the hallucinations and violently paranoid.

So much for helping soldiers in battle, she thought.

Several of Hector's disciples volunteered to act as test subjects, believing this to be a holy endeavor. Cannabis use by the Rastafarian people has long been a religious rite and a way to reach spiritual enlightenment, not to mention the fact that any chance to sample more potent weed was often welcome by the lifetime smokers. So, when the great Hector called upon them to test the limits of their spirituality, they were all too happy to oblige. The only difference between the test subjects and the real subjects was that the testers were given the antidote, what little was left of it.

In addition to her aid in the military experiment, Mia was also forced to relinquish all of her notes. Her work completed, Summer and Natalie departed to the main house and left her with Hector and the general.

"Why are we producing so much of this and why in a pollinated form? Why not liquid? It would be much easier to control."

Mia's question was a valid one for a scientist who didn't know the intended application. Hector shared with her what his plans were, and Mia lost her breath.

"A whole village?"

She was stunned. She'd just unknowingly produced the world's first chemical agent designed to save soldiers. Now, as great research is so often thwarted, Sonny's and her work would be killing rather than saving. She felt sick to her stomach. Oh, where was Sonny when she needed him most? He may have been riddled with anxiety and have the confidence of a groundhog, but he was brilliant and gentle. He'd never stand for this.

"Look at it this way, you're saving soldiers' lives. There's nothing more valuable in a war than the life of the soldier fighting it. We target terrorist cells about the size of a small village and prevent soldiers from even having to fight at all," the general said.

He was aloof and she could tell that he was disinterested in her opinion, yet he still tried to validate his position.

"What about wind? How do you target only terrorists? This will surely kill innocents."

Mia begged him to reconsider. She told him the agent in its pollinated form would affect wildlife, ecosystems, and any human within a breath of it.

"Casualties of war, Mrs. Hannassui," the general barked, then stormed out.

"Which village is isolated enough to contaminate?" she thought aloud.

"A tiny one at the base of the mountain," Hector answered her without being asked directly.

"The only village at the base is Batasee? You're not . . . but the children?"

"I am liberating them to the one true Zion," Hector said proudly.

"Your religion is a front. How much are you making off dese people's lives?"

"Take her away. Her work is done here."

Hector signaled to one of his guards who quickly jumped into action. "Where to, your holiness?"

Hector walked over to Mia and placed his palm on her forehead. He looked directly into her eyes and said, "My wife."

He paused for a brief second. Mia squinted her eyes and shook her head, knowing what was coming. "I liberate you to Zion as well. I hope Sonny Flowhas was worth it. He'll be joining you dere soon." He turned to the guard. "Take her to de cliffs and throw her over."

Hector then turned to Mia before leaving, smiled, and sang, *"We can't go on together with suspicious minds—"*

He laughed and blew her one last kiss before closing the door.

"Rot in hell, Hector Hannasui." Mia shouted as the heavy door slammed.

The guard grabbed Mia by the arm and led her out. She slipped a vial of the agent in her pocket as they passed the workbench.

They made it to the cliffs. Mia could hear the waves crashing against the rocks below and knew she needed to act fast. Just before they reached the edge, she fell, pretending to twist her ankle. She grabbed it and rocked in pain.

"Ah. My ankle. I tink I sprained it."

The guard instinctively leaned down to help her.

"You're here to kill me, remember?" Mia asked him sarcastically.

"You should have just dragged me by my hair to the edge. What difference does a sprained ankle matter now?"

The guard looked confused. With his defenses lowered, Mia waved the vial in a quick sideways motion across his face. The liquid worked like mace, stinging his eyes and mouth, entering his bloodstream within seconds. Enraged, he reached a hand down to strike Mia when she growled at him ferociously. She raised her hands in front of his face and formed them into claws.

"Show me tiger," she said, imitating a fashion model posing on a shoot.

The gunman went white with terror and stumbled backward. Mia kept up the charade even swiping at him a time or two before he finally met the edge of the cliff.

"You are liberated to Zion," she shouted and threw her two open palms into his chest, sending him plummeting over the edge to his death.

Chapter 34

Rufus sat in his cell, beaten and bloody, waiting for his turn to die. He knew the day he kissed Dehlia for the first time that he was in a lot of trouble, but he was willing to die for her. His only regret was that he wouldn't be there with her when she got to meet her father.

With his right eye practically swollen shut, he strained to see who was opening the door. He heard the knob turn, expecting this would be it.

Max entered the room slowly, studying Rufus from every angle as he circled his one-time friend like a shark circling a wounded fish. Rufus knew the look. Many a Jamaican boy had tried and failed to win the heart of the beautiful Dehlia Storm. It was as if her voodoo powers not only left each of them completely dejected and heartbroken, but also attached a scar that left them unable to ever love another. Rufus didn't need his vision to see the hurt in Max's heart. Rufus had seen Max hurt before. He was there when Hector took Max in after the death of his parents. He knew that Max was at his most sadistic after heartbreak.

"I don't regret it, Max."

The gangly mute uncovered a switchblade and flicked it open in front of Rufus' good eye. Rufus sat quietly awaiting whatever horrific torture Max had in store for him. Rufus had seen Max work one too many times not to expect something awful, so when Max cut his hands free, Rufus confusion laced his surprise.

"Can you give me a ride home?" Rufus asked almost begging Max to reconsider if, indeed, he was about to free his prisoner.

Max sneered and shook his head. Rufus knew it was too good to be true. Max, the sick son of a bitch he was, wanted to give Rufus a fighting chance. Rufus knew he was no match for the lanky artisan, but raised his hands in defense all the same.

Max was swift in his brutality, unleashing punch after punch to Rufus' face and ribs. Max was the toughest soldier Hector had, having been trained by Hector himself, and Rufus felt the sting of every shot. Max, seeming to gain strength with each blow, let his broken heart mend a little with each spattering of blood.

After several hard hits, Rufus fell to the floor and curled up in a ball, praying for death to come quickly. He couldn't bear the beatings any longer. His cracked ribs made breathing a painful chore, almost certain one of his lungs had been punctured. Blood dripped from his mouth and the hazy picture, barely visible from his good eye, turned black as he drifted off into the unconscious abyss, thinking only of Dehlia as he did.

Max had beaten him within an inch of his life and as Rufus faded, "Dehlia" was all he could mutter.

"Rufus! Oh my God. What did they do to you?"

Rufus, blind, both eyes swollen shut, tried to move his broken lips to speak but could not.

"Don't talk, baby," Katrina said in the softest, most nurturing tone she could muster.

Her eyes filled with tears looking at the beaten face of her once handsome husband. She held a wet washcloth over his forehead and fed him ice chips. Cold compresses covered his eyes and she used her kitchen shears to cut the bloody t-shirt from his battered torso. His dark Jamaican skin was badly bruised and she knew he was bleeding internally.

"Just rest, my darling. Just rest."

"Mommy? What happened to Daddy? Is he gonna be okay?"

Molly, Rufus and Katrina's seven-year-old daughter, wasn't supposed to see her father like this. Katrina shooed her away and assured her that he would be just fine. She struggled to wear a brave face for her daughter but stammered several times as she spoke.

"H-h-he'll be okay, baby," she said, waving Molly off, suggesting she go play with her dolls.

Katrina was despondent, knowing all too well what Hector was capable of when someone crossed him, and, while he wouldn't tell her for a few hours, Rufus knew she would ask him what happened. She had always suspected that Hector was

involved in the death of her cousin, Max's, parents. He knew that
she wouldn't forgive Max, though, nor would she forgive her
uncle for their brutality. He also knew that she would never
forgive him when she learned of his love for Dehlia.

"I love you, Rufus Jones. Come back to me."

Hearing her say that was almost more painful to bear than
the beating.

The morning faded into afternoon, and afternoon into early
evening, by the time Rufus awoke. He stumbled across the
living room floor. Katrina was relieved to see him alive, some
sight having been returned to him. He clutched his side as he
walked and drank a glass of water.

"What the hell happened, Rufus? What did you get yourself
into?" she barked as she held him gently, caressing his head and
kissing his swollen cheek.

"They found out about Dehlia and me," he muttered.

Katrina's eyes widened and her lower lip trembled. She
struggled to hold back the tears, but couldn't. Her sadness,
combined with the rage of being played for a fool, was too much
for her to handle.

"You son of a bitch. You lying, cheating, whoring, no
good—"

"Please, Katrina. Dere's no time. Someting is going to
happen. I know it. You and Molly have to go."

"We have to go? *We* have to go? I tink not. You are the one
who'll be goin' straight away."

She pointed to the door and Rufus limped out. He didn't know what Hector had planned for him and his family, but Max left him alive for a reason. He watched his wife's heart break in front of him and his hurt for her, but he knew the greatest kindness he could do for her in her moment of sorrow was to get her out of Batasee, but convincing her to go was looking like an impossible feat.

Chapter 35

Mia Hannassoui hiked back the way she came, wondering where exactly she was and where she was going. Her muscles ached, having not been used in weeks. Boy, what she wouldn't give to have Juan, the sexy Spanish masseuse working on her right now. With Hector presuming her dead, she was safe for the time being, so she stopped in a small clearing along the trail and plopped down to relax her aching body and hatch a plan.

It's what Sonny would do, she thought.

Sonny— where was he? She wanted so badly to see him, to hug him and hear him tell her it would all be okay somehow, but she couldn't even be sure he was on the island. She felt overwhelmed. All of those poor unknowing souls in Batasee would soon be meeting their demise. Mia wanted so desperately to help them, to warn them, but how? Would it even do any good? They'd just find another village, or worse, a city like Port Antonio or Kingston.

She closed her eyes and thought about the night prior. Natalie and Summer had made it to the island. She didn't remember hearing Sonny's name in the lab, but she felt it in her heart, in her gut, that he was in Jamaica and that he was alive. She hoped he was sitting at a parish bar enjoying a rum drink.

"Oh my sweet, Sonny, where are you? I need you," she whispered, praying that her plea would be carried to him on the Jamaican wind.

Mia leaned back against the shade tree and closed her eyes, letting her mind drift and her muscles relax. It was the first time she'd really felt like herself since the whole ordeal began. Smiling to herself, she silently embraced her new freedom but it was short lived. Her smile faded as she heard a twig snap. Someone was approaching.

Mia stood quietly and crept around the tree, ducking under a nearby shrub. She watched as the figure approached, praying it wasn't another of Hector's guards coming to find the one she killed.

It was a female, and from what Mia could tell, she was alone. The stranger drew closer and Mia's heart raced. The vial she used on the guard was her only weapon, and it was gone. *I should have grabbed his gun before I pushed him,* she thought, angry with herself for not thinking ahead. The stranger stopped in the clearing, giving Mia a clear look. She breathed a sigh of relief when she saw who it was.

"Boo!" Mia shouted playfully as she jumped out from her hiding spot.

Dehlia Storm, startled out of her wits, was quick to produce the cleaned, sharpened dagger from the *Serpentine Orchid* wreck. She flashed it in front of Mia and took a swipe, barely missing her shoulder.

"Whoa, girl," Mia exclaimed. "It's me."

Dehlia lowered the dagger and embraced her friend for the first time since the accident. They cried and hugged for a long time before letting go.

"You're okay?" Dehlia exclaimed.

Mia nodded. "They found the antidote."

"Thank God. Do you have it?"

"No, why?" Mia replied.

"It's Sonny. He's at my place, all crazy like you were."

"Sonny is here?" Euphoria washed over Mia.

"Yes, dey didn't tell you?"

"We need to get to de lab right away," Mia said.

The duo worked out a plan. Guessing that the lab would be closely guarded by any number of Hector's men, they decided to try and use Dehlia as a distraction and prayed it would give Mia enough time to slip through unnoticed. Once inside, she would unlock the side entrance and let Dehlia in.

As they spied the location, it was just as they suspected; two armed guards stood watch at the main entrance, both of them puffing joints and singing reggae songs, using the butts of their rifles as makeshift drums.

"It's Thomas and Jeffery. I know dem," said Dehlia.

Dehlia stumbled out from the forest, panting and limping. She cried for help and watched the predictable pair come rushing to her aide. She collapsed to the ground and acted as if she were lying at death's door. Mia crept past, marveling at Dehlia's dramatic performance. She cracked the door and slipped inside, forgetting the loose hinge. She took exactly three steps before the door slammed behind her.

"Shit," she muttered and scrambled to find a hiding spot.

Thomas spun and ran toward the lab. He opened the door and saw the room in exactly the same condition which he left it, dark and vacant. He patrolled the main floor, walking up each of the aisles, keeping an eye out for anything out of the ordinary and stealing a bud from one of the healthier looking pot plants. Satisfied and smiling, he headed out the main entrance and signaled to Jeffery, holding his discovery high in the air for Jeffrey to see.

Mia crawled out from under the desk and retrieved the flashlight she hid under it in case of an emergency. She unlocked the side door and performed a quick visual inventory of the main work area. The entire chemical agent was gone, but from what she could tell, no antidote had been manufactured. She wondered why and then looked at the Blood lily.

"They don't know about it?" she whispered to herself "Then how was I revived?"

She was completely puzzled, but relieved as the Blood lily she had was the only one in the entire lab. It was an extremely rare flower that only bloomed once a year. That in itself wasn't too much of an issue, but the fact that it resided at the peak of a very inaccessible part of the Blue Mountain chain was another problem altogether.

She counted the bulbs of the plant and saw where two of the three bulbs had been harvested. Depending on the severity of the dosage, one bulb was needed to manufacture enough antidote for a single person.

"Oh, no," she said.

"Oh, no, what?" Mia hadn't heard Dehlia come in.

"You have a plant like dis at home?" Mia asked her

"Not like dis one."

"It's okay. I think I have enough here."

"Well, hurry up." Dehlia barked

Mia knew what Hector had planned for the village. She knew Dehlia's interest

was Rufus. Dehlia had no idea Rufus was going to be dosed with the agent in a few short hours, and Mia didn't have enough of the Blood lily to save him. How could she tell Dehlia Rufus wouldn't be saved?

A single tear ran down Mia's cheek as she prepared the antidote and thought, *I*

hope someday she'll forgive me.

Chapter 36

The general's hour had finally arrived. The dignitaries sat around the grand table in the main house, feasting on jerk chicken and ackee rice. Hector regaled the men with stories of slave struggles and Jamaican strife. He applauded them for their contributions to his people and offered high praise to each of them individually for being such forward thinkers. He was really on his game and the military men ate it up, accepting stroke after stroke, not realizing it was just one big sales pitch. Hector was nothing, if not a diplomat, although, he preferred deity.

The general let Hector warm up the crowd, then stepped in to deliver the knockout punch himself.

"Gentlemen, what we have in store for you today will prove beyond any doubt that the necessity for traditional warfare tactics has now become obsolete."

He watched their reactions as they ate and listened. Renau, the fat Frenchman, slathered a slice of cornbread with heavy butter and stuffed it all in one bite, bloating his cheeks like a chipmunk. Wayne, the Middle Eastern emir, nodded as he sipped a glass of red wine and placed slices of cheese on a baguette. Mr.

Lee, the North Korean sat silently, eating and drinking nothing, his arms folded and his eyes sternly focused on the gluttony before him.

There were several others in attendance: a small Pakistani official, a few African warlords, and a Russian, whom the general was certain was drunk already. General Chamberlain confided in Hector that he thought the Korean was the best potential buyer, but Hector had other ideas.

"My African brothers, it is time to cleanse the civil strife of our homeland and bring peace to all. We shall wipe the land clean and create the one true Zion."

The general cringed as Hector spoke, and the African warlords stood and applauded. Civil strife and unrest were common themes in Africa, and militant groups like the ones represented at Hector's table were the epitome of rouge leadership common on the continent.

The others stared in silence until the Pakistani ambassador jumped in, "We will use this for defense. You will use it for genocide."

The African warlord called Zawe stood and drew his sidearm. He aimed it at the head of the feisty Pakistani. "Our money. Our decision."

"But…" the little man interjected.

Zawe cocked the hammer back and waited for the man to speak again.

A very commanding, yet feminine, voice broke the tension. "Gentlemen, good afternoon. My name is Natalie Flowers, and I'll be briefing you as to what you can expect to see today."

Natalie began speaking as if nothing out of the ordinary wa happening, shaking her hips as she walked past them. Zawe stared at her for a moment and then lowered his weapon. The Pakistani ambassador excused himself and didn't return.

"What is the meaning of this? A woman?" the Korean shouted.

"She is quite capable, I assure you," Hector advised.

Natalie, a former marketing exec, was practiced in the art of presenting to a corporate audience. It was one of the main reasons Hector had asked her to take part in the project. With the wave of a remote, Natalie sliced through slide after slide, explaining how MOjo 55 worked once it entered the bloodstream. She paced around the table as she spoke, showing the syringe of the compound and explaining how a single cc of the compound would incapacitate a full grown man and leave him completely and utterly paranoid— violently paranoid, unless injected with the antidote, which, she advised, had been produced, but was not yet available.

"Show us then," Zawe exclaimed.

"You'll see a full demonstration in a short time, gentlemen," she whispered and continued speaking.

"After ingestion of the compound— "

Natalie was interrupted again by Zawe. She protested and asked him to refrain from any further questions until the end of the presentation. Hector didn't interfere. Zawe stood and approached Natalie, snatching the syringe from her hand. He stared at it for a second, then plunged the needle deep into her neck, squeezing a quarter of its contents directly into her vein.

"Let's see how it affects a weak woman?" he shouted.

The others at the table protested his rogue action, but Zawe and his counterpart, Basa, produced pistols and assured the men they would not hesitate to use them.

"How did they get through with guns, General? We surrendered ours at the gate," the Korean screamed.

"They were diverted as special guests of Mr. Hannassui," Chamberlain barked.

The Korean pounded his fist again in anger, but reluctantly took his seat as the warlords fired a warning shot across the table.

Natalie saw the men around the table and knew all eyes were on her. She heard music playing in her mind as the MOjo 55 took hold of her, an R&B number she hadn't heard in a long time. She moved with the music and felt each note slide down her arms and legs. She hummed softly and closed her eyes, swaying and humming.

Zawe stared at Natalie. Sheer repulsion turned to lust, which would soon become evident to all.

"Violent— I think not," he said, laughing, and reached for Natalie, placing his hands around her hips from behind, pulling her into him, grinding with her to the imaginary song. Natalie turned and saw Zawe's face. He looked like a lizard— a giant

Godzilla— a man creature that was about to feast on her, his snake tongue flickered back and forth.

She clawed him hard, digging her nails deep into his flesh.

"Ahhh!" he screamed and back-handed her across the table.

She fell, but bounced back quickly, cursing and scowling at him. Fueled by lust and rage, Zawe pinned her to the table and tore her blouse. Hector moved to restrain him, but was thwarted by Basa.

"You savages. You are out of line," Hector barked.

"Take me instead." Summer approached. "Take me instead of my mother."

Summer was cleaned and radiant, her hair flowing, her lips soft and crimson, and the air of confidence with which she moved stopped Zawe dead in his tracks. The warlord nodded, and Summer sauntered over to him. She caressed his cheek and slid her hand down his arm, grasping his hand and placing it on her shoulder. Instinctively, Zawe forced Summer to her knees. She obliged and flashed a glance to the general as she did. The smirk on his face told her he was receiving his silent revenge.

Summer smiled back at him and watched as Chamberlain's face went white. His jaw dropped as Zawe screamed. She pulled the needle out of his testicle and stood to face him.

"Was it as good for you as it was for me?" she said and spit in his face.

He didn't have time to respond. He was dead. Zawe's cohort, Basa, barely had time to figure out what happened before he felt the sting of the needle and the warm liquid course through his veins, sending him to an early grave as well. Summer collected their guns and injected Natalie with the remaining dose of antidote.

"Anyone else need convincing, or shall we proceed with the actual demo?"

The men sat silently.

"Good. Let's get on with it then, shall we?"

Chapter 37

Mia worked as expeditiously as possible. Dehlia stood guard and waited impatiently, eager to begin her search for Rufus. She blamed herself for being preoccupied when Max crept up behind her, but it wasn't her fault. Even the best, most highly trained, sentry would not have heard Max enter. His steps were soft, like a tiger, lurking in the tall grass.

The voodoo priestess tried to yell for help, but Max had her mouth covered with his hand and the knife pressed tightly against the side of her neck. He didn't say a word— he never did. Dehlia had known Max all her life and had watched him grow from an innocent, sweet boy, into the troubled angry man that stood before her. She had always done her best to keep him as calm as possible, but she was now certain that he knew about Rufus. He would never hold her, the woman he loved, at knifepoint otherwise.

Max didn't see Mia working at the lab counter. Dehlia guessed that he, like the others in Hector's employ, had been told some lie about his aunt so that, when he heard her speak to him, he was taken aback.

"Let her go, my sweet boy."

Dehlia prayed Mia could keep him from hurting her.

"Put the knife down, Max," Mia said calmly.

Max lowered the knife and released his grip on Dehlia, almost as if Mia had induced a hypnotic spell over him. He started to speak, struggling and mumbling. Frustrated, he walked to the desk and retrieved a pad and pencil. He jotted his thoughts quickly and handed them to Mia.

Thought you were dead? I wanted to find the guard that did it and kill him.

Max's eyes welled up as he stared at Mia.

She pulled him in and embraced him. "You're such a good boy, Max. Why do you do such terrible things?"

Max scribbled the note and handed it to Mia. A tear ran down her cheek as she read: *Hector. He is the chosen one, and I do what he asks. I owe all to him.*

Max had been so misguided and so taken advantage of for so many years. Mia simply couldn't stand by and watch any longer. Dehlia listened, but kept her distance, unsure what Max might do.

"There are some things you should know, Max," Mia said. "Hector swore he would kill me if I ever told you the truth, but now I'm dead, so what does it matter?"

Mia took a deep breath and then told Max where he came from and what really happened to him as a young boy. Max's father, John, and Hector were brothers. Hector had just returned to Jamaica after attending school at Oxford in England. He declared himself the reincarnation of Hailee Selassie I, the Rastafarian Jah, shortly after his return— about the time they lost their father.

The family farm was to be divided equally, but Hector wanted it all. He wanted to stop producing sugarcane and start growing marijuana— the spiritual tool of the Rastafarian and lucrative cash crop for exportation.

"That's what a business degree from Oxford does, eh?" Dehlia caught herself saying out loud.

Mia shushed her and continued. John, a faithful Rasta, called Hector a fake and further declared that, should Hector cultivate his half of the land with marijuana, John would burn it all in sacrifice to the true Jah.

Hector became enraged, so one evening when Max was only five years old, Hector ordered a small group of radical Rasta followers to destroy everything, including John and his wife, Martha. What he didn't plan on was Max. Hector didn't know about Max. John kept him a secret, hoping Hector would simply grow disinterested after a while and go back to England.

The radicals moved in and burned the sugarcane fields, burned the house, tortured and raped Martha, all while forcing John to watch. Once they were done with her, they slit her throat and beat John to death.

Dehlia watched Max cringe as Mia recounted what had likely either been his worst or repressed memory. Tears streamed down his cheeks as they did on Dehlia's. Max scribbled that he remembered hiding in the closet, watching the men hurt his parents. He remembered when they opened the closet door and found him.

Mia shuttered as she watched him write it out: *They cut out my tongue.*

"Do you remember why?" she asked.

Max shook his head and looked down.

Mia gently lifted his chin and looked him in the eyes. "You fought back, Max. You bit them and called them evil."

Max had repressed as much as he could about that night and didn't remember fighting. He only remembered his parents, and the pain he felt as the men cut his tongue from his mouth.

Mia continued her confession.

"Hector walked in before they could finish you off, Max. He never knew you existed and even a man as self-absorbed and narcissistic as Hector couldn't allow a small boy, his blood, to be tortured and killed. So, rather than order de men to stop, which they would have, he killed them. He killed them in front of you. He became your savior and liberator. You've known only his love since den, and have honored him as your father, when, in fact, it was he that took your parents from you."

Max shook his head, not wanting to believe a word Mia said to him, but Dehlia felt that he knew in his heart that Mia spoke the truth. Mia hugged him and he broke down.

"I'm so sorry, Max. I should have told you long ago."

Max recomposed himself and scribbled: *How did you know?*

"I found his journal shortly after we were married. It's all in there."

Max paced the room frantically. His universe, and all he thought he knew, had just crumbled. All he believed in was now a lie. All the lives he'd taken in the name of his uncle, all the horrible things he did to people, all the stories of his parents and how he came to be— all lies.

Max turned to Dehlia and scowled, faced with yet another lie. Dehlia tensed. She knew how much Max loved her. She was the only one he'd ever loved, and he felt that she had rejected him.

Mia spoke again. "Hector drove you away from Dehlia."

Max turned his attention once more to his aunt, as did Dehlia.

"What you talkin' 'bout, Mia?" Dehlia demanded.

Mia paused, wondering if now was the best time to tell them, but weighing the alternative— Max killing her, she confessed, "Max, Dehlia is your cousin."

Max furrowed his brow and shook his head. Dehlia did the same, not believing it for a moment.

Mia told them how Hector had an affair with Dehlia's mother shortly after returning to Jamaica. Believing harm would come to her and the baby once his followers discovered her existence, he thought it best to keep things quiet. She told them how Hector used Rufus to steal Dehlia's heart. Rufus was one of his most loyal followers, and Hector thought once Max found out Dehlia was in love with someone else, he would move on.

He also knew Max might be heartbroken and kill Rufus. He said it was a win for him no matter what. He wanted to keep Max angry and doing his killing for him. If Max fell in love, and that love were returned, he would surely go soft and be of little use.

Dehlia's voice trembled as she interjected, "No. Dat's a lie. Hector is not my fatha. My fatha owns a plantation home in New Orleans. I'm going dere to find him. Rufus is comin' wit me."

Mia reached out and touched Dehlia's shoulder, looking at her with soft sincere eyes. "Your grandmotha hated Hector for what he did. She told you dat story 'bout your fatha to keep you from ever knowin' de trut. You needed a fatha and de one she made up was much better than de actual one. I'm so sorry."

Dehlia sobbed as Mia hugged her. Max tapped Mia on the shoulder and handed her another note: *Medical school?*

Mia shook her head. "He was never goin' to let you go, Max."

Max's entire being filled with rage, the rage of a broken man who had been pushed to his limit. He grabbed the machete on the table and screamed at the top of his lungs, unable to release the anger pent up inside of him.

The front door swung open and the guards rushed in. They were surprised to see Max and lowered their weapons in his presence.

"What's goin' on in here?" Thomas asked.

Max stared them down, both men a product of his uncle, the man he now despised. Max motioned to them to leave. They refused.

Thomas called to Jeffery, "Radio to de main house. Tell dem to get Hectah."

Thomas barely finished the sentence when Max swung the machete and separated Thomas' head from his body in one swipe.

"Come again?" Jeffery said, stepping in to the lab, plenty stoned from the bud they'd swiped earlier.

Max made quick work of Jeffery and motioned to the ladies to follow him. "Dehlia, you go with Max. I'll help Sonny."

Dehlia nodded. "Max, we have to find Rufus."

Max stopped and looked at Mia suspiciously. Dehlia became anxious. What wasn't she being told? What did they know of Rufus?

Mia sighed and called Dehlia to her. "Take this. You'll need it."

Mia handed her a syringe. Max looked at Mia and squinted, likely wondering what the syringe contained.

She looked back at Max, but spoke to Dehlia."This is for Rufus in case he's dosed with the MOjo 55. I don't think it will fix his bruises and breaks, but it will keep him sane."

Mia kissed them both.

"In case we don't see each other again, you two take care of each other. You're family."

Chapter 38

The general and his dignitaries finally reached the elevated platform on the mountainside. It was a beautiful Jamaican day, the wind blowing a gentle five miles per hour, and the village of Batasee one mile below was a beehive of activity— well, as much as could be expected in the Caribbean.

The crop duster flew over the village once to find his mark, then circled back to make another pass. He kept low to the ground for maximum effect, per the general's instruction. It was late afternoon, and most of the villagers were outside tending to their crops and finishing their daily chores.

The dust hung in the air for some time, floating gradually to the earth. Most of the farmers kept about their daily business, while other villagers stopped to watch the plane, wondering what was happening.

Exactly five minutes after the dust was dropped, the general officially dubbed project *Jamaican Flowers* underway.

Merry Bindi, wife of Marcus Bindi, was one of the first residents to be infected. She was tending to her afternoon laundry in between bites of a cheeseburger, a guilty pleasure brought to her after Marcus's trip to America. She chomped and hummed a happy tune, when a tickle in her nose caused her to sneeze. She took a deep breath after the sneeze and realized something foreign, something dusty, had just entered her lungs. She coughed, but it was no good. She had been dosed with MOjo 55 and would not live long enough to tell the tale of how she'd been told to kill her husband that afternoon by her talking cheeseburger.

The general and the men on the mountain were duly impressed and satisfied with the potency of the agent as they watched it take hold of the Bataseeans below. One of the men suggested actually making a sport of the event and passing wagers.

"Zat's right. We'll draw names from a hat and see who lives zee longest," the Frenchman suggested.

"Bloody brilliant," Wyane, the emir, chimed in.

They drew names and watched through telescopes and binoculars. They drank Jamaican rum and smoked cigars. It was a real gentleman's club outing. They called the villagers names like "yellow shirt farmer," "horse," and "fat woman in red flowered dress."

They cheered loudly and bills changed hands quickly as villagers fell.

Chapter 39

Rufus Jones had just been thrown out of his house. He limped out the front door and took several steps down the pathway, then doubled back around the side of the house as quickly as his ailing body would allow him. He knocked on Molly's window and smiled.

She threw her arms around Rufus' neck and cried, "Oh, Daddy, you're okay. I was so worried. What happened?"

"Noting, baby. We need to work fast."

"What are we doin', Daddy?"

Rufus passed her a crowbar and spade through the window. Molly struggled with the large shovel but managed to get it in without making too much noise.

"Rememba when we played hide and go seek?" Rufus asked his daughter.

Molly nodded and smiled.

"Well, now we going to make you de best hiding place evah."

She sat on the bed and watched her father work, prying floorboards and tossing them aside. Once he had a space big enough to comfortably fit Molly, he dug. He dug a hole in the dirt under her bedroom floor. He hurt with every scoop of dirt and had to stop several times before finishing the job.

Once the hole was deep enough, he laid out Molly's blanket in the loose soil and had her lay in it to make sure she fit. She giggled, looking up at her dad, thinking this was the most fun they'd had together in some time.

"Put the sheet over your face while I slide the wood over you like a blanket. You stay in this spot as long as you can. You'll be safe there."

She did as her father instructed and Rufus carefully placed the floorboards loosely over top of her. She smiled at him through the crack in the floor and he smiled back, blowing her a kiss.

"I'll be back for you, my love."

He tossed the shovel and crowbar out the window and closed it behind him.

Rufus started toward Dehlia's, exhausted and dying, but didn't get far.

He heard the yelling coming from the main square and limped over to investigate. What he saw was total bedlam, people wielding farm tools and throwing rocks at one another.

"What's going on?" he yelled

"Go to hell, devil." he heard his wife scream before she threw the grapefruit sized rock at his head.

He ducked and screamed back. "I told you I was sorry."

Katrina was moving closer, displaying an unnatural look in her eyes he hadn't seen before. She was carrying a bat and looking like she was going to use it. He limped off into the neighbor's yard, praying she wouldn't catch him.

Rufus only took five steps on the main road before it hit him, but hit him it did.

Katrina found him and bolted toward him. What he saw was a witch, a witch with feet of flames. His pain was gone and his adrenalin pumped. He grabbed a rock and aimed. As a former baseball standout, she didn't have a chance. Katrina fell to the ground, her head lying in a pool of her own blood. She was dead, killed at the hand of her own husband's wicked fastball.

Rufus picked a machete up off the ground and skulked forward, wary of the danger surrounding him. A pack of menacing wolves appeared out of nowhere and surrounded him. They had blood filled eyes and drool hung from their hungry jaws. They worked in unison, the leader attacking first. Rufus swung the machete hard and sliced his attacker in two. The yelp of the animal sounded like a hellish howl to Rufus' tainted ears.

"Damn you, beasts." Rufus shouted.

He stood his ground and fought each, slaughtering the village dogs one by one. The new leader, a German Shepherd that belonged to his neighbor, circled him and growled ferociously, appearing to have a saber-tooth tiger-like appearance. The pit bull terrier looked like a hyena, and the teacup poodle appeared to Rufus as a small troll with sharp teeth and spikes all over its body. It didn't matter, though— Rufus killed them all. He spit blood and carried the head of the poodle in his hand as he walked toward the main road. All of the villagers were dead, all except one, a dragon man named Gregory Mandu, a close friend of Rufus in real life, but under the influence of the MOjo 55, a fierce enemy.

Rufus held the head of the little dog troll high in the air, presenting the trophy to his foe, declaring that his head was next. Gregory tried to duck out of the way when Rufus zinged the poodle head at him, but his quick feet were no match for Rufus' sinker. Gregory screamed, believing the troll head to have taken a chunk out of his leg when it made contact.

Gregory, wielding an ax, sprung up and struck back, whipping the blade across the torso of Rufus. Rufus jumped backward, dodging the blade by inches.

"Not today, dragon! Today I spill your blood and keep my soul."

With that, Rufus dropped to his knee and spun around, extending the machete, slicing the hamstring of his dragon foe. Gregory fell to the ground and Rufus delivered a swift, fierce blow that quickly separated Gregory's head from his body.

Rufus crouched, still in attack mode, waiting for the next evil to strike.

Chapter 40

Dehlia and Max hid behind some bushes on the outskirts of the village. They wore the surgical masks Dehlia took from the lab and watched the scene unravel before them.

"Dis is what I was afraid of," Dehlia whispered to Max, still a little shocked about the revelation that they were blood related. She shuddered again at the thought that Hector was her father.

Max nodded as he and Dehlia watched people they knew, friends some of them, kill each other in a paranoid rage.

They waited for a while, Dehlia praying and hoping for a glimpse of her love, Rufus. She heard the dogs howling in the distance, but had no idea her gentle sweet Rufus was the one slaughtering them. They waited.

"Does Rufus really love me, Max, or is it all an act— Hector's plan?"

Max looked at her and didn't have to say a word. The look in his eyes told her what she longed to hear. Rufus' love was true. Her heart leapt when suddenly the village went silent. They held their breath and waited. While it may have started as something contrived, there was no denying what they shared.

"What if he's...?" Dehlia couldn't bear the thought.

Max poked her arm and pointed. Like a well-directed scene from a movie, Rufus crept around the corner of the church square, holding a machete and the head of a toy poodle. Dehlia squirmed and squeezed Max's arm, repulsed by Rufus' appearance. His battered face and bloody body made her true love look like the living dead— a real life zombie.

Dehlia began to move in, believing she had the antidote. Max stopped her, pulling her back down and pointing to Gregory Mandu. She couldn't watch and buried her head in Max's shoulder. She heard Rufus yell at Gregory and then scream to the heavens once he had overtaken his foe.

Max acted quick. He stood and threw a tennis ball sized rock at Rufus' head. He hit him square, but Rufus didn't fall. The MOjo55 pumped adrenalin to his muscles that made him almost impervious to pain. Max dreaded the idea of facing Rufus in his condition. Rufus spun to see who hit him and as he did, he stumbled. The gunshot sounded like a firecracker pop off in the distance. Dehlia and Max barely heard it. Max, thinking the rock had taken effect, was happy to see Rufus fall to the ground.

Max ran out from the bushes and pulled Rufus as fast as his body would let him back to his and Dehlia's safety zone afraid there may be other villagers or animals still lurking.

Dehlia cradled her love and injected him. She waited patiently for the magic elixir to work its way through her lover's veins and revive him, but saw no result. She gently slapped his face and begged him to wake up. She tore the mask from her face and pressed her ear to Rufus' mouth— no sign of breath. She felt for a pulse and found none.

"No! No! No!" she cried and pulled his head close to her breast. She squeezed him hard and wept as she gently rocked him back and forth.

Max tapped Dehlia on the shoulder and pointed down to Rufus' chest. Dehlia sobbed as she touched the spot on Rufus where the bullet entered.

"They were watching the whole time, Max," she cried.

Max reached out and held her hand in his. She knew Max felt her pain. She could see in his eyes that he wanted so badly to make it his own, but he couldn't.

Dehlia stopped crying and pushed Rufus away from her, letting his head fall to the ground. She stared at Max for a second. Her face relaxed and looked almost peaceful. She leaned over and kissed Max on the cheek. He smiled softly and squeezed her hand.

He didn't see Dehlia retrieve the Jameson dagger with its glimmering jeweled gold handle, or the polished sharpened silver blade. He only heard her mutter her last words, "I will nevah love anotha as I did my sweet Rufus. We will go to dat plantation home together in the aftalife."

Dehlia plunged the dagger deep into her own abdomen, thrusting the blade upward to her heart. She gasped in pain and then smiled softly as her last breath drifted toward the heavens.

She fell to the ground while Max watched in total disbelief.

"No!" he yelled and held Dehlia as she had done with Rufus only moments earlier. Max couldn't take any more. His world was crumbling before him. The memory of his parents, the loss of his love and the anger he felt welling inside him was too much. He was about to explode.

He held Dehlia and wept. He didn't see the armed soldiers start to comb the village for survivors. He heard the gunshot and looked up to see one of Hector's soldiers shoot a man writhing on the ground. The villager's arm had been severed and his skull fractured by a rock, but he was still alive.

The soldiers dragged the bodies to the middle of the town square and began piling them up. Monk, Marcus Bindi's horse, still ran free, kicking and bucking anything in his path. The immense draft horse caught one of the soldiers in the torso and sent him flying ten feet. Max silently rooted for Monk, hoping he could take several more, but the other soldiers were quick to empty their machine guns into the crazed equine. The old boy fell hard and the soldiers joked as to which one of them was going to drag him to the center square. They left him and continued collecting bodies. Max watched in disbelief, saddened that he was once a leader of this unholy army.

He wondered what to do? The only woman he ever loved lay dead next to him as did his one-time friend, set up by his uncle to protect him. He thought about ending it all, of joining Rufus and Dehlia in the sweet afterlife, but then he heard her voice.

"Come out, come out wherever you are."

Molly walked down Main Street as if nothing out of the ordinary was happening, looking for whom Max could only guess was Rufus, her dead father. The soldiers hadn't seen her yet, but Max was certain that once they did, they wouldn't leave her alive.

Max pulled the dagger from Dehlia's chest and tucked it in his belt. Without thinking, he sprang into action, darting toward Molly, trying to reach her and keep her safe before the soldiers had a chance to act.

"Max?"

Max stopped in his tracks, fully expecting to be peppered with bullets .

"Where you off to, mon?" the sergeant asked.

Max didn't say a word. He looked over the sergeant's shoulder and followed Molly. She had stopped playing the game and looked frightened. The sergeant looked back and caught sight of the seven-year-old. He raised his rifle and took aim.

Max reached around and lifted the sergeant's chin with his left hand and let the blade of the Jameson dagger slide across the soldier's throat with his right. He tried to keep Molly from witnessing the same monstrosities he was subjected to as a boy, but given the circumstances, it was his only choice. Molly screamed and ran toward her house.

The other soldiers heard her and looked at Max. Seeing their officer in charge dead, all four of them started in toward Max, drawing their weapons and taking aim. He lifted the sergeant's rifle and dropped to one knee. He fired four shots, one bullet for each aggressor, hitting each of them with the precision of an expert marksman. They fell quickly, not a single one of them able to get off even one round.

Max threw the rifle to the ground and chased after Molly. He caught up to her and tried to settle her down.

"Who were those men, Uncle Max, and where is my daddy?"

Max couldn't help it. No matter how hard he tried, he couldn't hold back. He hugged Molly. As the tears ran down his cheeks, he silently vowed to keep this little girl from harm. All the sadness, love, hate, and longing inside of him now had a different purpose, a new meaning. He picked her up and headed toward Dehlia's house, praying Mia would still be there.

Chapter 41

Mia walked softly up the pebbled path leading to Dehlia's main entryway. She clutched the antidote in her hand tightly, praying nothing happened to it before she could inject her sweet Sonny and bring him back to life.

She opened the door. Based on Dehlia's description of the events that occurred, she expected to see him lying immobile on her bed. What she found was an empty bed and an empty cottage. She set the antidote down on the kitchen table and started hunting frantically.

"Sonny?" she shouted, hoping to hear his voice and see his face appear around a hidden crevice or corner. He always liked playing games with her, hide and seek, tickling her from behind. She loved his playful nature. It seemed he was always so relaxed when he was with her. She ached for those moments to return.

She called his name again— silence.

Scouring each room of the house, she mumbled the Saint Anthony jingle Sonny

had taught her. *The paralysis must have worn off,* she thought.

Mia was at a loss. She had no idea where to look. She wasn't about to start trudging around the island, giving possible witness to the fact that she remained alive. To the world, she was dead, and she wanted to keep it that way.

She poured herself a drink and dropped two ice cubes in it. Swirling them in the glass, watching the ice dance in the rum, she remembered the day Sonny told her he was in love with her. It was over a rum drink at Wavy Davey's, a beach bar in Port Antonio. He said it with such passion, as though, if he didn't, his heart would never forgive him. She remembered feeling the rush of happiness when the words passed his lips. They kissed and life, as she knew it, would never be the same. Mia sipped her drink and smiled— then she heard him.

"Who are you, and what do you want?"

Startled, she dropped her glass and watched it shatter. She turned to see the man she'd been longing for, but in some twisted state of himself. She knew this is what she must have looked like only two days prior.

Sonny was shaking and twitching violently, something Mia hadn't seen in all of her tests. She wondered how much he'd ingested. He was backed in a corner, crouched down in a squatting, defensive position, almost waiting to be attacked, ready to strike. Mia studied him, trying to figure out how to best approach him with the needle— the syringe. Where was it? She looked over to the table where she set it down and discovered it had vanished.

Her gaze moved back to Sonny and saw him holding it. Her heart sank. If anything happened to that syringe, it was all over. She had no more Blood lily, no more antidote, and zero options from there. He had obviously taken a much higher dose, in greater volume than she had. His behavior was highly paranoid, but she moved toward him anyway, hoping some part of him recognized her.

Sonny Flowers jumped out from his position and swung the needle at her fiercely, believing it to be a dagger.

"Stay away!" he shouted as he moved back into his crouch.

Mia knew she had little time to waste. If she left, he might bolt for real and catching him before one of Hector's men did would pose a greater challenge than she was capable of handling. She looked around the room, hoping to find some kind of inspiration, some tool that might help her. The frying pan might prove useful if she could get close enough to conk him on the head with it, but Sonny was much too strong for her to challenge physically.

Her only option was to manipulate him to either surrender the syringe or inject himself with it.

"Sonny? Do you know who I am?"

"You're one of them! You're here to kill me."

"No. Sonny. I'm your daughter, Autumn."

Mia knew about Autumn as she and Sonny were working together when the call came that she died.

"Autumn?" Sonny looked confused and agitated.

"Yes, Daddy. It's me."

"You look different."

Sonny was testing her. In his paranoid state he wasn't stable, but Mia had to keep trying.

"I miss you, Daddy."

"I miss you so much, sweetheart." He began to weep. "Come over here and let me see you."

"I can't. I'm not really here."

"I don't understand."

Sonny's eyes were squinted and his head cocked, trying to put the puzzle pieces together.

"I sent you something— special medicine that will let us be together. It's in your hand."

Sonny looked down and opened his palm. Where moments ago he saw a knife, a sword, or a stick, it now held a syringe full of a glowing gold elixir.

"Stick it in your arm and push the plunger down. Then in a few minutes, we'll be together."

Sonny excitedly jabbed the syringe into his forearm and depressed the plunger. His hand dropped to his side and his head fell back. The antidote rushed through his veins and to his brain where it went to work ungluing all of the highly concentrated MOjo 55 formula, sending the compound through his bloodstream to his excretory system.

Mia rushed over and removed the dangling syringe and wiped the puncture wound with a washcloth. He was sweating profusely, and she held him as he trembled. Sonny was crashing from an extreme response to the drug. His adrenal glands stopped pumping and his muscles relaxed.

"Open your eyes, baby."

"Autumn?" Sonny mumbled, still caught between worlds.

He half opened his eyes and strained to focus, exhausted and disoriented. "Mia?"

"Yes, Sonny. It's me."

"Where am I? How? How did you?"

"Shhh. Don't strain yourself right now. Just rest. I'll explain everything."

Mia led Sonny to the bed and propped his head on one of Dehlia's pillows. He took deep, slow breaths in an effort to help his body readjust. He couldn't fight it. Worse than when he was plucked from the sea by the pirate, Bishop, every muscle in his body had been completely worn down. He needed rest. He tried to talk, but stammered, unable to finish the sentence. He paused, and then it all went black.

Chapter 42

Mia walked in a few hours later to find Sonny sitting upright in the bed reading a letter.

"Well, hello, handsome," Mia said smiling.

Sonny glanced up and gave her a smile that acknowledged her, yet told her to hold on for a moment longer while he finished reading.

"What has you so engrossed?"

"Dehlia left this for me."

"Anything interesting?"

Sonny nodded and solemnly folded the letter and placed it in his back pocket. He motioned for Mia to come over. She smiled the bright beautiful smile Sonny remembered in his dreams and sat next to him on the bed.

Sonny mustered the energy to suppress his need for food and rest a bit longer and addressed the one need he'd been longing to satisfy since arriving on the island. He took Mia in his arms and embraced her lovingly. He cupped his hand against the side of her face and drew her in. Their lips locked for minutes, both of them wishing it would last an eternity. Mia's sweet jasmine scented hair and her milky soft skin took him back to their first kiss— the first time he truly fell in love with her that day at Wavy Davey's.

The estranged lovers had finally found one another, and the rediscovery of Mia was more of a treasure than any he'd ever find.

Mia whispered to him as they lay wrapped around each other, "Thank you for coming back for me." Sonny caressed her hair and kissed her forehead. It was the first time Mia felt true happiness since being left alone those months ago. "You figured out de anagram. I knew you would."

Sonny raised his eyebrows.

"I didn't have much time," she said. "I used the *Serpentine* anagram to throw Hector. He'd almost certainly read de note I left for you."

"He did," Sonny said. "I don't understand. What happened after I left?"

Mia sighed and recalled all of the events that took place after he left the island to get back to his family. She told him how she continued his work, making some great breakthroughs in his effort to find cures for bipolar disorder. She told him how the general and Chris Smith kept pushing her to work on the control agent.

"I just kept delaying and pretending that I couldn't do it without you."

"That's why Chris came back for me. But how did you overdose?" Sonny asked.

"Like this," Mia motioned to her elbow and pretended she was injecting herself. She closed her eyes and let her tongue fall out of the corner of her mouth. Sonny laughed and drank an imaginary shot. "I did it like that."

They both laughed and kissed some more. Mia went on to explain that after a while, Hector and the general lost faith in her ability to produce anything of value and decided to bring Dr. Hodges in to finish the job. She told Sonny how she regularly changed numbers in Hodges' formulas and kept him from discovering anything.

"What happened to him?" she asked Sonny.

"I don't know for sure, but I think Hector had him killed."

"Doesn't surprise me," she said. "He had me killed, too."

"Huh?"

Mia smiled and continued. She explained that Hector and the general were growing suspicious of her activities and wanted to know why progress wasn't being made. Meanwhile, Mia told him, she was able to not only perfect the MOjo 55 compound, but she also discovered the cure. She feared that leaving any trace of the cure would give Hector too much control if he ever learned of its existence, so she never wrote anything down. The closest thing to instructions she left was the note for Sonny.

One day shortly after discovering the antidote, she had overheard a conversation between Hector, the general, and Christine. They were convinced that the only one capable of giving them what they wanted was the infamous Sonny Flowers.

"Of course, Christine volunteered to go fetch de great scientist. She was so obviously in love wit you, Sonny," Mia said in her best dramatic voice.

Sonny stopped her.

"So let me guess, you realized you were expendable, so you dosed yourself, knowing I'd fix you?"

"Kind of— I dosed myself to protect myself from possibly being tortured by Hector and giving up de formula before you arrived."

"Ah," Sonny nodded. "A fine husband he is indeed."

The soft Jamaican breeze washed over them, the sun started to set on the horizon.

Sonny got out of bed to find some food.

"Whatever the reason, I'm glad we're both okay, but we need to get Summer and

get the hell off this island." He peeled a banana and went to bite it, but the banana opened its mouth and looked like it was ready to bite him.

"Jesus!" he shouted, throwing the fruit to the ground, stomping the life out of it.

Mia shouted, "No, Sonny. It's a flashback. You're going to have dem for a while."

Sonny breathed a sigh of relief and peeled another banana— cautiously.

Chapter 43

I ate my banana and grooved on Mia's energy. The general negative weight of the universe was absent in her presence. She radiated only love and positive energy, at least for me. She was what I wished we could all be like. I'd often wondered if *she* wasn't the second coming. The sun crept through the window and formed an aura around the left side of her body which only made her look more angelic. I wanted to crawl right back in bed with her and never ever leave, but thoughts of Summer and what had happened in Batasee left me uneasy. I was a dad after all, and Summer was out there somewhere. My paternal instinct had overridden my desire instinct so I got dressed.

"There's something else, Sonny."

Her tone made me nervous.

"Well?" I said

"It's Summer."

"What about Summer?"

"She's in on it somehow – working with Hector. She's been playing everyone, including you."

Was this a flashback? I looked at my arm hoping to see it on fire. Summer would never. She couldn't. I shook my head in denial.

"Sonny, I'm not joking."

"I'm not calling you a liar, but I'm sure she can explain whatever her involvement is."

"Go find her den and ask. I hope I'm wrong, my love, but you should be prepared to face dat what I'm sayin' is de trut."

I kissed her once more before leaving.

"I won't be here when you get back, Sonny."

"Why not?"

"I'm leaving de island. I'm going to take a boat to de Caymans and fly out from dere."

"Why?"

"Dey all tink I'm dead. I want it to stay dat way."

"I have to go Mia. I have to find Summer. I'll come back for you— I promise."

"Hurry, Sonny. I can't wait long."

I closed the door and contemplated Mia's words. How had Summer been forced to work for Hector? He had to be blackmailing her. The asshole probably told her he had me locked up. I rubbed my medal, recited my jingle, and headed back toward the lab.

Chapter 44

Mia curled her legs into her chest and rested her chin on her knees. "I love you, Sonny," she whispered.

She had been in the cottage long enough to get dressed and fix herself a drink, but not long enough for Hector's men to have figured her out, so she was startled when the door swung open.

"Aunt Mia," the little voice cried.

Molly charged toward Mia like a rampaging rhino. Mia caught the little girl mid-stride and twirled her around.

"Wee," she said, watching Molly's bright eyes light up as she giggled.

"Are you here wit your daddy?"

Molly's lower lip jutted out, trying to be a big girl and hold back the tears. Max appeared in the doorway and shook his head. Mia knew then that Rufus and Katrina were gone.

"Don't worry, sweetheart. Auntie Mia is goin' take good care of you."

Molly clung to her and relaxed enough to let her aunt know that she felt safe.

"Max, you're not going after Hector, are you?" Mia asked.

Her special boy, visibly heartbroken, just stared at her. He didn't acknowledge the question. Mia could see the hurt behind his eyes. She knew there was nothing she could say to stop him. She silently pleaded him not to go, but he went anyway. He blew a kiss to Molly then disappeared into the dense jungle.

Molly blew him a kiss in return and asked him to hurry back. Mia feared the worst. Max, while quite capable, would still be no match against Hector. She only prayed that the hurt he carried inside would be fuel enough to let him do what he felt he must.

"C'mon, Molly. Let's get ready for a boat ride."

Chapter 45

The general sat in the courtyard, puffing on his cigar, one of Havana's finest. He kicked up his heels and blew smoke rings in between sips of rum. His guests had all either retired for the evening or decided to head out and enjoy some of the Port Antonio nightlife. The general just wanted to relax alone and enjoy what he considered his swan song – the crowning achievement of an illustrious career.

"Good evening, General."

His uninvited guest pulled up a chair next to him and made herself comfortable, slipping a joint from Hector's cigar box and lighting up alongside the small-footed militant.

"You know, I think you and I are more alike than we might admit," Summer said, shaking the lit match and tossing it aside.

"Sweetheart, you and I are nothing alike." He took another puff, gloating in his own self-righteousness.

"The way I see it, you betrayed your country in an effort to improve your own financial position, just as I betrayed my father to better mine."

Summer took a long drag and held it. The general started to speak when she exhaled. The pot smoke enveloped his face, souring the flavor of his cigar. He fanned the smoke away with one hand; Summer smiled as he did. He could tell she liked pushing people's buttons, especially those she despised as much as him. Yes, he was growing to like her.

"I served my country faithfully for over thirty years, and all I got was a medal and a handshake. No bonus, no retirement home, no parade into the sunset. I deserve this."

He puffed again, blowing the smoke in Summer's face, a tit for tat power play. "But you— you are a treacherous little thing, indeed. Willing to sell out your family and your soul for a chance to win the keys to the kingdom."

He flicked his cigar ashes to the ground and looked at Summer sheepishly, awaiting some clever retort.

Summer stood, pacing slowly, like a little girl in a faraway dream. She spoke softly as she took her steps, "It's too bad, really. I think you and I could have worked well together."

The general smiled and closed his eyes as he took another puff and blew another smoke ring.

"See, the only problem I have is that you blew off MY FUCKING HAND!"

The general shot up, startled.

He watched Summer signal three armed guards, who quickly surrounded the general and held him at gunpoint. He knew in a flash that with or without Hector's permission, she would have her revenge. She had gumption. That, he admired.

He didn't stand. He simply sat back again, relaxed and as poised as he'd been during their last meeting.

"You don't honestly think you can do anything to me, do you?"

He flicked his ashes to the ground and took a sip of his drink.

"Without me, young lady, to whom will you sell your weapon? I'm the negotiator, remember?"

He took another sip when a thought came to him. "Also, correct me if I'm wrong, but you did just kill my daughter, did you not? I believe I was justified in taking your hand. Were Hector not there to save you, it would have been your head."

He swiped his hand in the air, motioning for the guards to disburse. He did it as he had probably done a thousand times. He was cool under fire, the quality one might expect from a man in his position. The guards looked to Summer for guidance. She shook her head, a signal that meant stay put.

" Apologies, General. Your daughter was a casualty I hadn't expected. The nosy bitch put it together. She had somehow learned of my new deal with Hector." Summer was calm as she spoke, the general coolly admiring her panache. "I was close to discovering the antidote on my own, and her timely arrival gave me a great excuse to eliminate my father from the picture, so I dropped a couple depth charges."

Summer took a long drag on her joint, closing her eyes and holding the smoke in for several seconds before exhaling. "I was planning to keep Chris alive. She was useful, and plenty sexy if I do say so myself— killer legs."

The general shook his head in disbelief. Summer appeared so fragile, so innocent, yet here she was, a mastermind the likes of which he'd rarely encountered during his career as a military man. She had ambition and reminded the old man of himself at her age, but her desire to turn on her father – her family - didn't sit well with him. He knew that her ambition would be her undoing.

"She tried to stop me, so I had no choice. I had to shoot her. Besides, you killed a whole fucking village, General. Who is the real tyrant here?"

"The cost of war, Ms. Flowers," he said with little emotion.

"This, too, General, is the cost of war." Summer snapped her fingers. The big guard snapped the titanium band in place around the general's neck and handed Summer the remote. "Let me try to remember how this works again. The green light turns red when I hit this button and— boom, or is it the red light turns green? I can't remember."

The general dropped his cigar. She wasn't serious? Had he underestimated her? *This is it*, he thought.

"What will you tell our guests?" he asked, trying desperately to gain some kind of leverage.

"I've already negotiated a deal," Summer replied rather arrogantly.

The general shook his head.

"You conniving little bitch. I've survived three wars and have fought my fair share of battles over the years. I never would have imagined my end to come at the hand of a little girl, a scientist nonetheless."

"Step back, boys. I would hate for you to be hit with any of this vile shrapnel."

She smirked as she said it and waved the remote in front of the general's face. "Bye bye, General."

The general smiled and motioned for her to wait a moment while he retrieved his cigar. He stood, closed his eyes, took a long puff, straightened his uniform jacket, then said, "See you soon, Summer Flowers."

Summer pressed the button and watched the green light blink twice, then turn red. The explosion was small, but effective. He stood headless for five seconds, swaying gently as his small feet struggled to balance his big body. Finally, his lifeless legs collapsed.

"Feed him to the flock," Summer ordered as she flung the remote to the ground, wiping the bits of skull, brain, and blood from her face and hair as she walked away.

Chapter 46

Natalie rolled off Hector, completely exhausted, naked and sweating.

"That was amazing," she whispered, trying to catch her breath. Hector lit a joint and stared at the ceiling fan, relaxing and enjoying the moment, dreaming about the money he'd soon be making with, not only the MOjo55 formula, but also the high potency herb he'd be sending to market.

"I think I'll call it Rasta Magic, or better yet, if it were crack, Jailhouse Rock."

"Call what?" Natalie asked. "Oh—" She watched him take another hit. "I guess it's my cross to bear— destined to be with a pothead forever," she chuckled.

Hector rolled over and grabbed her by the throat. "I am no pothead. Dis is a spiritual tool."

"Jesus Christ, Hector." She brushed his hand aside. "Don't be such a psycho."

Hector reached back and put his arm behind his head. He closed his eyes and hummed "Fools Rush In" like nothing had just happened.

"So, now what?" Natalie asked.

"Now, we go to sleep."

"No, I mean about the Korean deal, the business, Summer, me?"

"I know what you meant," he took another drag. "I do believe dat daughter of yours would kill her first born to rule an empire." He exhaled and watched the ceiling fan blades catch the smoke, whipping it into the night. "She's going to run the business stateside, and I'll head up operations here in Jamaica."

"And me?" Natalie asked, leaning over, caressing his chest. "Am I to stay here with you?"

She kissed him softly, stroking his neck and arm as she did.

"Impossible. I am a Rasta God. You are simply my plaything for de moment."

Natalie shot up. "It was you who courted us. It was you who asked us to help you. You said—"

"What I said was dat I would make it well wort your while— dat's it."

He may have been a god, but he was still a man, a man filled with the same jealousy and rage as other men, maybe more. It wasn't enough to kill Mia and Sonny. His ego wouldn't be soothed until he won the love of Sonny's wife and returned the injustice he felt he'd endured when Sonny stole Mia's heart from him.

"What the fuck did I ever see in you?" Natalie barked.

Hector laughed. "I tink you saw me in you— literally."

She screamed at him at the top of her lungs. "You're no god. You're nothing more than a slimy, selfish, drug-dealing, murderous cocksucker!"

Hector sprung off the bed and caught her with the back of his hand, sending her reeling and slamming against the bedroom door. Sliding his trousers over his waist, he buttoned them and drew the loose belt from his waist. Wrapping the flat end around his fist, he snapped the leather and moved toward Natalie.

"How dare you say such tings to me, woman."

He swung the belt high above his head and brought the buckled end down hard on her midsection.

She screamed and started crying, clutching her side in pain. "You son of a bitch."

Hector raised the belt again, but before he could land another strike, the door flew open.

Sonny Flowers stood there, sober and strong, looking downright courageous. Hector wondered where the anxiety ridden coward had gone. Perhaps his adversary had faced death, insanity, and loss and had risen from the ashes anew? It mattered not to Hector. He was actually happy Sonny had arrived in time to see his estranged wife. She had been sexually used and then beaten. What better exclamation point to punctuate Sonny's defeat.

"Natalie?"

Sonny was stunned indeed. Hector raised the belt and smiled.

"Sonny. Watch— " Natalie couldn't finish.

Sonny turned as Hector thumped him on his left temple. He stumbled sideways, and dropped to one knee, clutching his head. Hector unleashed a vicious right hand to Sonny's head, sending him down with swiftness. The deity reveled in his savagery as Natalie struggled to her feet, trying to reach the doorway and get help. She made it across the threshold but hit a barrier that separated her from her freedom— Max.

"Maxi, grab her," yelled Hector.

Chapter 47

Natalie sobbed and silently pleaded with the stone-faced Max. He looked her in the eyes and felt contempt. *She probably deserved all of Hector's rage*, he thought, and were it a day earlier, he would have complied with his uncle's order and stopped her, but today was different. Today, Max had more contempt and rage for his uncle than any other human being on the planet.

Max allowed Natalie to pass and placed himself in the path of his uncle.

"What de fuck are you doing?" Hector yelled.

Max stood like a statue. His face was expressionless; his fiery stare blazed a trail directly into the heart of his uncle that stopped Hector dead in his tracks. Max could sense that Hector knew why he was there. His dark past had been revealed, and now it was time for Hector to pay for his sins. Max knew that he had him. He stared into the eyes of the devil himself and watched his pupils dilate. The mighty man-god was scared.

"Maxi, please, let me explain—"

Max sliced through the room as though he were sliding on quicksilver. He didn't hesitate. He executed his strikes with precision and force. Hector tried swinging the belt and catching Max with the buckle, but Max was too fast. He raised an arm and watched the belt wrap around it. He tugged hard, summoning the strength of ten men and forced it away from his uncle, leaving Hector's hand bloodied.

Max unwound the belt and in a few quick steps, had it wrapped around Hector's neck. He slipped the loose end through the buckle and yanked it tight, cutting off the air supply to Hector's lungs. He thought about killing him right there on the spot, but that would have been far too swift and merciful. Max had other plans.

While Hector gasped for air, Max pulled him out of the room like a dog on a leash. Hector stumbled and tripped over Sonny on the way. The young henchman continued toward the main staircase, his intensity unwavering. Without pause, he shoved his uncle down the stairs and watched him tumble.

"What you doin', Max?" Hector begged as he lay beaten and bloody on his own foyer floor.

Max didn't offer a reply. He just retrieved the belt and dragged him through the house toward the courtyard.

Chapter 48

I cracked my eyes and struggled to my feet. My head felt like it had been crushed in a vice, so I sat on the bed and collected myself. Blood oozed from my temple.

"That's gonna leave a mark," I mumbled. What the fuck happened? I tried and failed to piece it all together. Where was Summer? I stood on my own, but had to sit again. My head was throbbing. Lighting the joint on the nightstand, I took a drag hoping it would numb the pain. I wasn't panicking. I blamed my bloody temple. After three puffs, I closed my eyes for a second, letting the THC take hold of their respective neurons when I felt a hand on my shoulder.

I opened my eyes and saw Summer.

"Where did you come from?" I asked, wondering if I was imagining her.

"Daddy, are you okay?"

She hugged me and buried her head in my chest. I didn't care if it was a flashback. It felt damn good. We'd found each other.

"Yeah. I'm better now." I reached for her hand to help me to my feet. "What the fuck? Where's your hand?"

"The general," she said.

"I'm gonna kill him."

"I already took care of that," she replied.

Her voice was different, sinister sounding. When we'd been in the lab together, she broke down and cried for the first time in ages. I thought it was a breakthrough. Now, she sounded like her old cynical self, but angrier. While she'd always had a sharp tongue and short temper, she wasn't an angry person, so my whole body tensed as I listened to her.

"What do you mean you took care of it?"

She smirked and her eyes narrowed. "You saw Mia, didn't you?"

I felt the familiar pit form in my gut and recalled Mia's word of warning.

"Start talking, Summer."

She laughed. "You're a smart guy. I think you can figure it out."

"Please tell me you weren't part of this?"

"See? Like I said - a clever guy. Was I part of it? Yes. Proud of it? A little, maybe."

Her indifference sounded more like bragging. My mind raced to piece the puzzle together, the rock in my gut growing heavier by the second.

"It was always about Autumn and the research with you."

I heard her, but couldn't believe it. Jealousy? Really?

"I made you more money than you'd ever dreamed, but did you even care? Did you ever even say thanks?" She walked over and leaned in close. "Well, did you?"

"We were working in the name of science, Summer. You turned us into common drug dealers."

Summer shook her head. "Even after all this, you still don't appreciate a damn thing I do. And who are you to talk about science? I'm more of a real scientist than you'll ever be. Besides, I thought I was rid of you."

"Rid of me? I don't understand."

"There you were. You popped right out of the water after two fucking depth charges. How the hell did you make it out alive? That whole ship was destroyed."

I lost my breath. "It wasn't Chris at all, was it?"

"Are you kidding? She was so in love with you, she would have sacrificed everything. She would have thrown it all away—for you."

My chest tightened. *I'm going to have a heart attack*, I thought.

"I'm your father. I love you. I know I haven't said it much, but it's true."

"Love? " Summer became even more agitated. "You loved Autumn. You used me. Hell, the way you swooned all over that voodoo bitch – you probably love her more than me. You should have seen yourself, all enchanted and bewitched by her. It was like watching you and Autumn all over again. I was actually holding out hope for you until that display."

"Summer, you don't really believe that?" Had I really driven her to this? "You planned it all?"

"Not at first. Hector approached me after the Bishop slaying. I declined his offer to partner with him after we finished the formula. Then, after Dehlia's house, I not only accepted, but offered you and Mia in exchange for a piece of the action."

I fell back on the bed. This wasn't happening. Natalie appeared in the doorway.

"It's my fault, Sonny."

I lifted my head. "I thought that was you with Hector. I just didn't want to believe it."

"I've been on the island since I left you. Hector called after the funeral and told me about you and Mia. I was angry, Sonny."

"Hell hath no fury, eh, Nat?"

Natalie nodded. "I just wanted to do whatever I could to hurt you."

I shook my head. How could I have been so stupid? It was all starting to make sense. Hector probably would have let Mia die. He just wanted me to cure her so that he and Natalie could watch us burn together and feed his ego.

She walked over to Summer and tried to embrace her; Summer pushed her away "What do you think you're doing?"

"We've gone too far, Summer. It's over."

"Over?" she shouted. "Nothing is over. It's all just beginning. I'm building a new empire."

Natalie shouted back, "None of this will bring her back, Summer, or change what's happened in the past."

"Spare me your parental psychobabble. Autumn was a flake. I've always been the brains in this family."

I leaned over the bed and puked, heaving hard, unable to control the anxiety. It hit me with a fury.

"We're leaving," Natalie said, helping me to my feet.

"You're not going anywhere," Summer shouted, summoning the guards from the courtyard to hold us.

"Feed him to the flock" she barked.

"What of de woman?"

"Take her, too," Summer said.

Summer disappeared, and I threw up again. The guards prodded me with their rifles and kept their distance. Getting puked on probably wasn't what they had in mind when they signed on for the job.

"I never meant— " Natalie started.

"It's on me, Nat. All she ever wanted was my love – same as you."

Chapter 49

Summer met her new business partner at a quaint bed and breakfast called Moon San Villa in the center of Port Antonio. It overlooked the famous Blue Lagoon, and Summer thought about how little of Jamaica she'd actually seen since she'd been on the island. She remembered family vacations when she was a little girl. She pictured her parents fussing over Autumn, and it made her sick. *Well, at least I don't have to deal with them anymore,* she thought as she knocked on the Korean's door.

"Welcome, beautiful Flowers," Mr. Lee said, shooing away the hooker and inviting her into his suite.

He offered Summer a drink, and she made herself comfortable.

"Shall we discuss our arrangement?" she asked, as Lee passed her the White Russian.

"Very well." Lee produced an envelope and handed it to Summer. "Three million U.S. has been transferred to the numbered account in this envelope. Do you have the samples and formulas?"

Summer handed Lee a small box containing the notes for the MOjo55 compound and a vial containing a liquid sample. Lee smiled and leafed through the box, but his smile faded and his face tightened. Summer tensed. What had she forgotten? What was he looking for?

"Where is the antidote?" Lee asked impatiently.

"The antidote wasn't part of the agreement, only the agent."

Summer began to sweat, hoping the deal hadn't become unglued.

"Young lady, how do you expect me to give you three million dollars for the agent without the antidote? The antidote is our control. Without it, chaos could ensue."

Summer swallowed the lump in her throat. She had no idea how to produce the antidote. She was unconscious when Sonny figured it out, and she used what he had developed in front of the men to cure Natalie. Having just sent her father to his death, and Hector having sent Mia to hers, she would be unable to reproduce it on her own. Summer Flowers, the genius, knew that she'd just made a mistake that could cost her everything.

"Mr. Lee, I had other offers, and my agreement to guarantee you exclusivity drove them away. I'm counting on you to follow through with our arrangement."

Lee paced, extremely agitated. He loosened his collar and began mumbling under his breath.

"Where is the general? I want to speak with him."

Summer's face started burning. She felt the heat radiate throughout her entire body. She was in trouble.

"Sir. The general is indisposed. He has complete faith in me to negotiate this deal. Beside, I'm the one who invented the agent. I can get you the antidote."

Lee paused and looked at her. He rubbed his chin and pursed his lips.

"Your ambition will be your downfall, Ms. Flowers. Do not fail me."

With that, Lee opened the door and motioned for Summer to leave.

The young scientist made a hasty exit and ran back to the Hannassoui compound as fast as she could, praying Sonny hadn't yet been thrown to the piranha.

Chapter 50

Max was like a robot who, when programmed to complete a mission, was unstoppable. He'd been offered many a bribe by men about to die: a wife, a daughter, money, gold; he'd heard it all, but no matter the plea, the bribe, or the threat, he simply would not deviate.

"Please, Maxi. I didn't know you existed. Your fatha never told me."

Max used a zip tie to fasten Hector's hands behind him on the courtyard whipping post. He used some nylon rope to fasten his legs at the ankles.

"You don't know what you doin'. I am a god! You will be damned for dis."

Max ignored Hector completely, unrolling his medical kit on the ground next to the post. He took an inventory of his instruments and silently rehearsed the procedure in his mind. He'd read it so many times he knew it by heart. It was extremely complex even in a normal operating room.

An experienced surgeon would have a small chance of success in the courtyard. Max felt confident, though. He knew that a surgeon would have been working under the premise that the patient needed to stay alive. A surgeon would have used anesthetic, clamps, vital sign monitoring equipment, and would have had a team of people there to help. Max had no use for these things. He was just hoping his patient would remain alive long enough to experience the torture he'd forced so many of his victims to endure under his reign.

Max retrieved the belt he used to drag Hector into the courtyard and strapped it tightly around his uncle's neck. He buckled it tight behind the post and was satisfied that it would keep the head immobile. The amateur surgeon flicked a switch and the halogen lamp pulsed waves of hot light on the face of Hector.

"What you plannin' to do to me?"

Max ignored his uncle and studied the area on which he needed to work. As he reached down to retrieve the scalpel, he saw a small pouch in his case that looked unfamiliar. He picked it up and studied it for a moment and then remembered what it was— the pollen Dehlia gave Hector to use on Dr. Hodges. He remembered how effective it had been, and decided to give it one last use on his whimpering, whining uncle.

He unfolded the pouch and held it in front of Hector's face. Hector blew hard, hoping his breath would reach the pollen first and paralyze Max, but the effort was in vain. Max shook his head and waved his finger in Hector's face. He blew softly and steadily. The pollen floated off the paper and directly in Hector's face. Hector held his breath, but he couldn't hold it forever.

The pollen dissipated, and Hector took a deep breath. Max grimaced and blew the rest of the pollen directly into the deity's mouth. Hector coughed and uttered what would be his final words. "You ungrateful son of a bitch. I should have killed you dat day."

The words were music to Max's ears. It fueled his hatred and motivated him to hasten his action. He donned his surgical gloves and grabbed the scalpel. His first cut was at the left corner of his uncle's mouth. He slid the instrument slowly until the blade reached the bottom of the ear. He sliced the tendons, nerves, and muscles that connected the mandible to the skull. He repeated the action on the right side, and then smiled as he displaced Hector's jaw. Hector wailed, in spite of his paralysis. Max continued to work, immune to the tears streaming down his uncle's cheeks.

Max, not without a sense of humor, began humming one of Hector's favorite tunes, "A Little Less Conversation".

"Hold it right dere!" Max heard from behind.

The three armed guards, who were escorting Sonny and Natalie, appeared. Max turned slowly, staring them down, almost daring them to try and stop him.

"Step back, Max," the lead guard shouted.

Max shook his head and turned back toward his uncle.

The guards looked at each other, not knowing exactly what to do. They'd taken orders from both men, but ultimately concluded their loyalty should stay with the Holy One.

"Max, dis is blasphemy. He is Haile Selassie incarnate. You cannot do dis."

The lead guard raised his rifle and took aim.

"Hold on," Sonny shouted.

"Reach in my back pocket and pull out the envelope," Sonny shouted to the guards.

They were curious, so they did as instructed. The head guard opened it and retrieved the letter from Dehlia and the two photos that accompanied it.

Dear Sonny,

While you were unconscious, I called on the guidance of my Grandmother's spirit to help me. I didn't know what to do. She came to me in a vision and told me to do nothing. She said someone else would come to your aid. She also told me you needed to know about Hector.

Hector is not the reincarnation of Haile Selassie I. He is the son of a Jamaican farmer, and no more Selassie than you or me. The photos included prove it. She had them hidden in an old book for safe keeping. She told me where to find them.

Tell the men who follow him and tell Max.

Love, Dehlia

The guards stared at one another and passed the photos. The first showed Hector brandishing a bottle of rum, obviously drunk. In the place on his right bicep where the Ethiopia birthmark had been imprinted were three tattooed Greek letters, an obvious sign of membership in a college fraternity.

The next photo showed who they all assumed to be Dehlia's mother, tattooing a purple shape over the letters. The birthmark was a forgery designed to win the loyalties of the true Rastafarian believers. He'd duped them all.

"You know how she died?" Sonny asked them.

They all shook their heads.

"Hector said she went crazy, the voodoo made her mad, and she threw herself from the cliffs into the sea. I'm sure he did it, especially after discovering Dehlia was his daughter."

The guards looked shocked. They grew angry and started toward Hector. Max halted them. They threw down their weapons and cut Natalie and Sonny loose.

Sonny said, "Tell the others. Take the photos to prove it. Then, go home to your families."

Max watched and smiled as the guards left. He knew that he was now free. He was free to do as he pleased to Hector without fear of reprisal from anyone, free to live his own life, and free to love whomever he chose.

He went back to work and sliced the remaining connective tissues that held the lower jaw to the skull. Hector had passed out and regained consciousness several times from the excruciating pain, but Max kept at it.

Using the steady hand and precision an actual surgeon would have been proud to witness, Max cut the tongue from Hector's mouth. He was sure to sever the organ at the very root of its origin in the deep recesses of the throat. Once it was completely removed, he turned to Sonny and smiled. He held the tongue in his hand and displayed it— a trophy of his victory over Hector and his accomplishment as an amateur surgeon.

Natalie threw up, but Sonny, even though he was disgusted, smiled to let Max know he was proud, in a disturbing sort of way. Max carefully wrapped the tongue in medical grade plastic and placed it in a small cooler filled with dry ice. Max finished packing the tongue and removed his gloves. He started walking away when Sonny stopped him.

Pointing to Hector, he asked, "What about him? Is he dead?"

Max nodded, but he needed to finish the job. He grabbed the dirty scalpel and stood in front of his uncle. He recalled all that Mia shared with him. He thought of his parents, of Dehlia, and of his life, and the terrible things he'd done for this imposter. With one quick swipe, he severed Hectors airway. He knew his uncle was already dead, but it gave him great satisfaction and the closure he needed to move past the pain.

Max made quick work of the corpse, cutting him down and tossing him to the flock of piranha. The water bubbled and teemed in a frenzy of activity. Within minutes, the self-proclaimed man-god was gone.

Chapter 51

Summer rushed in to the empty house, frantically searching for her father, mother, Hector, or anyone who might be able to help her. She saw Max driving off and asked a passing guard what was happening.

"He gone to de Cleveland Clinic. Doctor dere goin' to do a tongue transplant."

Summer was confused. She figured the old guard was stoned and pushed past him. "Hector?" she shouted.

The guard turned back to her. "Ain't no more Hectah."

"What the fuck are you talking about?" she barked.

The guard smiled at her as he said it. "It be Hectah's tongue dey sewin into Maxi. Hectah's dead."

With that, she watched him walk out the door

What happened while I was gone, she thought, as she continued the search for her father.

"Looking for me?" she heard his voice say.

She turned and saw Sonny, pack in hand, heading out the door like everyone else.

She exhaled a sigh of relief. "You're still alive? I need the antidote."

"I've been a crummy father to you. I've also been afraid for a very long time, afraid of failing, being abandoned, and afraid to say the things that lived in my heart. I love you, Summer. I love you as much as I love Autumn. You are my little girl. I'm sorry for all the pain I've caused you, but I will not help you out of this mess. Too many people have died because of you, because of us. Come with me and start over, you and me?"

Summer's bottom lip trembled, and she wiped away tears, tears of joy that she'd finally heard her father tell her what she had been so longing to hear, but she couldn't leave, not now. She was so close to finally realizing her dream of ruling an empire and running her own operation.

"I'm staying, and you need to help me. You owe me that," she barked.

"I owe it to you to be a better father. I'm walking out. Please come with me, Summer."

Sonny started toward the door. Summer panicked. She needed him.

"Dad, I admit it, I made a few mistakes, but Hector is dead. Max is gone. All of this can be ours. I'll run the business, and you can continue your research. You can live here with Mia in peace."

He stopped and stared at the exit for a few seconds before turning around.

"I don't want all of this, Summer. I never did. I came back here for you. I'm walking out that door. Please follow me," he said, not knowing if she would, rubbing his Saint Anthony medal and silently praying his daughter would come to her senses.

To hell with him, she thought. *I can find the antidote. I can have it all. He'll come crawling back when he is home alone, wishing I was there.*

"I couldn't help but overhear your conversation."

Mr. Lee appeared in the dining room. He'd come around through the courtyard. Summer gasped. She looked around, hoping someone would be there to help her. The rooms were empty, the halls silent, the house abandoned.

"Mr. Lee, I can explain."

"No need. You have confirmed what I suspected."

"What are you going to do?"

Lee smiled and shook his head. " You've given me little choice. I'll have to honor our terms and take the MOjo55 compound with me."

Summer breathed a sigh of relief. She needed a miracle and found one in Mr. Lee.

"I understand," she said and waved Mr. Lee to the front door. He obliged.

"Before I leave, however," Mr. Lee said, "I would like a guarantee that what you have already given me is authentic. You have shown your dishonesty once, so how am I to believe what you actually gave me is the MOjo 55?"

Summer's heart began to race once more. "I assure you, Mr. Lee, it's authentic."

Lee retrieved the vial from his jacket pocket and swirled it softly in front of Summer. Her pupils dilated, and her face went white. He nodded and turned toward the door.

"Goodnight Mr. Lee," she said.

Lee turned around and said, "Well, just to be absolutely sure."

Summer screamed as Lee doused her in the face with the agent. The liquid penetrated her eyes and mouth. He threw the vial to the ground and stomped on it.

Summer paced knowing her rational mind would only be with her a few more seconds. *He wouldn't waste it like this, would he?*

He had the written formula. She looked down and saw the ground beneath her start to move. She dropped to her hands and knees and crawled to the corner. She curled up in a ball and screamed. Then she screamed again. She sat screaming over and over. Nobody came to help her.

Chapter 52

I raced to Dehlia's house, praying Mia was still there. She wasn't. I looked for a note—something— anything.

Nothing.

"Where did she say she was going? The Bahamas? Anguilla? Fuck!"

This can't be happening, I thought. She left. She warned me about Summer, but did I listen? Hell no. Now, she's gone, Summer's gone, Natalie's gone, and Autumn is gone. All the women I've ever loved are gone, and I'm alone. I squeezed my eyes shut and prayed hard to my favorite saint. Then I set out to find the one woman I truly loved.

I woke up to the prodding of a fishing pole in my ribs. The old Jamaican fisherman probably thought I was dead or had passed out from a drunken night at the marina bar. I sprung to my feet and scanned the docks for any sign of Mia.

"Mia!" I called out.

The fisherman sat at his perch and cast his line. He looked at me like I was crazy, but I didn't care. Nothing was more important to me than finding her. As I scanned the docks, I saw that all of Hector's fleet had disappeared. Irony kicked me in the nuts as I gazed upon the only remaining boat - *The Mia*, a forty-foot sailboat. It was a sign. I'd comb every island in the goddamn Caribbean until I found her. With the turn of a key, the engine fired up and I motored out of the dock. Once out in open ocean, I raised the mainsail. First stop, Anguilla. I breathed in the salty ocean air and looked forward to my life ahead.

I sailed day and night, alone on *The Mia*, dreaming of the moment we'd be reunited, praying that Summer would find her way to us somehow. I made a dozen ports of call and came up empty at each one. I didn't give a shit. I was determined.

It'd been fifty days, and there was still no sign of her. Defeat was settling in. I'd been staring at the cigar box in the cabin for weeks. The temptation to smoke my mind useless presented itself every time I came up short in my quest to find Mia, but I resisted. I should have thrown it overboard, but keeping it and resisting it made me feel stronger.

Today, though, was my fiftieth day. I opened the box and lifted a joint to my lips. I didn't light it, though. I just held it in my mouth and thought about where I was – Summer, Mia, Nat, and even Regina. I'd faced the worst of what life had to throw at me and survived, in spite of myself. I leaned back on the bench and let the warm Caribbean sun envelop me. I flicked the joint overboard and rubbed the medal around my neck.

I thought of Autumn and said to her, *I'm not so lost. I've been found. Thanks sweet Autumn, for looking out.*

I smiled as the waves rocked me to sleep. I was happy. I'd finally let her go. The journey ahead could take forever, but I was ready for it. I was ready to become the man Mia needed, Summer needed, and, most of all, I needed.

Chapter 53

"Oh, my God. It looks like he's back."

It felt like I'd only dozed off for a minute, but I was struggling to open my eyes. It had to be a dream – the voice. As I struggled to see, I prayed pirates hadn't boarded.

"Sonny?" I heard the voice ask. It was a familiar, but one I couldn't immediately place. "Sonny, look at me. Open your eyes."

I was so groggy, but somehow managed to pry them open. The light was overwhelming. The sun must have been high in the sky already.

"Son of a bitch, it's bright."

"Yeah, he's back."

"What time is it? I asked.

"Hit the lights," the voice barked, and the lights went out.

"What the fuck? What's going on?"

I was disoriented again. The familiar rocking of the boat and the breeze I felt when I'd dozed off was gone. I couldn't see. My head pounded and my eyes strained to focus. Had I been kidnapped? Was I dead? I heard the scratch of the lighter and saw the flame across the room. A candle had been lit and my eyes finally started to adjust.

"Where am I? Where's my boat? What have you done with my boat, God damnit?"

I placed my hands at my side and realized that I was on a bed. It felt like a hospital bed, the uncomfortable electric beds with guardrails and built-in tabletops. Why was I in a hospital bed, wearing a hospital gown that bunched up around my neck, cut into my armpits, and left my ass open to the breeze? I sat up and felt light-headed. Swinging my legs over the side, I stood. My feet hit the cold linoleum and sent shock waves up my spine. I forced myself to stand, but my legs were rubbery and gave out under the weight of my upper body. I fell back on the bed. An IV became tangled in the mess of blankets and bed and tugged against my skin uncomfortably.

The familiar voice spoke again. "It's me, Sonny. It's Mike, Mike Maserati. We've been using electrodes to keep your muscles from experiencing atrophy, but it will take some time, and a lot of physical therapy, before you're back to your old self, I'm afraid."

"Mike?"

Mike held the candle in front of his face; it *was* him.

"Mike? What's going on? Where am I?"

Mike smiled warmly. "You're at the clinic, Sonny. You've been here a while."

"Huh?"

"Take it easy, old friend. No need to conquer the world in your first five minutes."

"Why do I feel like I just got the crap kicked out of me?"

"We need to talk, Sonny, but I'm afraid what I tell you may put you in a serious state of shock."

"Quit being a drama queen asshole and tell me what the fuck is going on."

"Sonny, you've been in what we've deemed to be a delusional coma for the past five months."

"Come again?" I said.

"You've been in a delusional, paranoid state of mind for the past five months. You just came back to reality, so to speak."

"No, no, no, Mike. I was just on a boat in the Caribbean. Before that, I was in Jamaica with Summer and Mia. Natalie was there, too."

"You were in Jamaica five months ago, Sonny, but you went alone. I don't know who Mia is, but we'll figure it all out."

This wasn't real. This couldn't be real.

"You're telling me I'm goddamn Dorothy from the *Wizard of Oz*?"

Mike nodded. "Get some rest, buddy. We'll talk in the morning."

Mike blew out the candle and closed the door. I just lay there, aching and terrified, trying to make sense of what was happening. The room felt real, as did Mike, but Jamaica and Mia, the boat and my search – it was all real, too. At least it felt real.

"Sweet Jesus," I mumbled, then fell back asleep.

Chapter 54

Sunlight crashed through the window and woke me from my slumber. My eyes were cooperating a little better, and I could see clouds, birds, and heard the noises from the street. I thought of Jamaica. I couldn't remember seeing any clouds or birds on the island. Maybe it was the stress of the job? Maybe I just hadn't paid attention? Maybe it was like Mike said, all just one big fucked-up dream?

My body still ached, but I managed to get to my feet and walk to the bathroom. I pissed for an hour and felt relieved. I couldn't remember pissing in Jamaica. I was starting to accept that what Mike said was the truth. I'd been in a fucking coma for five months. Holy shit.

Everything hurt. What had I lost over that time? How much of my mind was gone? I looked in the mirror for the first time and almost cried. I looked like a shell of my former self. I looked like an AIDS patient; my face was shallow and sunken. My ribs protruded. I didn't recognize the face that looked back at me. Where had I gone?

"Well, good morning."

Her voice was chipper and familiar. I was nervous to leave the confines of the bathroom and face my new reality.

"Hi." I scooped a mouthful of water and licked my lips. "Sorry, it's a little hard to talk."

"Oh, honey, no need to apologize. I bet you'd like a bath? Let me help you."

She was a nurse, but I couldn't see her name tag. She slid past me and ran the water.

"I'm so happy to see you up and about. We didn't know if you'd ever be back."

"You've been taking care of me?"

"Sure have. All five months. The name is Katrina."

Why did it sound familiar? Rufus' wife?

Was she real, or part of the delusion? My heart started racing. I took a deep breath and tried to calm myself.

"Any idea how I ended up here, Katrina?"

"Sorry, sweetie. I can't help you there. You'll have to ask Dr. Maserati."

I nodded and immersed myself in the warm water. I dunked my head under and closed my eyes. It felt good – safe. Then, in an instant, I was at the *Serpentine Orchid* wreck site. I felt myself under the fallen bowsprit. I shot up and exhaled, blowing water like the humpback whale after the plane crash. It was all so real. I felt myself starting to tremble. What really happened in Jamaica?

Chapter 55

It took a couple days, but I started acclimating to my new reality. The neurons in my brain started firing at their normal, rapid pace. I worked for hours trying to piece my two worlds together. Very little of it made sense to me because my mind saw both existences as equally real. Had I done it? Had I actually created a new realm of consciousness? Had I proven out my own theory? I was ready to talk to Mike.

"Well, hello stranger," Mike said.

I didn't bother to change. I just strolled into his office in my robe and slippers. He laughed at me. I gestured to the robe and said, "I read that muumuus were in this season."

"Glad to see you still have your sense of humor."

"How the hell did I get here, Mike?"

I peered over his desk, hoping to see the call girl of the week. I was both happy and sad to see him fully trousered. Mike's face tightened as he put on his glasses and flipped the file folder open.

"Why don't we start with what you remember, Sonny? Think as far back as you can."

I rested my head on the back of the chair and stared at the ceiling. "I remember working with you and Jane. I remember Agent Tuley asking me to come to Jamaica."

I told him the whole story – Hector, Chris, Summer, Mia, the general, and the genocide.

"What the hell is that?" I asked.

Mike was at his white board, popping open caps on different colored markers, plotting what looked like a time-line.

Mike smiled, proud of his handy work. "It's the Jamaican Flowers project."

"The Jamaican Flowers project?"

"I have hundreds of hours of audio and video spanning the last five months."

He placed the small red dots as he spoke. One went next to Jane, and one went next to Agent Tuley.

"I created this chart and timeline to correlate what you tell me now with what I captured from your ramblings during your delusional state."

I was amazed, still shocked that I'd been here for five whole months, and now shocked again that I'd been rambling the entire time.

"What's real, Mike? What is my real life?"

"That just it, Sonny— I don't truly know."

Mike went on to explain that the only things he could accurately account for was the time leading up to my original departure.

"So I was in Jamaica?"

"Yes. That's how I knew where to find you."

"Huh?"

"Five months ago, I received this with an anonymous letter stating your whereabouts and telling me that I should get you back to the states."

Mike handed me the familiar brown leather journal. I leafed through it, nodding at some of the pages I recognized, and puzzling over others.

"There's some truly fascinating stuff in there, by the way. The notes on MOjo 55— very impressive." Mike said excitedly.

"MOjo 55— it really exists? That's what happened? I was dosed with MOjo 55 and have been delusional for the last five months? I wonder if I dosed myself."

"Your being dosed would be the most likely explanation. Whether you did it yourself, we may never know. Now that you're back to reality, we can at least try to figure it out together. You may be up for the Nobel Prize in science if this is true, Sonny."

"The antidote? You were able to manufacture it? That's how you revived me?"

"No," Mike said matter-of-factly. "You just woke up."

I was perplexed. How did I just wake up? How did I get dosed in the first place?

"Best I can tell, based on your notes, MOjo 55 lasts five months. MOjo 44 would last four months and so on." Mike kept writing on his white board, making small side notes in between pauses to speak. I walked over for a closer examination. Mike continued to write frantically, ignoring my inspection of his work.

"It's a shipwreck," I said, pointing to the spot on the chart that read *Serpentine Orchid*. Mike had it noted as a plant.

"Huh?" Mike stopped to look.

I explained that the *Serpentine Orchid* was both a ship and an anagram for the cure. Mike was fascinated, looking like a kid that just discovered the map to Treasure Island.

"This is good work, Mike."

I took my time and studied all of his notes. For the most part, it seemed accurate. There were several key points missing, but pretty good otherwise.

"What's this down here?" I asked, pointing to the bottom right corner of the board where Mike had been writing earlier.

"Those are my unknowns— the things you talked about that I couldn't plot on the chart. Names, places, events."

I looked at the list and had to laugh. Christine Smith, Autumn, Rufus Jones…

"Why are you laughing?" asked Mike.

I pointed. "Autumn. You have Autumn written on your list of unknowns."

It was obviously a mistake, but Mike still looked confused.

"Who is she?"

"C'mon, Mike, seriously? My daughter? Autumn? You knew her, man."

I was annoyed. After the hell we went through following her death, Mike was the one who really helped me cope. Mike should have known better than to pull a stupid prank like this one me. Maybe after another week, but not now, not when I was still trying to figure it out.

"Sonny? Are you serious?"

Mike looked scared.

I didn't like the way he was looking at me. It was the look I'd given to more than a few patients of his over the years – like I was crazy with a capital C. I reached for my Saint Anthony medal. It was my constant reminder of her. I patted my neck and chest.

"What the fuck happened to my Saint Anthony medal? Did one of those nurses steal it?"

Mike was silent. He watched me search frantically for a medal that he suspected never existed. I was digging myself a nice hole. He'd have me in a strait jacket soon enough.

"Sonny?"

I couldn't stop. I had to find it. It was the only thing I owned that meant anything to me. That medal and the box of keepsakes were all I had left of her.

"Sonny. Listen to me. You only have one daughter, Summer. You know that, right?"

"That's impossible," I heard myself shout.

This was a cruel fucking joke indeed. Then I remembered the tattoo – the one on my back with their baby footprints and names and cherry blossom tree.

"Look," I said, dropping my robe and pointing over my shoulder.

"Why don't you go take a look, Sonny?"

Mike pointed to the door with the full-length mirror. I approached it naked and angry, pissed that I even needed to prove it to him. Facing backward, I peered over my left shoulder and stared at the tattoo on my back. My eyes must have been playing tricks on me. The tree was there. The cherry blossoms were there. The footprints were there. Even the banner with the name was there, but it was only Summer's name and it was only her set of footprints.

It didn't make sense. Where was Autumn's name and prints?

"Sonny?"

I just stared in that goddamn mirror, waiting for my eyes to adjust. They didn't.

"Sonny, there is no Autumn."

The blood drained from my face. I fainted.

Chapter 56

"Tell me about her, Sonny."

I heard Mike's voice as I opened my eyes. I was back in my room and had no idea how I'd gotten there. I traced my memories and started hyperventilating when Mike's words echoed in my ear – *there is no Autumn*. He gave me a paper bag and waited for me to calm down.

"She was Summer's twin," I said.

I explained to Mike what had happened. I shared vivid memories of Autumn as a child, her struggles as a teen, and her untimely suicide. I caught myself reaching for the medal around my neck several times. The pain and realization stung. I didn't want to accept the idea that she had only been a figment of my imagination. Was it all some kind of fucked-up game? Had my ego consciousness really experienced an extreme time and space alteration? The theory was so sound on paper, but I'd never given any consideration to the ramification of the brain's ability to re-acclimate to its original state of time and space consciousness. I was experiencing just that and prayed I wouldn't suffer a full-blown psychotic break.

"Sonny, what I'm about to tell you will probably come as a huge shock, so I want you to prepare yourself."

"I don't think I could possibly be any more shocked, so lay it on me."

"You said that Autumn was bipolar and committed suicide?"

I nodded.

"I think Autumn in your hallucination was your mind's projection of yourself."

I wasn't shocked. I was confused. I rolled my eyes and reached for the medal again.

"Sonny, you are the one with bipolar disorder. You've had it as long as I've known you. Our work together with Jane and the others has been to find a cure, yes, but a cure for you, Sonny."

I would have accused him of lying, but the look on his face; the pain with which he shared the news, told me that he was being honest. Al I could think was, *how fucked up am I?*

"Tell me everything, Mike."

"I'll tell you, Sonny, but only because I believe you can handle it. I don't know what happened in the last five months, but news like what I just gave you would have historically slid you into an immediate depression."

"Do I have anxiety? Panic attacks?" I asked.

"Sometimes, but nothing a beer and shot doesn't cure."

Mike told me that the real problem I'd been struggling with for years was bipolar disorder, and a fairly severe case of it. He said my mood swings were epic. Natalie had left me because of it. I tried to remember, but all that kept coming to mind was Jamaica. The story he told sounded like the tale of a different man. He could have been reading a dossier on a new patient. This wasn't me, was it?

"You had a troubled relationship with Summer. You were hard on her but she never gave up on you, Sonny."

Wow. It was hard to hear. I sounded like a monster. Poor Summer. I can't imagine how she must have felt.

"In fact, that was why she became a scientist— she wanted to find a cure as badly as we did."

"What about meds? Was I on them? *Am* I on them?"

Mike shrugged his shoulders. "We tried a lot of variations over the years, but you didn't respond to much. The weed helped, though. It's what got us working with it in experiments and trials. You were the original test subject."

It was the first thing he'd said that made sense to me. The weed was something I could definitely relate to. I was puzzled why I hadn't smoked anything since coming out of the coma?

"We don't have you on any meds now, Sonny. Believe it or not, you seem stable."

"What happened to Natalie?"

"I don't know."

"And Summer?"

"She still lives in your house. She took a fellowship with Melvin Hodges. You two went to school together, right?"

"Hodges?"

I wanted so badly to remember. I just couldn't. Mike continued to fill me in but I was too preoccupied with thoughts of Summer.

"I need to go home, Mike. I have to see Summer."

"Sonny. You still have a long way to go— physically, mentally, and emotionally. You're nowhere close to being ready to leave."

I started to dressed. "I'll take my chances. How much more fucked up could it get?"

"What about your meds? We should wait a while before you see her, Sonny. She's fragile. I don't think she can stand another heartbreak from you."

It killed me to hear him say it, but I was in a good state of mind. If I was going to revert back or become unstable at some point, I needed to at least try and talk to her while I could.

"Mike, one question before I leave – where do I live?"

Chapter 57

I paid the cabby with money I'd borrowed from Mike. As I watched him pull off, my anxiety increased. There was no turning back now. I looked at the scrap of paper in my hand, the one on which Mike had scribbled my address. I couldn't even remember my own goddamn address. The number on the paper matched the house number, so I threw my backpack over my shoulder and made the long walk to the door. I felt like a stranger. It all seemed so foreign.

Next door, a middle-aged man with a balding scalp and gap between his front teeth backed down the drive and unrolled his window.

"Glad to see you home, Sonny. We've missed you."

I waved and thanked him. Fortunately, he appeared to be in a hurry, so he didn't attempt to make small talk. Thank God, because it would have been embarrassing to admit that I had no clue who the hell he was. I reached for the doorknob and twisted, taking a deep breath as I did. It was locked. I dug through my pockets but couldn't locate a key. I nervously rang the bell, the nip in the fall air started to work its way down my back. I was chilled.

After a minute of silence, I rang again. I heard her approaching.

"So help me, Clemens, if that's you, I'm shooting you where you stand."

Summer opened the door and froze, looking like a deer in headlights.

I smiled, relieved that I recognized her, and even more relieved to see her. She was lovelier than she'd been in my dream, and my soul felt like it was reconnecting with the part of it that had been missing.

She stared at me for a long time, looking like she'd just received a visit from a dead relative. I waved my hand in front in front of her face.

"Earth to Summer?"

She nodded, her Glock 9mm in hand.

"Dad?"

I must have looked dreadful. "Do I look that bad?"

She smiled and shook her head. Her lip quivered and tears formed in the wells of her eyes. She threw her arms around me and buried her head in my shoulder.

"Hi, sweetie," I said kissing her several times on the cheek.

I closed my eyes and held her tightly. It was a moment I wished I could have bottled up.

"When did you wake up? How are you feeling?"

"How about I fill you in over a cup of coffee? I'm freezing my ass off out here."

She laughed and wiped the joyful tears from her cheeks. I breathed a huge sigh of relief as she took my hand in hers and led me through the doorway. I didn't tell her how happy I was to see it still securely attached to her wrist. Two hands, two feet, ten fingers, ten toes – it's what I'd wished for the day she was born and happy to see it still granted.

As she led me through the foyer, I felt like I was in a museum. Pictures of the three of us adorned walls and shelves. We looked like a normal happy family. The only thing I recognized outside the girls was Buster, our old blind broken-down Doberman. Summer bought him when we started growing pot as a deterrent for would-be robbers. Buster looked the part, but was the world's worst watchdog. The only way he'd have hurt anyone was by licking them to death. It was nice to have an actual recollection from my real life.

"Where is old Buster anyway," I asked.

"He died three years ago. You took him to the vet, remember?"

"No." I didn't remember and felt terrible. Not only had I not recalled his death, but I was sad, fully expecting to see him on his old bed in the family room waiting for a scratch behind the ear and a pat from me.

"It's okay, dad. It'll all come back. Just give it some time. Your brain has been through a lot. It's probably just doing what nature intended it to do, protecting itself."

She was right, but I hated not remembering. The world was a much bigger, much scarier place without my memories. I had no ground. I was a loose electron.

Summer led me to the family room and instructed me to relax in what she said was my favorite easy chair. I sank into it, and it felt great. The old leather recliner had been perfectly formed to my frame. I kicked up my heels, and it felt like the chair was welcoming me home. Summer flicked on the television for me and bounced into the kitchen to start the pot of coffee.

I waited for her and watched a commercial for an organic garden fertilizer. The spokesperson advertised a triple growth rate over other fertilizers. I shook my head and scolded the man on the screen,

"You dumb ass, higher phosphorous will give you bigger blooms, but the nitrogen will increase growth post-germination."

"Well at least you still remember your science," Summer said, handing me my cup of coffee.

The words had just come out. I wasn't consciously thinking about it. I felt a sudden rush of optimism.

"You look different," she said.

"You look beautiful," I replied.

She blushed.

"So I spoke with Mike."

"Yeah?"

She tried to act indifferent, but I could tell she was anxious to hear all of the details. I told her what I knew. I told her about

Autumn and Jamaica. I told her about the details of my delusion and my new reality.

"I had a twin sister?"

"The worst part of it," I said, "is not knowing which reality my memories are coming from. I feel crazy and scared and happy and sad all at the same time."

Summer tensed. "Did he tell you what you were like?"

"About me being bipolar?"

She sighed. "Did he tell you what your triggers are?"

"No."

"It's your work," she said.

She told me that when I'm involved in a project that I go into some sort of manic superhuman mode then crash for days afterward.

"We were working on some alternative treatments and a possible cure, right?" I asked.

Summer nodded.

"Did we discover anything? Is that what happened in Jamaica?"

"We made several breakthroughs, but never found a stable long-term treatment."

I sipped my coffee and thought about what it must have been like for her to live with me. Hell, I'm surprised she let me through the door.

"Your mom left. Why didn't you?"

"Because I had faith in you to beat it."

She cuddled up to me. I didn't deserve her.

"So then, what about Jamaica?" I asked.

"What about it?" she replied.

"How did I end up there in the first place? Were the Feds really onto us?"

"You got a call from a Dr. Hannassui. You rushed out the door, hopped a plane, and I saw you at Mike's clinic a month later in a delusional coma."

"Did you go with me?"

"No," Summer said.

I wanted so badly to know more. I hugged her again and told her that I was happy to be home. We sat there quietly for several minutes until a news story caught our attention.

"This just in...intelligence sources are reporting that a small village in the province of Yanggang-Do has been obliterated. According to reports coming in live, it appears that the residents themselves have turned violent, injuring and killing one another.

It has not been determined if the violence is the result of a chemical attack. Some experts believe that extreme conditions such as starvation or disease may have been to blame. The village has been quarantined, and further reports will be given as we learn more.

Kim Blough, reporting for Channel 3 News."

I felt sick to my stomach. "Was that real?" I hoped it was a flashback.

Summer nodded. "That's a crazy story."

"I have to go, Summer."

"Go where? You just got home."

"Jamaica."

Summer grew irritated. "Well, here we go again. Why did you even come home at all?"

"I'm sorry, sweetie. I have to."

"If you go, I won't be here when you get back— if you get back this time."

"Where will you be?"

"I'm moving to California. I was offered a spot at Berkeley."

Fuck. It could have been the highly paranoid thinking from the MOjo 55, but my gut told me that I had something to do with the attack in North Korea. I needed to understand what had happened to me and what my involvement had been. Summer was here, though, and the last thing I wanted was for her to feel I'd abandoned her again.

"Please wait for me. I'll only be a couple days."

"Here. You'll need this." She unlocked a wall safe hidden behind a picture of her and Natalie and handed me a stack of $100 bills.

"Good luck, Dad. I hope you find whatever it is you're looking for."

She kissed me on the cheek and slipped out of the room. I tried to catch her. I wanted her to come with me, but she hopped in her car and sped off before I could.

Chapter 58

I stepped off the commercial jet and the Jamaican sunshine washed over me. The flight was incident free. I stayed pretty relaxed even through a spot or two of turbulence. As I headed toward the terminal, I couldn't help but feel a strange familiarity about this place. In a strange way, it felt more like home than the house I'd just left.

"Good mornin', mon. Where to?"

"Good question. I'm not sure."

I hadn't given much thought to my plan of attack once I'd actually arrived. I went with my gut and leaned on the only memories I could – the ones from my coma.

"Port Antonio, please."

The cabby nodded and started off, piping some local reggae through the speakers.

"You like de ganja, mon?" he asked, offering me a joint.

I held it in my hand and glided it under my nose like I'd done on the boat that last day. The smell reminded me of Chris and our making love on the boat after being kidnapped by Bishop. I hadn't even thought of smoking since waking from the coma. I passed the cabby ten bucks and tucked the joint in my pocket.

We pulled into Port Antonio, and I decided to make camp at the Moon San Villa. It looked nice enough, and I had a funny feeling I'd been there before.

As I reached the front desk, I was welcomed by several smiling faces, none which I recognized.

"Flowah mon. You back?" The concierge ran around the front desk and hugged me. Well, that answered the question as to whether or not I'd been there. Now if I could only recall who this friendly bastard was?

"Where you been, mon?" the concierge asked.

"I've been laying low for a few months."

I glanced down at his name tag. It read Rufus Jones.

"You've got to be fucking kidding me?" I heard myself say out loud.

"Something wrong, Sonny-mon?"

"Rufus?"

"Yeah, mon. It's me, Rufus."

"Do you know a girl named Dehlia?"

"You okay, Sonny?"

"Yeah, yeah, I'm okay It's just been a long flight." It was a lie, of course. I was anything *but* alright.

Rufus smiled again and patted me on the back, "Let me take your tings. Your usual suite, Flowah mon."

I thanked him and slipped him a twenty. He was about to walk away, and I was afraid I might not get another shot at him. "So when was the last time you saw her— Dehlia?"

Rufus scratched his head. "Come to tink of it, probably de last time I saw you."

Oh for Christ's sakes. This dude was worthless. Oh well. I'll figure it out somehow.

"Flowah mon?"

I looked over at him just before walking through the door.

"When was de last time you saw her?"

Rufus looked inquisitive. He'd obviously guessed something wasn't right.

"Honestly, Rufus, I can't remember."

"Well dat was some kinda fight you two had. You should try to see her. I'm sure she'll be happy."

A fight? With Dehlia? I had to play it cool.

"I wouldn't be too sure about that, Rufus. You know women."

I smirked, hoping he'd buy it.

"Where do you think she's staying?"

"Don't know, Flowah. She your niece. You tink you'd know."

Rufus turned and walked away.

My niece? Now my head was really spinning. I thought about lighting the spliff from the cabby but instead just jotted down the few scraps of info I'd been able to gather and tried to plan my next move.

Chapter 59

As I walked the streets of Port Antonio, more than a few friendly faces smiled and said hello. I gave them a wink and a nod and wondered if I was related to any of them as well. It was a long shot, but I was eager to head to the lab, to Dehlia's house, and then down to Hector's. Where had I been before? What role did I have in creating the Mojo55 strain, and, most importantly, is that what was used in the North Korea attack I'd heard about on the news?

My first stop was to the marina. I needed to see for myself if the *Mia* really existed. It had been the freshest in my mind and I just wanted to believe so badly that my experience had some reality to it. I wanted to feel like I hadn't just made it all up. I needed an explanation. I passed boat after boat, manically scouring the names of each. No sign of the *Mia* anywhere. Then another sobering thought occurred to me. What if Mia wasn't real? Mike hadn't been able to validate her existence, so it was very possible. My heart sank at the thought. If there was one thing I wanted to hold on to from my delusion – even more than Autumn, it was Mia.   Knowing Autumn didn't really exist was strangely comforting. I liked knowing that I hadn't lost her - that she hadn't killed herself. I loved Mia, though, with the innocence of a teenager and a heart deeply longing to be with her. If she wasn*'t real, there was a good chance I'd be checking myself back into the clinic for good. I'd be Mike's guinea pig for the rest of my days. Hell, maybe I could get my hands on some MOjo55 and just wake up in another five months with new stories to tell? Maybe I could live in my delusion forever?

I spent the rest of the morning hiking through the trails of the Blue Mountains. Each trail was laid out exactly as I'd remembered in my hallucination, which was great because it offered a tether from one reality to the other. Perhaps the landscape was the constant? People, events, and time could move, but mountains, trails, wind, and oceans did. While my optimism was strong, I couldn't help but feel uneasy that Summer wasn't with me. She'd been with me almost every moment of my delusion. I felt lonely and disconnected without her. Maybe she was a tether as well?

As I thought of her, I couldn't help but wonder if she'd be waiting for me when I came back. She probably thought I'd be back sooner than five months the last time. What if she really had moved on? How badly had I fucked things up for her? What was her life like before? I was suddenly regretting my quick departure. Maybe I should have spent more time with her? An idiot, as always, I never seem to learn. I'd get my answers and then get back to her. If she really did leave, I'd move to California. I wasn't going to let her go, not ever again.

I stopped along the edge of the coast where Summer had first met Hector and wrestled Max for her luggage. I plucked a sea grape from its vine and admired the Brassavola cordata growing in the foreground. The native Jamaican orchid was Summer's favorite. She loved the white heart-shaped blossoms and said that when it came to fragrance, no other could match it. She'd taken about a thousand photos of them in my dream.

I'd finally made it to the clearing that I'd hoped would give me a clear view to the lab and greenhouse. It did, but the lab looked dilapidated. What was an immaculate greenhouse in my delusion was actually and ivy-covered neglected greenhouse with a dozen broken windows and overgrown landscaping. The frame of the structure was heavily rusted, and the six- acre farm behind the lab where workers had tended to Hector's prized marijuana was completely overgrown and looked as though it had never been cleared or farmed. A lizard scuttled across my feet and a black-billed Amazon parrot screeched at me for disturbing him as I muscled my way through the door. A desk still resided in the place I remembered, but it was beaten up. The rows of plants I'd inventoried with Summer had been invaded by weeds and vines. I looked for the spot where I'd discovered the Blood lily. A broken ceramic pot was in its place.

As I trudged on, I became even more frustrated. I seemed to be continually coming up with more questions than answers. What did it mean? Had I been to this spot years ago? Was the hallucination a memory of long ago simply repressed, or had it been a projection of different time and space elements all meshed into one bad dream? I was now walking through my life with an ever-present sense of deja vu.

It sucked.

Dehlia's cottage was more of the same. It existed, but in shambles, appearing to have been abandoned and neglected for some time.

"Brings back some memories, don't it?"

I jumped out of my skin. "What the fuck? You trying to give me a heart attack?"

"I thought I'd find you up here. You always did like dis spot— all your stories about great discoveries happening right here."

She spoke with some sarcasm, but he could tell she was happy to see him.

"Dehlia?"

"I was wonderin' if you'd be back?" she said.

Thank God. She looked exactly as I'd remembered her: tall, lean, light brown skin and the most beautiful smile. I couldn't help but stare. It was like I was seeing her for the first time all over again. I wanted to run up to her and hug her to death, but I had no idea if she'd be welcoming of it. She might hate my guts for all I knew? Fuck it, I said, and went for it. I pulled her in and hugged her like a parent hugs a lost child. To my amazement, she squeezed back just as hard.

"I missed you, Flowah."

I pulled back and held her shoulders. "I need your help, Dehlia."

She laughed. "Dat's notin' new, Flowah mon."

"No?"

She shook her head. "When have I evah said no to you?"

She buried her head in my shoulder and hugged me again. I was thankful and relieved to have finally found an ally.

Chapter 60

Dehlia held my hand and led me back down the path. She listened as I told her about the delusion. She was both bothered and amused at her part in my story.

"You thought me an 'lo Rufus?" She laughed as she said it. "You tried to fix us up once, but you knew Max was da one I loved."

"Max? Is he here? Did the transplant take?"

Dehlia laughed again. "You stoned, Sonny?"

"Goddamnit," I said, frustrated that my reality had been so distorted.

"Tell me about Max."

"Why don you just ask me who you really wan to know 'bout?"

I blushed and stammered. How do I ask if Mia is a real person? Do I love her in real life, or was that the dream? These are questions people don't typically have to ask those with whom they're close. I was truly out of my element and feeling like a jackass because of it.

"My mother is well. She misses you, though."

"Mia? She's your mother?"

Dehlia stopped. "You really don't remember?"

I shook my head.

"You seem well, Sonny. You takin' your meds?"

"No meds. I feel good."

"You look great. My mom isn't going to recognize you."

"About your mom… what's her story?"

Dehlia just smiled. She wouldn't give in, thinking it best that I just find out for myself. I was as nervous as a kid at prom. I had no clue what to possibly expect. I reached for the Saint Anthony medal, and was about to recite my jingle, when it hit me again. I still didn't really even know who I was.

Chapter 61

Dehlia escorted me through the front door of the old plantation house I'd seen in my delusion. It was the same: grand, well maintained, and the odor of jasmine flowers hung heavy in the air.

"She's out in de courtyard," Dehlia said.

I sighed. My anxiety had been pretty transparent. Dehlia pulled me down and gave me a kiss on the cheek.

"For luck," she said, then pushed me toward the double french doors that led out to the courtyard.

Mia sat reading under the gazebo. She sipped a drink and flipped through what looked like an issue of *Scientific Mind* magazine.

"Is this seat taken?" I asked.

It was a cheesy line, for sure, but it was all I could muster. Mia looked up at me and about choked on her lemonade. I gave her a few slaps on the back and waited for her to catch her breath, not sure if the tears in her eyes were from the choking or the joy of seeing me?

"Is it you? Is it really you?" she cried.

All I could think about as I hugged her was that night we'd spent in Dehlia's house. I promised I'd find her again, and while the trip was a roundabout one for sure, I'd found her at last.

"Oh, Sonny."

It was all she could say. She shook and sobbed and hugged and kissed. A full ten minutes passed before the realization that I was, indeed, there, actually settled in.

"Mia, I don't remember anything."

I felt terrible admitting it to her. Our past together was as clear to her as the fictional night we'd spent together was to me. The only difference was that her memory was factual. Mine wasn't.

"Sit down. I'll tell you everything from the beginning."

For the first time since waking in the clinic, I relaxed. The answers were finally going to come. I'd soon learn, for better or worse, who I really was and, hopefully, what had happened. I trusted Mia.

"You know Hector is dead, right?"

I shook my head. "Mia, until you just mentioned his name, I couldn't even be sure he existed."

"You two were best friends, Sonny. You went to college together and were even in the same fraternity."

"Oxford?"

Mia choked on her lemonade again. "Don't make me laugh like that. No, Ohio State."

How in *the* hell had I come up with Oxford? I asked her to continue. She did. She said I'd been crazy fun in college, having grown up for real in the hippie commune.

"You were way more liberal than most in the science department, clamoring on about higher vibrations, quoting Einstein, '*Reality is an illusion albeit a very persistent one.*' You loved Einstein, especially the work he conducted in his later years."

The quote she'd recited resonated with me. The memory of it rushed back. His concept and my aunt's guidance are what drove me to study the mind in such detail. I remember wanting and needing to understand human perception of time and space. What if thoughts are things? What if our thoughts leave our minds in the form of energy and contribute to a collective consciousness?

"Keep going, Mia. It's starting to come back." I was excited to hear more. I felt as though I was discovering the things and people I loved all over again.

"Hector was a foreigner in a strange new world. You were both biology majors, but you tripled majored with both chemistry and physics. Hector said you were the most brilliant man he'd ever known and that you regularly made him feel like an idiot."

I didn't remember that, and the mere idea that he and I had been friends after my delusional experience was unsettling. He was the scary one, not me.

Mia laughed. "Hector used to say that equations danced for you like ballerinas, always fluid and perfect."

"Did he also say that Mary Shelly probably said the same thing about Dr. Frankenstein?"

She squeezed my hand, sensing my insecurity about the condition I'd been told I had in spades. "Hector had always known about your bipolar disorder. It was he that started you down the road of using cannabis for research. He said you'd been self-medicating with it for a long time, so it must have some positive effects."

"Hector sounds like the brilliant one, not me."

"Oh, Sonny. The two of you had a symbiotic relationship. What one of you did always seemed to either help or hurt the other. You were two souls that had probably been carved from the same stone."

Mia went on to explain that Hector had to leave after grad school and head home to Jamaica. One of his brothers had died and the other was ailing, so Hector took over the family sugarcane farm. He ran the operation and began farming cannabis in field behind the greenhouse. She said that I sent him formulas to manufacture from the states, and he conducted the research in Jamaica where it was lower risk to work with what was a highly controlled substance in the US. Hector would send samples, via courier, to me, and I would test them on myself and other volunteers

"My work with Mike?"

Mia smiled, "Precisely."

She went on to tell me that our work together continued for a couple years with little success. We both started to run out of money so decided to partner and sell some of the marijuana to support our research. Hector handled the growth and importation, while I handled the distribution. Hector catered to the Rastafarian crowd in Jamaica and developed a loyal following, often hiring Rasta men to guard his expanding farm.

She said we split everything 50/50 and were doing so well, selling commercially, that the bipolar research took a back seat.

"You met and married Natalie. Hector met and married me. You were the best man."

She looked at me longingly. My guess was that she'd hoped something would register for me. It didn't. I took a wild guess.

"That's when you and I fell in love?"

Mia smiled. "That's right."

She explained that Summer was born the following year, but she and Hector had trouble trying to conceive. While they adopted and raised Max as their own after Hector's brother's death, it wouldn't be until eight years later that she would become pregnant with Dehlia.

"So Dehlia isn't really my niece? Rufus just said that because Hector and I were like brothers?"

"Correct. Dehlia is not your niece. She's actually your daughter, Sonny."

I choked on my drink. It was my turn now. "She's my . . ."

Mia nodded.

"Does she know?"

"Yes, I told her the last time you were here— after Hector's funeral. She was angry, and you two fought."

"How did I not know?"

She squeezed my hand and told me how happy Hector was to finally have a child of his own. She told me how Hector called me right away to ask if I'd be the godfather. It wasn't be until Dehlia was twelve that Hector discovered she wasn't his.

"Why did we do that, Mia? Why would we hurt him like that?"

"No, no, Sonny. You say this now, but you and I were very much in love. I couldn't be with you the way you wanted. I could never handle your mood swings. Your bipolar disorder was too hard on me. It killed me a little every time I saw how you had to suffer, but it I still loved you. I still do."

"So how did he find out?"

"Dehlia was bitten by a shark while swimming one day— a tiger shark. She needed a blood transfusion and a kidney right away. The doctors asked Hector to donate. He agreed of course, but wasn't a donor match. Dehlia's blood type is A-positive. Hector and I are both B type"

"I'm A-positive."

"I know."

Mia told me that they'd found a donor and that Dehlia survived. Hector was furious and demanded a paternity test. He wasn't the father and was crushed.

"I told him the truth, and he was so devastated."

"I'm starting to remember. That's the real reason Natalie left me, isn't it?"

"Yes. We told Dehlia and Max that Uncle Sonny was very sick and wouldn't be coming back to the island."

It was all coming back to me as Mia recounted my life's events. I wanted to know for better or worse. This part was definitely for worse.

I said, "Natalie told Summer she couldn't handle my bipolar anymore."

Mia nodded.

"I remember that I was so distraught, I stopped taking my meds and poured myself into my work."

Mia confirmed my memory and went on to tell me that Hector cut all ties with me and swore never to speak to me again.

"He struggled to keep the money flowing, having only the Jamaican Rastas to supply. He was too angry and stubborn to ask you for help," she said.

I nodded. That's when Summer started helping. I had the lion's share of the market in the states but couldn't keep up with demand. Summer stepped in and delivered the Elks distribution and expanded our operation in Ohio.

"Summer's been through hell with me. I've been a shitty dad to her and the guilt I feel now for what I've done to her, Hector, Dehlia, and you is almost too much to bear. I'm beginning to wish I hadn't learned the truth. I'm not liking myself too much right now."

Mia frowned. "Summer loves you so much, Sonny. After your accident, she was the first one here."

"Summer was here on the island?"

"Yes. She didn't tell you?"

"No. In fact, I asked her directly. She denied it."

"Hmm. I wonder why?" Mia asked.

I had too many other things to mentally digest. I'd save that puzzle for another day.

"So what ended up happening to Hector?" I asked.

Mia looked down, looking almost ashamed to tell me the rest. She admitted that Hector had a hard time surviving without me. She told me how he started bidding on experimental bio-science projects for various government contractors. Word got out that he'd made a couple strong breakthroughs cloning orchids and marijuana plants for use as biological warfare agents. It was really small-time stuff compared to some of the more potent chemical agents derived from different animal venom like cobra and jellyfish. All the same, he attracted the interest of a crazy U.S. Army General named . . .

"General Lawrence Chamberlain?" I interrupted.

"Yes, you remember?"

"Bits and pieces." I said.

Mia went on about how the general wanted the Jamaican Orchid project to be his swan song— his big contribution before retirement.

"Hector owed a lot of people a lot of money, so he double-crossed the general and made a deal to sell the agent to North Korea," Mia said.

"The story on the news. It was Hector?"

"No, Hector hadn't finished the formula when the general learned of his betrayal. The general had him killed, thinking the agent was complete."

Mia had to stop. Her voice cracked, and her eyes welled up. She took a breath and continued, "When he learned it wasn't complete, he threatened to kill all of us unless we could finish it."

"I saw the story on the news, so it obviously worked. Who finished it? Max?"

"Max tried, Sonny, but he just didn't know what you and Hector knew."

Like a bolt of lightning, it hit me. "It was me, wasn't it? I finished the formula?"

"It wasn't just you, Sonny. Max helped." Mia paused for a long time before she finished. "So did Summer."

"Oh, God, no. It was me? I killed all those people?"

Chapter 62

Mia tried to reassure me that it wasn't my fault. She said that I was just trying to protect the people I loved. That meant cleaning up Hector's mess.

"Is Max okay?"

"Yes, you kept all the notes in your journal. After the accident, I sent the journal to Mike. Without the journal, and without you, the project was dead."

"So then how did North Korea…?"

"You made the deal, on your own, for three million. One million to go to the general, one million to go to Hector's debtors, and the last million was going to be for us to retire, settle down, and have the life together we'd always dreamed of."

I struggled to take it all in. I did this?

"So the general has his money? We're all square?"

Mia shook her head and told me that when I went to make the deal, I took a sample to a Mr. Lee and never returned.

"Lee dosed me?"

Mia said she couldn't confirm it but that was her guess. She said they found me in a delusional state and assumed that I'd been accidentally dosed, or the deal went bad and Mr. Lee dosed me.

In my delusion, Summer was dosed by Mr. Lee. If I was projecting myself as Summer, then perhaps I'd been projecting Autumn as someone else, but who? Then it dawned on me. Dehlia was the daughter I'd learned I had with Mia. She and I fought in real life. Maybe I extrapolated that in my hallucination to suicide?

"Dehlia." I shouted.

Dehlia came bouncing down, smiling.

"Is everyting okay?" she asked.

"Did I ever give you a Saint Anthony medal?"

"Yes, I wear it every day."

She grasped it in her hand and held on tight. I could tell she treasured it.

"May I see it?" I asked her

She handed it to me and there it was, an engraving carved in the back;

SD0055

"What is it Sonny?" Mia asked

"It's a password," I replied.

"What for?"

"I'm not sure."

I sat in silence, trying to recount any other detail that might help me remember something— anything.

"I think I have the money," I said. "I need to talk to Max."

Chapter 63

Max was hard at work, cataloging plants and jotting notes, when I entered. He looked good. His lean frame carried some added weight and his hair was close cropped, a change from the long dreads I remembered. Max was singing a reggae version of "Fools Rush In". I smiled, remembering Hector's love of the King.

My memory was coming back in bits and pieces. Mia helped immensely, but I still felt uneasy, curious as to what actually happened with the development of the MOjo55 agent.

"Hey, kid," I shouted.

Max looked up from his clipboard and smiled. At least, it appeared he was happy to see me. "Flowah mon," he said, smiling.

I caught him up, and, after he let my craziness settle in, I asked him about the formula. "I've made some good progress," he said.

"Good means?"

"I'm close to finishing MOjo 66."

I walked the aisles and looked at the strains of marijuana listed on the shelves: Koosh, Diesel, and Rasta Magic.

"These are all commercial strains. Where are the research plants?"

Max tensed and then got agitated. "Just come out wit it, mon. What you want to know? Dat I stopped doing de research and am back to commercial production?"

I nodded. "That's what I thought."

Max stood tall, defending his executive decision.

"Now that I think of it, you actually wanted to become a medical doctor, right?"

Max clenched his jaw. I sensed that he felt an accusation coming his way so I didn't hold back.

"It was you Max, wasn't it? It was you that dosed me?"

Max stammered a bit and looked like he didn't know what to say. Just based on his reaction, he knew something more than he was letting on, even if it wasn't him who actually plunged the syringe into my skin. I had to push him.

"Why did you do it, Max? Did you hate me because you found out that your Aunt Mia and I were in love? Were you angry? I wouldn't blame you if you were."

"No," Max said. "I hated you because my uncle adored you. He said you were his brother. He spent the better part of his life trying to cure you, and you broke his heart."

Max was angry, and rightfully so. He went on.

"You didn't have to watch him struggle, watch him whore himself out to the government, and watch him weep when he couldn't solve a problem he knew you could."

Max was right. I hadn't been there. I'm sure that, if I was as bad as they said, I was either manic or depressed anyway. It was a disease, but it wasn't an excuse. I needed to own up for my sins of the past. Now was probably too late.

"Max. I'm sorry."

Max just shook his head and paced. Maybe I knew a while ago that Max was carrying this anger? Maybe that's why I'd imagined him to be a violent mute?

"Why dose me, Max?"

"Dose you?"

"Yeah, I delivered the agent to Mr. Lee and woke up five months later."

"I didn't know where you went. I thought you left wit de money and took it all."

"I came back to help you. Why would I skip out with the cash, man?"

Max shrugged his shoulders. "Don't know."

"I'll tell you what happened."

Her voice echoed off the high lab ceiling. I recognized it immediately.

"Summer? What are you doing here?"

"I came back to finish the job I failed to do five months ago."

"What are you talking about?"

I was, once again, perplexed, and then it hit me— my

delusion. In the end, Summer *was* the one. She orchestrated it all. Was that part real? God, I hope not.

"Sonny Flowers, the crazy son of a bitch who just had to have it all."

"Summer. What is this?"

"When I opened the door two days ago and saw you alive on the doorstep, coherent and smiling, I about died."

Here it was, the deja vu all over again. Hadn't she and I just done this dance? I told myself I was emotionally ready this time but I wasn't. It hurt just as much.

"You were the one?"

"Yep. You ruin people's lives. Don't you see that, Sonny?"

She walked toward us with purpose, her fists clenched, looking like she was going to take a swing at me. My God, I'd really done a number on everyone. I deserved whatever I had coming, I'm sure.

"You successfully drove you wife, daughter, and best friend away and in the process, alienated the one person who actually loved you— Mia."

I listened to her and knew she was right, but I'd changed. Since waking up, I'd been even-keel. I couldn't even describe a slight change of mood. The coma really had changed me. How would I ever convince Summer and Max and Mia of that, though?

"I'm better, Summer. I swear. Let's just try and fix this and get our lives back."

Summer reached behind her back and pulled the gun from her waistband. That goddamn Glock again. It was like her American Express. She never left home without it.

"The money?" she said

"Seriously, the money?" You don't need it. We don't need it. We have millions."

"The government seized all of our plants, froze our accounts, and took all the cash. We have nothing."

"We have each other?"

It wasn't what she wanted to hear. I couldn't believe I'd said it.

"Don't give me that bullshit. You never wanted me. You only care about yourself."

"I honestly don't know where the money is, and whether you like it or not, I do love you, Summer, and always will. You're my daughter, for Christ's sake."

"Lee transferred the money to a numbered account. Where's the account information?"

"I don't have it, Summer."

"Well then, I guess you're as useless as always."

She raised the gun and pointed it at my head. She honestly wasn't going to shoot me, was she? Who could shoot their own father? She cocked the hammer. I almost pissed myself. This is how it was going to end? How fucking poetic.

"Hold it right there, Summer," the voice shouted from the entrance.

Summer was startled and turned. Max grabbed the wrist that held the gun and twisted it, forcing Summer to the ground.

Three armed authorities rushed in and cuffed her.

"Christine?" I said, not sure if what I was seeing was real? Maybe Summer had gotten the shot off, and I was playing the scene out after my death? Jesus, I was fucked up. I needed a break from the metaphysical.

"Hey there, handsome," she said smiling. "Actually it's Celeste— Celeste Hansen."

Celeste re-holstered her weapon and walked over. "I'm with Army CID. I've been working undercover investigating General Chamberlain. The Army suspected he was up to no good for some time. The Jamaican Flowers project just proved it."

Max clutched the file folder containing the contents of our research.

"Confiscate the files," she barked to the MP. "Sorry, Sonny. Sorry, Max. I'm sure you understand. The formulas need to stay with us."

I nodded. Max played tug of war with the officer trying to seize them.

"But... North Korea. I saw it on the news."

"Lee was a plant. He was one of ours. The exchange was real. The money was real. The village, unfortunately, was real."

"But, all those people. They are all dead because of me."

"That Korean village was harboring the leaders of a terrorist cell and a few hundred of their followers. That news won't reach the public, but sleep well, knowing you performed a great service for your country, Sonny. There were no innocent casualties."

"What's going to happen to my daughter?" I asked, watching the men take her.

"Many hours of therapy and a mandatory sentence working for the government in experimental science. You may see her again in ten to twenty years."

I'd driven her to this. All of her anger and rage, it was all aimed at me and for good reason.

"She made her own decisions, Sonny, no matter what you did."

"The money?" I asked her.

"You've been in a coma the last five months. You've suffered some horrible trauma. Like you said, you just don't remember. If the account number comes to you, give me a call."

She winked at me and smirked. I was awestruck. Was she for real? She started to walk away, file folders in hand.

"Celeste?"

She turned back and raised her eyebrows. "Yes?"

"This is going to sound crazy, but did we ever—?"

She walked back to me and whispered, "The boat? You were amazing, Sonny Flowers. You're my hero."

I blushed as she walked away.

"What you gonna do now, Flowah mon?" Max asked.

"I'm thinking of retiring, Max. Maybe settle down here in Jamaica— get to know my other daughter. I also have some fences to mend with you. I may never win your trust again, but goddamn it, I'm gonna try."

Chapter 64

It'd been a few months since waking up to my real life. I was finally adjusting and decided to make a go of it in Jamaica with Dehlia and Mia. I'd tried visiting Summer, but she wouldn't see me. Mia joked that I'd retired, but that I was far from it. My experience only fueled me to continue the work Mike and I had started, but now Mia was involved, so we ran formulas in Jamaica and legally shipped vials of the liquefied serums to the states.

Jane was in the third week of her extended coma, and it would be three more before we'd be able to publish the results. But the community had caught wind that my experience was powerful enough that, after four months, I'd not experienced a single mood swing. The worst after-effects I'd experienced were flashbacks and confusion about time and space events from the coma.

Most mornings were spent in the courtyard with my two favorite ladies. We drank the famous Blue Mountain coffee and ate fresh fruit while telling stories, laughing, and just being happy with our new life together. Mia swam most mornings, and while it was a pool with no real piranha, I had yet to dip a toe. If I were to have a flashback while swimming there, I could drown. Mia joked that I was a chicken.

Dehlia would just hold my hand and tell me that she understood and was happy that, because of my fear, we had an excuse to spend some good one-on-one time together. She loved hearing about my life, my childhood, and my experiences. She said she wanted to be a psychologist. I told her she'd be an excellent one, but that she was forbidden from working with Mike.

Dehlia surprised me that morning when she handed me the joint I'd been given by the cabby my first day back on the island.

"Found dis in de laundry."

I took it and ran it through my thumb and finger like I'd done a thousand times. I hadn't smoked since waking up and didn't really have any desire to start up. Not only did life appear more colorful and vibrant sober, but I'd been stoned for so much of my life that I wondered what I'd missed.

"So you gonna smoke dat?" Dehlia asked sarcastically.

I shook my head and handed it back to her. She toked up and exhaled in my direction. I actually choked on the secondhand smoke and wondered what Summer would say.

"Tell me the story of Jameson and Maria again," I asked her.

Dehlia laughed. "You mean dat pirate story you used to tell me an' Summer when we were little girls?"

I smiled. "That's the one."

Dehlia recounted the story of Jameson and Devanagari, fighting for Maria's love. She told me how the Spanish galleon sank the *Sea Orchid* and Jameson with it.

"Wait. The *Serpentine Orchid*, right?" I asked.

"What you talkin' 'bout? It's de *Sea Orchid*."

My mind started spinning. Something wasn't right. Why had I invented the *Serpentine Orchid*? The story was familiar enough that I should have known the real name.

"It can't be that simple, can it?" I asked.

"No idea what you talkin' 'bout," Dehlia replied. She looked at me like I was crazy, but she was stoned. I didn't hold it against her. My mind was sharp and the final answer to the puzzle had come to me.

The account name and password fields appeared on the screen of my computer for Saint Antony's Bank in the Cayman Islands. I worked out the words *Serpentine Orchid* on paper and counted the number that corresponded with the letter. It was a simple cryptogram.

"You see?" I asked her "The letter S equals the number nineteen. We use the second digit for numbers with two decimals. The letter E is the number 5, and so on."

Dehlia watched as I typed out the sixteen digit account number: *9580540945583894*

"Let me see that medal again," I asked her.

She handed it over, and I typed the password in the field. We sat in silence and stared at the account balance— three million dollars U.S.

Mia stepped in and stood over us, asking if what she was seeing was real. "What are you going to do with all of it, Sonny?"

It took a few minutes for the weight of it to settle, but as I stared at the money, I knew what I had to do.

"Well, for starters, I'm sending Max to medical school. Then— "

The phone rang.

"Sonny, it's for you. It's Mike Maserati." Mia said, holding the receiver in the air.

"Hey, Mike."

"Sonny, you're never going to believe this."

"What is it?"

"It's MOjo55. It works."

I didn't understand. Jane wasn't due to wake up for another three weeks.

"Mia sent me a new formula to trial. It's a two-week treatment."

"And it works?" I asked

"So far, so good. I used it on Jane instead of the MOjo55. She's been up a week and isn't showing any signs of paranoia and hasn't had a single swing."

My heart leapt. The news had been better than discovering the money. Jane was better. She could live the life I hoped she'd one day be able to live.

"She's been asking for you, Sonny."

"Tell her Mia and I will fly home next week."

I squeezed Mia's hand and told her the news. She beamed with exhilaration.

"Just like Viagra, eh, buddy?"

I remembered the story of Viagra, how the scientists who discovered it were never looking for an erectile dysfunction drug. It was an unintended, yet favorable side effect. I'd inadvertently cured myself, well, Summer and I had. I wished she were here to celebrate with us.

"I'll be damned," I mumbled.

"Of course, we'll have to do some more testing," said Mike.

"Yeah, of course," I replied.

My mind was still working in overdrive. I couldn't believe it. We'd really done it. It hadn't been just me or Summer. It was Summer, Mia, Hector, Max, Mike, and, yes, me.

"I wish Hector could see this," I said

Just then, a gust blew through and flipped my journal open to a page I hadn't read in ages. It was one on which Hector had written:

Adversity is sometimes hard upon a man; but for one man who can stand prosperity, there are a hundred that will stand adversity.

Elvis Presley

Mia told me that it was Hector's favorite quote and one that he'd recite to me after every failed experiment. Today was our day to be prosperous. We'd actually done it. We changed the world - together.

26147798R00187

Made in the USA
Charleston, SC
26 January 2014